Wilson Mooney
Almost Eighteen

Wilson Mooney
Almost Eighteen

a novel by

Gretchen de la O

Re-edited by Tiffany Barkman Grayson
Cover design and graphics by Sommer Stein with Perfect Pear Creative
and Toski Covey
Photography Art by Liza Aharonovich

 Wilson

Mooney

is dedicated to

all the women who

want to remember what

it felt like when their

butterflies fluttered

south for the

first time.

When I become so entrenched in the process of living life sometimes I forget to look up and smile at the people who make my life worth living. This moment is my opportunity to thank those who have inspired me to be the person I am, and the writer I keep striving to become. They are the people who gave me the confidence I needed to jump off the crumbling edge, feet first, into the refreshingly deep, crystal clear waters of my creative discovery.

My Shout-outs...

The Wilson Mooney Book Club: Allison, Becky, Brittney, Debbie, Jennifer, Karley, Lisa, and Nicole: Thanks for the insight into Wilson and Max and the dinnertime discussion of the characters you loved—and even the ones you didn't love so much. You all hold a very special place in my heart.

April: Your belief that I could write a good story means the world to me. Thank you, sis, for giving me the push I needed to publish Wilson.

Eunice: Thank you for stepping forward when I needed someone to help me. I am so grateful for your time and generosity.

Toski & Sommer I am so glad you were willing to work with me. Your flexibility and willingness goes above and beyond. Thank you for your encouraging words and gentle manner.

Liza: Thank you for your creative eye, and finding our perfect Wilson and Max! It was wonderful meeting you and working with you!

Dorothy: Thank you for your wisdom, excitement, and the faith you have in me. I appreciate your wealth of grammatical knowledge.

Karley: Thank you for your endless cheerleading and your total belief in what I was doing. I am completely grateful for your support, input, and the late night readings.

Debbie: Thank you for your eyes, ears, and voice; for putting up with the countless times you were forced to listen and read aloud. I appreciate the brainstorming moments and directional shifts that kept me focused and moving toward my goals.

My Family—Ed, Jared, Kyle, Nate, and my mom (Grandma K): Thank you for giving me the space I needed to create, and the moments in life when you had to fend for yourselves. Thank you for believing that, beyond my righteous titles of wife, mother, and daughter, you saw me as an author. Thank you for making Sunday mornings our family time. You guys are my world and I love you.

Becky: No words exist in *any* language in the modern world today that can express the limitless gratitude I have for you. I am beyond blessed to have you in my life. You are my twin in consciousness and my sister in greatness. Thank you for your unconditional love, your fabulous dreams, and the absolute reassurance that I am worthy. (REALLY, REALLY!)

CHAPTER ONE:

I wish I could remember my childhood. The vivid memories and deliberate words just didn't work for me. I remember small pieces—chunks of events that took up residence in my head—but details of who took whom to the fifth grade dance or how it felt when Christian Sibley, one of the most popular boys in middle school, broke up with me…well you could just forget it. My mind was blank. It was like Swiss cheese; cheese that left a pukey, pungent flavor in my mouth after I swallowed.

Okay, so maybe I was being a little melodramatic with the Swiss cheese reference and the Christian Sibley thingy—but it stung. If I thought really hard, I could remember some of the couples at the fifth grade dance. But if you've lived a life like mine, you tend to make it a habit to forget the crappy parts and a struggle to retain even the mediocre ones too.

My name is Wilson Mooney and I'm a senior at Wesley Academy. I knew from an early age that my life was different. Think about it, how many girls do you know named Wilson? Then saddled with the last name Mooney? Odds were stacked against me from birth, I was going to be the butt of someone's joke. If I had money for every time someone called me Looney

Mooney, I wouldn't need to work another day of my life; but life's not fair.

Unlike most of the girls at my school, I wasn't born into privilege. I was the product of a one-night stand between two under-aged, pimple-faced ninth graders. My father was a no-show from the second my mom told him she was pregnant, and my mother had made it her life's work to live off of the state of California. That's why I'm here. My grandparents thought I would be better off at a school away from my misguided, loser of a mother. Oh yeah, Wesley Academy is a boarding school for girls.

***

The grimy dust from the dry-erase pens always covered my hands—evidence that I was one of "those" kids. I'd been erasing the whiteboards for twenty minutes straight and it sucked. Not only did I have to use the crappy black brick eraser to wipe away the chicken scratches of my fifth period teacher, Mr. Swanks, but I also had to use a wet wipe to clean the residue that made my hands look like I belonged in the first grade again. What teacher in their right mind had to use every color pen that came in the economy-sized box? Weren't black and red enough? After I erased the trig problems, in all different colors, I had to clean Mrs. Clouser's boards. She was my English Lit teacher. At least she stayed to the two-color maximum.

When it's all said and done I spend sixty minutes every day of my life cleaning the whiteboards of six of my teachers, three of whom I hate with a passion and two who I can barely tolerate. At least I have Max Goldstein. He's the young new student teacher who came to Wesley last year to teach government.

Today Mr. Goldstein came into Mrs. Clouser's classroom while I was cleaning the whiteboards. His strong hands pushed his straight black hair away from his face. His electric green eyes watched me erase. Back and forth they danced. I caught him staring.

"Hi, Wilson, I'm looking for Mrs. Clouser, have you seen her?"

My heart fell into my stomach. He was actually talking to me as an equal.

Don't be stupid, answer him using sophisticated words. Think, think, think—okay, I got it.

"No." I felt the dry eraser brick catch under my hand and stumble across the whiteboard as it flew to the ground toward him. My cheeks flushed red, *how embarrassing.*

"Here let me get that." He bent down and his hair fell toward his sharp, well-built nose. The tip of his tongue wet his lips as he held out the eraser.

Don't stare, I kept repeating to myself as I opened my mouth and tasted the sweet aroma of his French Vanilla coffee across my tongue. A hint of Crew hair gel found the spot in my body reminding me that I was a woman. *God, he is so hot! Man, I wish he wasn't my teacher. Maybe I should just brush his fingers when I grab the eraser. I could make it look innocent enough.*

"Here you go," his voice shattered my thoughts. He held out the eraser giving it a little adjustment in his hand.

"Thanks." I reached for it and my fingernails caught the back of his hand scratching across to his knuckles.

I can't believe I scratched him. "Oh, I'm sorry." *Why wasn't I more careful?*

"I think I'll survive." His lips parted; he smiled and I melted.

"If you see her, could you tell her I came by?"

"Sure." He turned away and left through the big beige metal door.

I tossed the black eraser onto the aluminum tray, grabbed the wet wipe, and finished the job that helped bankroll my stay at the academy, thinking about him the entire time.

I'm seventeen—I'll be eighteen in another month—and he's twenty-two. Four years is nothing; it was actually considered normal now. I figure with the maturity gap between males and females, I am about the right age for him.

I was born on Christmas. Yeah, it sucked for me. I never understood the hypocrisy of people getting presents for someone else's birthday. How could I justify getting presents for someone who died for my sins over two thousand years ago? *Here, sacrifice your life for me. And, by the way, look at the new iPod Touch I got for your birthday.* Besides, I always got stiffed. I never had a real birthday party with my friends. It always amounted to my grandparents singing "Happy Birthday" to me as I opened my one birthday-slash-Christmas present that was surely wrapped in dreary solid red paper. I'm not complaining; my grandparents did the best they could with the cards they were dealt. They didn't intend to emotionally damage me with the Christmas thing—they loved me.

When I lost my grandma six months ago I didn't expect my grandpa to follow her five and a half months later (almost to the day). He went out to get the newspaper and suffered a massive heart attack. He was dead before he hit the driveway. He just gave up and died of a broken heart. They'd been married sixty-four years.

Some people tried to comfort me into believing my grandparents were together, sitting in heaven, looking down from their celestial space in the sky. Me? Well, I didn't know what to believe. Part of me wanted to think they were sitting right next to Jesus, but I couldn't. I just wasn't convinced the legs of their chairs weren't going to fall through the soft, puffy clouds. Besides, what were they going to do on a picture-perfect, clear day?

The school assigned me a grievance counselor; someone who could help me with all the "pain" I buried deep in my soul. When I didn't show up for my first session, they called me out from seventh period and cornered me in the hall outside the classroom. *Talk about a real awkward intervention.* Principal Rose, Vice Principal Hardbough (known to most as Mrs. Hardballs), and the guidance counselor, Mrs. Jenkles, swarmed around me and bounced in rhythm. They kept chanting strange words about letting go of my disappointment and embracing the small, lost child within. Lesson learned that day? Fake it 'til you make it. If I'd just gone to the stupid appointment, I could have stayed in pottery and finished the ashtray I'd been making for my non-smoking best friend's parents. Instead I got shuffled into the guidance counselor's office every day for the next two weeks during seventh period.

By the time I convinced Mrs. Jenkles that I was mentally balanced enough, the trimester ended and I got a "D" in pottery. You want to know what the real kicker was? My grade was a result of my lack of attendance and incomplete projects. That was the bureaucracy of it all; nobody would claim the blame. The day I took my unfinished ashtray to Joanie's parents, I realized how much I missed my grandparents. The stupid, restless bowl of an ashtray helped me break down and understand that I was truly alone in this world. I cried hard that night into my pillow and vowed to never cry for my grandparents again; and I haven't.

Truth be told, I wasn't really alone in the world. I had Joanie, my BFF. We met when we were both dumped at

Bethany's Boarding School for Girls at the ripe young age of eight; wide-eyed and scared, we gravitated to one another. Joanie's the most amazing person I have ever met. She has this way of making me believe I can survive anything. You know the type: they dared you to kick the devil between the legs while holding an angel by the wings. She was my rock through the whole *death comes in waves* thing. While I was busy waiting for the other shoe to drop, she was there to remind me to blow my nose and wash my hands.

Flashbacks and daydreams helped lessen the tedium of my under-aged, slave-labor moments cleaning the whiteboards. By the time I looked at the clock, I only had Max Goldstein's board left to rub; I liked to clean his last. He had the really nice, enormous erasers that wiped the board clear in a couple of swipes. But that wasn't the only reason. He always stayed late to work on his lesson plan for the next day and he didn't leave until around four-thirty. If I planned my wipes right, I could spend thirty minutes in the same room with him. Thirty minutes of uninterrupted time with the hottest teacher in the entire school. No flirtatious inquiries from Bonnie Wente or stupid questions from Jacky Burlington. Only him and me, with boards that needed to be stroked and lessons that needed to be planned.

I pulled open the massive metal door to his room and shuffled past the pile of crumpled paper overflowing from his waste basket. I could smell his cologne, fresh, like he splashed some on his neck before I showed up. The hint of lavender hovered faintly in the air. He looked up from the planner he had spread across his desk.

"Oh, hey there Wilson, I almost forgot you were coming in today."

I froze; my heart crashed down into my stomach. His words damaged me like a wrecking ball plummeting into a building. *This wasn't the first time I came to clean his boards.*

"Did you need me to come back?" I asked.

"No, go ahead and do what you need to do." He pushed his finger into a black drawn square and started to write in the time.

How dare he forget I was coming to his classroom? The way he ignored me knocked me into the swell of my own self-pity as he continued to press his pen to the planner. *Fine, two can play that way.* I grabbed the humongous erasers and started clearing his board, the entire thing—starting with the part where he drew a square around and wrote in big black words, "DO NOT ERASE."

Okay, so it was immature and cruel; I would even go far enough to say rude. But I gotta admit, I felt vindicated. My emotions always ran hot and cold. That was me, that's how I rolled. I have heard people refer to me as a pit-bull. If you were part of my pack, I'd protect you to the death. Piss me off, and I'd turn on you faster than a crazed dog chasing an injured cat.

I guess it was time for me to apologize profusely and make it look like a total accident.

"I'm sorry, Mr. Goldstein. I think I just erased something you wanted to keep." I crumpled my eyebrows and twisted my lips. He paused from the planner and looked up. At first he narrowed his eyes and clenched his jaw. Frustration draped his face. *I've never seen him frustrated before. Wow, he is so gorgeous.* Then just as fast, his expression broke to forgiveness. His eyes rounded, his lips pulled across his perfect teeth into a smile and he shook his head back and forth.

He came over to me. "Don't worry about it, Wilson. I know you've had a lot on your mind lately." His hand pushed at my back. Shivers ran down my arms. My fingers clenched the eraser and I felt the ripples vibrate up through my scalp. He was touching me; his hand was so warm.

"I'm sorry about your grandfather."

He dropped his hands and slid them into the front pockets of his Levi's. His red-flannelled shoulders rose up to touch his ears, his dark blue T-shirt wrinkled by his waist.

What? What did he just say, I didn't catch that. I guess I was too busy watching his body move. Too busy listening to my inner voice practicing my new name, Wilson Goldstein.

"I'm sorry. I didn't hear what you said." He pulled his hands out of his pockets and grabbed my shoulders. "I'm sorry about your grandfather," he made sure I saw him speaking. I still couldn't focus on what he said. *Hello, now both hands were touching me.*

They always say teachers shouldn't touch their students. What a heap of steaming crap. Please, touch me all you want. How do you think he kept me coming back to my government class? It sure wasn't the curriculum. Who really cared about how a bill became a law, or the difference between the three branches of government. It was because I got to spend fifty whole minutes watching *him*. And if it was a great day, he would have brushed his hand across the top of my chair and I would have felt my shirt push across my back as he bent down to help me with something I didn't understand. Needless to say, I was always struggling in government. I looked forward to that moment where his smell would surround me; his one hand would rest on my chair while his other would anchor strongly onto my desk.

The edge of his eyebrow rose, waiting for me to answer.

"Thanks, but he died over two weeks ago." *Why didn't I just say thanks and move on?* His hands dropped from my shoulders and his face drained white. I felt the huge eraser I still had in my hand become too heavy and fall to the ground.

"I didn't know—you didn't miss any school. I assumed that it just happened."

"No. Don't be sorry, he lived *way* too long."

"Wow, well you seem like you're doing fine." He shook his head. I should have known when his eyes bugged out that I came across all wrong.

That was my downfall. I didn't know when to shut up. Open mouth and insert foot; those words should have been tattooed on the inside of my eyelids.

"Yeah, I'm fine."

I bent down and picked up the gigantic eraser. I needed to get some erasing done. I've been told the office had spies and narks and that, if they peeked into the window of Max's room and saw I was talking, I could lose my financial aid. With six months left before I graduated, I didn't want to mess it up.

Besides, part of me wanted him to be intrigued. Less was more. I wanted him to push. If I kept part of my life mysterious, he would take the bait. Although, the whole thing could backfire and he could lose interest, leaving me with the desperate act of flirting and asking stupid questions. *God don't let me reach that level of desperation.*

He stood for a moment longer before he headed back to his desk and pulled out a blank piece of paper. I could feel him staring at me. I wondered what he was thinking. *I knew what I wanted him to think.* I stole glances when I could, adjusting my arms to see underneath. He scribbled on the paper, folded it and stood behind me.

"Wilson, I know you're pretty much on your own. Well, I want you to take this…call if you need someone to talk to. Okay?" He pushed the folded paper toward me. He held it out in the open air between us. I watched it quiver. I looked around, and made sure nobody saw me grab it from him before I shoved it in the front pocket of my khaki shorts. I swear he saw my heart pound heavy in my chest. I heard it.

"Thanks."

Here we go, he's making his move. I'm so ready for this! I'll keep it cool for the next month, act like nothing is going on between us, and when I turn eighteen, nobody will be able to stop us. I will be a legal adult. My head spun off into images of us holding hands, walking down the halls at school, and sneaking away for lunch.

Christmas break—public schools called it winter break. I didn't know what the difference was, except one reminded me I shared a birthday with Christ, and the other made me think about dirty snow. I will be here at the dorms because, well let's face it—I don't really have any place to go. Maybe Max will be here with me and he could take me to meet his parents. That would work.

I watched him strut back to his desk. I couldn't wait to open the note. I continued wiping the boards while he packed up his books and laptop. He tossed a glance my way before he dragged his briefcase across the top of his desk.

"Want me to walk you out?" The way he looked at me melted my heart, causing it to drip into the pit of my stomach, teasing my butterflies, fighting to be free.

"That's okay. I still have the back board to clean."

"Here, let me help you. Get you outta here faster." He grabbed the huge eraser out of my hand, went to the back board, and started wiping. *okay, if that wasn't a sign that he liked me then I didn't know what was.*

"Thanks…," I stood and watched him for a moment before I had to turn and wipe his words from the board.

"You're welcome," he continued.

I wanted to remember this moment forever.

CHAPTER TWO:

I sat on my bed staring at the folded paper. There was a part of me that wanted to live in the moment when he had handed it to me. The butterflies in my stomach, the smell of the room, the letter quivering in his hand—I was there again, in my mind. They say that your imagination is the key to your soul. My deadbolt had been sprung wide open with my thoughts about him.

"Whatcha doin'?" a squeaky voice invaded my moment. It was Cindy Browler, my roommate. Typical rich kid. *You recognize her name, right? Browler?* Her grandfather is the owner of the hip food chain Browler Burritos; *thought you might know.* They only have about two hundred restaurants in the state of California alone, which makes them one of the richest families in the state. The food was edible; nothing to write home about. People eat up that trendy crap. All it took was a couple of movie stars and sports figures and, all of a sudden, it was the place to be. Anyway, Cindy was an okay person; needy, but who wasn't sometimes?

"I was just thinking about the test in trigonometry tomorrow; you ready?" Small talk was never a strong suit of mine. But after being roommates with Cindy for the last three and a half years I've started to master the concept.

"No, I was thinking: this weekend I'm flying out to see my dad in Aspen, *aaannd*...you're coming with me." Her eyes rounded, hoping she didn't cross the line with her demands. "I'll teach you how to ski. You have to say yes, because I won't go without you. *Please*." She flung her body on my bed. The folded love letter from Max catapulted up off the comforter and down onto the floor, landing between the bed frame and my nightstand. Panic rushed through my body as my eyes followed its flight.

Was I really going to get a chance to say no? After she whipped out a ticket in my name? I took a deep breath and held it before I answered her.

"When are we leaving?"
She squealed, bouncing up and down on my bed.

"Oh, we are going to have so much fun. We fly out on Friday night and come back Sunday afternoon." She jumped off my bed, grabbed her iPhone, and texted her dad that I was coming with her.

What that must feel like. Not the texting part, but the part where she got to tell her dad that I was coming. An experience that was foreign to me. I envied her; not for her money, her things, or even her looks. I envied that she was her daddy's little girl. Something I will never be. We're all dealt different hands in life; she got a full house and I busted with a pair of twos. Point was, if I sat around feeling sorry for myself I wouldn't be going to Aspen this weekend with my roommate.

"O-M-G, do you know who has a cabin in Aspen?"

"No idea, but I assume you're going to tell me."

"Yeah, *helloo* our one and only Mr. Maximillian Goldstein." She looked me square in the eyes.

"What?" A knot clogged my throat and captured my breath.

"I guess his family has owned their cabin since he…" her voice warped into the teacher from Charlie Brown. *Wah, wah… wah, wah, wah…*

My mind spun into a vision of Max and me finding each other; stealing hidden time from his family and my roommate to be together. Oh my God, what if he is up there this weekend? What was I going to wear? What was he going to think if I showed up there? What did the note say? What if the note was his number in Aspen? I gotta look at the note.

"Excuse me, Cindy. I need to go to the bathroom." I reached down, swiped up the note, and pushed it into my pocket on the way to the bathroom. My heart was leaping and excited, I couldn't wait to read it. I slammed the bathroom door, making sure to lock the knob. I couldn't open the note fast enough. The folds were tight and the corners stuck together. My pulse fluttered rhythmically before betraying me into beats that thrashed cruelly.

I was totally confused. Was this a joke? What did this mean? I stared at what he wrote, blinking to clear my eyes. I looked again. I mouthed it slow as my eyes took in what my mouth was saying.

"Matt Gladstone 555-2129. Who the hell is Matt Gladstone? Another damn counselor?" My heart shattered. My dreams burst before my eyes. I didn't understand. I replayed it in my head, him handing me the paper; *the love note.* He'd quivered as he handed it to me. He'd told me "call me, if you need to talk." That's what I remembered. "Call me"—that was what he said. *I am such a fool, like he would even want to be with me. What a frickin' idiot.* I crumpled the note and tossed it to the ground. I didn't cry. Fire could have burned from my eyes, and I still would have held it back. I learned a long time ago that nobody was worth crying over. Nobody! There was no Prince Charming to save me from my depressing life. The only person that could save me from tragedy was me. Maybe it seemed harsh, but it was the only way to save my sanity when I've had to fend for myself for so long. There was no mom to kiss it and make it better, daddy didn't exist, and as far as I knew I was an only child. That was my life in a boarding school's bathroom.

Cindy knocked on the door and I heard her clear her throat before she spoke.

"Wilson, are you still in here? Are you okay?"

"Yeah, I just needed to go to the bathroom. I'll be right out."

I looked down and saw the crumpled note. I picked it up and flushed it. It was my luck that it would clog the toilet, but instead I watched the black ink bleed purple into the water as the force of the flush sucked it into the sewer. *Goodbye, Matt Gladstone. And to you too, Max Goldstein.*

I pushed my hands into the freezing water from the tap, because washing them was the acceptable thing to do after you fake using the toilet.

"I'm so excited that you're going with me to Aspen." Cindy asserted through the closed door before pounding an enthusiastic rhythm with her hands.

"Me too," I answered unlocking the door and letting her into the bathroom.

"Let's get through school tomorrow, because after that it's you, me, and the hot guys of Aspen," she sang as she propped the door open with her foot and swung her hands through the air.

I pulled at the brown paper towels from the wall that dried my hands just enough to keep them damp. "Hot guys, that's exactly what I need," I mumbled.

***

It was lights out at 11:00 p.m. That was the time Wesley Academy expected us to be done with homework, bathing, and visiting. Well, sometimes—for a senior in high school—we're up pretty late. Studying for trig tests, looking over government homework, and writing scathing love letters; it all can take up quite a bit of time.

Tonight I was up late writing a two-page letter to *him* (after I studied, of course). It was four pages; two front and two back, to be exact. Nobody will find it and he will never see it. It was my fantasy written in pen and it was for my eyes only. *Don't tell me you've never written a letter to someone you loved, with the full intention they'd never see it.* Emotions too embarrassing blot the pages in roller-ball ink. His name with hearts to dot the i's. Fantasies of him teaching me in his classroom alone scribbled delicately on the back of page two. How his lips felt as they kissed me. My dream of him taking me away from the lonesome hell I called my life. How bummed I felt when I saw someone else's name and phone number on the note he handed to me. I never signed it—my love note. I folded it into a perfect square and hid it toward the headboard between my mattress and box springs.

Peaceful sleep came easy that night. Maybe it was because I'd written my feelings down, finally releasing all the pent-up emotion I had about him. No nightmares of huge gorillas chasing me with sock puppets or Billy Ray Cyrus being my long-lost father. For the first time in a long time, I dreamt I was a little girl again. I was about eight, it was summer, and I was wearing a bright yellow sundress with huge white polka-dots.

15

My long, blonde hair soaked up and splashed the sun across my face. The faint aroma of freshly cut grass was vibrant in the air. I was happy and my deep blue eyes were filled with hope. I was barefoot as I twirled in the grass at my grandparent's house. I had a toothless smile as I danced with my stuffed bear, Nemo. I cradled him in my arms; he was as soft as a field of dandelions. I knew we were safe; we had each other. Then, together, we dissolved into a swirl of primary colors.

I woke up before my alarm went off at six thirty. I thought I would be rejuvenated. I wanted to feel like I was eight again; instead I was totally wasted. I pushed the alarm off before it belched its awful, core-rattling noise, and stumbled to wake Cindy. She was already gone. Her bed was made and her bag at the end was already packed. Wow, she was so efficient. Kinda made me feel like I was already behind in a game we hadn't even started. She was down court, hammering three-pointers and I was still back, passing *in* the ball. I grabbed my clothes and the towel I was sharp enough to lay out the night before, and headed to the showers.

I liked to shower later in the morning because most girls stressed to get their make-up on and get their poufy hairdos to look right. I was fortunate to not have been given *that* chromosome at birth. The one that makes a freak out of you when you turn thirteen years old, turning you into a mirror-hogging, narcissistic bitch. Don't get me wrong, I care what I look like, I just don't need a two-hour block of time in front of a mirror. Thirty minutes was more than enough time. Usually when I've finished my shower and used the mirror, only a couple of girls are left to share it. It was so much more manageable without jockeying for position. I am the senior, therefore, the matriarch of the mirror at seven thirty in the morning.

My first period class starts at 7:55, plenty of time to run across the courtyard to Conversational Spanish. Señora Puttabaugh (don't say it, I know, she doesn't sound Latino at all. Trust me, she married to get that name) was one tough Señora. She locked the door at 7:55 and, if you were even a second late, you would miss the entire class. They might as well mark a big fat "U" for unexcused absence across the attendance record. Tardy and truant were words that didn't exist in her language. You were either there on time or not at all.

Now, I had it down to a science. As long as my feet were hitting the cement of the courtyard by 7:50, I was okay. I would be in her class, Conversando Español, with a whopping thirty seconds to spare. Today was no different. I hated her class, but I muscled through it so I could go to college and create a better life. That didn't come out right.

My life hasn't been torturous by any means. I didn't have parents that beat me or verbally abused me. I've been given an opportunity for a great education. I ate three squares and had clean clothes every day. I typed all my work on a school-issued MacBook Pro with wireless internet in my room. And, to top it off, I was attending one of the most prestigious boarding schools around, surrounded by some of the most influential people in California.

Señora Puttabaugh gave us a pop quiz on the Mexican history of Caesar Chavez—in Spanish. *Told you she was tough; hope I passed.* I slept through my second period class, Humanities. Mrs. Quest was the most monotonous, boring teacher at Wesley. What an interesting subject, the human condition, right? Survival of the fittest and the plight of the common man, right versus wrong, moral codes of conduct, studies based on the mortality of the human race, *how could that be boring?* She was the queen bee at making it unbearable. Sawed logs, that was all I had to say about second period.

I don't get lonely; *bet you didn't think I was going to say that.* Well, I don't. Most people think that, because I don't have *active* parents, I must be completely messed up; that I should be lonely, all filled with angst and hate. Why? So my life can be as miserable as theirs? Whether I believed in a guy on a cloud in lace-up, leather sandals holding a massive staff or a presence of energy that wanted to see itself so bad that it created us in its image, what right did I have to mess it up? Either way, I only had one chance to make this life of mine matter. *Sorry, wait, I'm sorry...my bad. This happens when I fall asleep in Humanities. Every single time, I get preachy. Sorry about that.*

My day was going as normal as it could. I had a small break between second and third period. I liked to get an orange juice and chug it before English Lit. I needed the sugar. Mrs. Clouser was another piece of work. Although I didn't hate her, I didn't particularly want to spend any extra time with her.

I was convinced she was from the Elizabethan time, it was a bit frightening. She was a Shakespeare freak. *Tell me you've had a teacher like her.* She was able to quote every line, by memory, of Juliet's balcony monologue while answering in a low, masculine voice for Romeo. *Didn't she know that the parts were all played by guys? Please, it was totally creepy.* It was so frustrating because I really hoped she rented the movie *Romeo and Juliet* from the early nineties. Leonardo DiCaprio, now he made Romeo worth watching.

Mrs. Clouser popped in a videotape from the late sixties; the thing couldn't go twenty seconds without looking like it was going to break and crack apart. The actors were all in tights. *So, of course, where did my eyes go?* You could figure *that* out. The guy who played Romeo was cute, but he was Lenard not Leonardo.

The special effects sucked, the dance scenes made me dizzy, and the music was so sappy I almost threw up. It was so bad, I couldn't even force myself to live in their fantasy. Maybe it was groundbreaking back in the sixties, but it was heartbreaking in the Y2K.

When the bell rang, I couldn't get out of there fast enough. As we left, Clouser reminded us that we had to write an essay on the first half of the movie over the weekend and turn it in or else we weren't going to be able to see the second half. *Was that a promise?*

Lunch, finally. I haven't seen Cindy yet and we have Government together. I was hoping to eat lunch with her and then head over to Goldstein's class together, or maybe she would agree to cut his class with me. I wouldn't need to tell her the rotten details, just that I wanted to pack and get ready, and that I needed her help. We had a substitute anyway.

Cutting wasn't the easiest thing to do at Wesley; even though they didn't watch you like a hawk or anything. They placed your education in your lap. They figured you should want to go to class so you could graduate and go to an Ivy League school. A lot of the students who attended Wesley were on a fast track to Stanford. All of the students were required to apply to at least three Ivy League schools. Let's just say, most people would get one of their three top choices. On average they send ninety-eight percent of their student body to higher education and eighty-five percent go on to Ivy League schools. Bet you could guess where I'd fit in; and it wasn't the majority.

"Wilson, there you are! I've been looking for you." Joanie, my BFF, skipped across the cafeteria toward me. Her smile filled her face. She was the only person in the entire world who knew *everything* about me, even how I felt about *you-know-who*. That explains why she was also very protective of me. She was the only person in my life who I came to trust with anything. It's not very common to have a friend you could tell your deepest, most intimate secrets to without fear they would end up on her Facebook page or in her tweets on Twitter.

"Oh, hey J. What's up?" I always called her by her first initial. It was so much easier than saying Joanie. She locked her arms around my neck and kept skipping, taking me with her. I was somewhat shorter than her, so I flew forward—but was lucky enough to catch myself. *I hated when she did that.*

She was a different bird to start with. Always smiling, always able to find something positive in the steaming heap of a mess I call life experiences. There had only been a handful of times when I could remember her ever being mad. She constantly found time to help people when they asked. She always saw the glass as half full, an optimist to the core. Maybe that was what balanced our friendship. I was the one always trying to find out what motivation people had for helping me, while she just bounced around trusting everyone.

"Oh my God, Wilson, Mr. Goldstein isn't here today. He left early for the weekend. I overheard him telling Mr. Weinstein he was going out of town and won't be back until Sunday night, something about skiing. I guess you're gonna miss your chance to get your fill before the weekend."

Great, this was awkward. How was I going to tell my best friend that I was leaving for the weekend tonight with our roommate, Cindy, and there was a slight chance Max could be going to his family's cabin and (an even slighter chance) that I am going to see him without her? Although she was optimistic, it didn't mean she wasn't easily tipped into becoming jealous. *Okay, here goes nothing.*

"Joanie, *CindyinvitedmetoAspenthisweekend.*" I blurted out in one strung-together breath. This was the part where I started making excuses. "She bought the ticket before she even asked me. Can you believe it? I wasn't gonna go, but she wouldn't have gone without me. Now, who am I to mess up her vacation with her father?"

She didn't say a word as her face went red. She just stared at the black- and white-tiled floor of the cafeteria. I knew she felt left out. Believe me, I knew exactly how she felt, and that was what was so messed up about it. I wish she had plans this weekend; it would've made my life a little less complicated and I wouldn't have felt so guilty.

"I probably won't have much fun. You know me and the snow." Joanie's head rose, she wasn't good at hiding the struggle that blanketed her face.

"Come on, Wilson, I think I can handle you taking off with Cindy for a weekend. I'll be fine. You better text me! I don't wanna have to go out there and kick your ass." She pointed her long thin finger at me. I bounced back and forth and held my fists in front of my face. She slapped my hands down.

"He's gonna be there, isn't he?" she asked. I stopped; suddenly I felt the gap between us.

"According to Cindy, his family has a cabin there. She doesn't know anything—about him and how I feel. I wish you were going to be there."

"Well, I'm not. You're gonna be on your own." One dig, then I waited for her to apologize.

Joanie grabbed me and pulled me into a bear hug. "I'm sorry. You text me the minute anything happens. You know I love ya, miss you already," she mumbled.

"Me, too."

Just as Joanie pushed me away, Cindy came running up. Her eyes wide and bright, a smile held captive by braces sparkled in the light. She grabbed my hands and pulled me to face her. I noticed Joanie's eyes narrow and the edges of her lips bend down. I knew it was painful for Joanie to see Cindy excited about me going with her for an entire weekend. Especially since Joanie only put up with Cindy because we all were roommates; heck, I think that was a mutual consensus.

"You'll never guess who's going to Aspen this weekend, too; oh, hi Joanie." She glanced at my best friend before she looked back at me. She didn't wait for an answer. "Chase Romero." Her eyes glazed over and I could tell this weekend was going to be all about him.

Chase graduated from Brown Academy for Boys last year and now goes to Stanford. Wesley and Brown have a long-standing tradition of arranging dances and social events between the two schools. The administrators and parents believe it give the students the opportunity to co-mingle with like minds and social standards. I think it's a way for the wealthy families to pick and choose who their kids are going to be allowed to bring into their own socially privileged networks and profitable empires. It was at our first dance in the ninth grade when Cindy fell in love with Chase. Four years later, she was still so infatuated with him that she got her father to agree to write a pretty hefty check to Stanford, a little insurance for her acceptance in the fall. It must be nice.

I really couldn't understand what she saw in Chase. Yeah, he was good looking. He had the slick, jet-black hair off his ears, ocean blue eyes, and a perfect smile, but his communication skills lacked the finesse to talk himself out of a paper bag. He thought "exacerbate" was a type of fishing tackle. Do I need to say more? "To each their own," that was what my grandma used to say. Besides, I had my own situation I wanted to focus on—Max Goldstein. He and I were going to meet in Aspen and have dinner, even if he didn't know it yet.

CHAPTER THREE:

I hugged Joanie goodbye and grabbed my bag. It wasn't an emotional goodbye, it was a *see you in a couple of days* goodbye. I promised her I would text her the minute we landed, and when I found Max. It was a remarkable symbol of our friendship. She had taken the place of a parent figure in my life; and as inconvenient as it felt sometimes, it was a peerless comfort that filled my soul when I realized it. We had each other in this world of ill-fated events. I knew she would be there for me, no matter what.

The dorm-room door flew open and Cindy stood at the threshold, waving her one free hand.

"Come on, we are going to be late to the airport." She strutted past me and forced a roommate hug goodbye on Joanie.

"We'll see ya when we get back. Miss you already!" Her words dripped with a spurious tone to make Joanie jealous. She turned and grabbed my arm, pulling me; I turned and watched Joanie disappear behind the door.

We all had our own stories of why we were at Wesley. For all the crap Joanie had lived through, she was still optimistic, trusting, and open; it boggled my mind. She was the youngest of four. Her oldest brother was forty-six, her other brother was forty-three and her youngest sister was forty. Twenty-two years later, hello Joanie. Her parents told her she was an accident because of menopausal sex. *Can you believe it?* They tried to sue the doctor for lack of information on how babies were made during freaking menopause. Her parents were so opposite of mine. They were married, older, established, and had already raised three children. None of her thirty-something-year-old siblings offered to take her. They all thought it best to send Joanie away to boarding school.

So at the ripe young age of eight, Joanie entered the boarding school system. That was when I met her. We both liked the scent of sweet peas and the taste of warm sauerkraut. Our favorite color was green and she loved beanie babies as much as I did. It was like some power greater than anything brought us together; if you believed in such things. We've been best friends ever since.

I tossed my bag into the trunk of Cindy's sports car. Her father bought her a 2010 Audi TTS Roadster. Fire red with black interior, it was an early graduation present. Heck, I think they go for at least sixty G's. It was beautiful. I slid my fingertips along the side of the car. It felt smooth, strong, and expensive. *Where was she going to park it so it didn't get jacked from the airport?* I guess it didn't matter too much to her. She was so rich, daddy could buy her a new one; must be nice.

The ride to the Oakland airport was all about how she was going to find out which cabin was the Romeros'. How, this time, she decided to go up to Chase and profess her love to him. She even worked out telling him how she dreams about them being together. Please—so desperate. Give me a vomit bag, the one with the metal tabs to seal it off. Her infatuation was totally different than my feelings for Max. First, she didn't see him every day. Oh, then there was the major fact that he liked Dena Larson. Who was, by the way, out of his league. Dena looked like a model for Victoria's Secret. Hello, tiny waist and D-sized boobs; there was no way Cindy could compete with that. She could almost fudge a B-cup on a cold day. The only thing Chase and Cindy had in common was that their names both started with the letter C and the fact that both of their families were over-the-top rich.

What was I thinking when I agreed to go to Aspen with Cindy? If the thirty-minute ride to the airport was any indication of how the weekend was going to be, maybe I should have faked the H1N1 flu and lived with the ramifications. Holy cow, that girl could talk. The only saving grace, my thoughts of Max Goldstein.

Cindy pulled into long-term parking and popped the back. She unloaded the huge suitcase and backpack that took up most of the trunk. I just had a duffel bag. I didn't fly much, but from what I've heard, it's better to take one bag and carry it on with you so they wouldn't lose it. Besides, it wasn't like we were going for a week or anything. A couple of pairs of jeans and a few shirts worked for me. I flipped my bag across my shoulder and was ready to go. She pulled the suitcase behind her and strapped her backpack across her shoulders. Price you pay for having more than you need, I guess. If the airport offered little slave boys to carry her bags, I wouldn't put it past her to do it.

I watched her fight the suitcase up the steps. "Oh my God, this sucks," Cindy griped as I grabbed the bottom of her suitcase and pushed.

"What do you have in here, bricks of gold?"

The suitcase had to weigh seventy-five pounds.

"No, just necessities."

We crossed the road and headed toward the Southwest curbside check-in.

"We can check in with this outside guy right?"

"Oh, Wilson, they are called skycaps," she chuckled as she looked back at me. That was the part of this weekend I wasn't looking forward to: how stupid she could make me feel because I wasn't as traveled as she was. Truth be told, this was only the second time I'd taken an airplane anywhere. The first time I went on an airplane, I was thirteen and my eighth grade class flew down to So-Cal to go to Disneyland for our graduation trip. That was a bust. I ended up with food poisoning and spent the whole second day of my flex-pass in the hotel room with Mrs. Sheath. A mother of three obnoxious boys, she wasn't nurturing at all. In fact, she accused me of faking it; even when I was up-chucking my guts and hugging the porcelain, she tossed me a towel and shut the door. I was just glad I caught it before it landed in my vomit. That was the worst trip ever. This trip has to be better than Disney from hell.

"Whatever, we can check in here, right?" I dropped my duffel at my feet and turned to her to help.

"Hi, ladies, welcome to Southwest Airlines, where are we taking you today?" a gray-haired, clean-cut, uniformed man said as he grabbed the tickets and loaded Cindy's suitcase on a carpeted metal wheelie cart.

"Aspen," my voice cracked.

"Actually, Denver," Cindy corrected me as she looked back and shook her head.

Strike two. I've never liked people who kept correcting the mistakes I made or kept tallies on the stupid things I did, just so they could bring them up later at an inopportune time or in the heat of an argument.

Anyone who would argue with me would win. I didn't have the space in my head or the ability to catalog the stupid things people did or hurtful words they would say. I guess I was the best kind of friend, because I wouldn't remember all the times they shat on me or screwed me over. Call it a blessing or a curse; it was just the way I was.

The skycap smiled and nodded. "Well, Ms. Mooney, have fun in Aspen and enjoy your flight."

"Thanks." I grabbed my bag and we headed through the faux security and up to gate 25. Lucky for us, it was one of the first gates we came to; not so lucky for me, I had to sit for an hour and a half listening to Cindy talk about Chase. How she loved his hair; how his gorgeous ocean blue eyes called to her; how she wondered if he was a good kisser; how her name would sound as Cindy Romero, then Cindy Browler Romero. I snapped.

"Cindy, I've gotta go to the bathroom," I hurried to the restroom across from our gate.

"I'll go after you. They start the pre-boarding pretty quick," she shouted as she adjusted her backpack on her lap, unzipping it to pull out a pen. No doubt to practice writing her name as Cindy Browler Romero. I didn't say anything; I just nodded and kept walking. I don't think it even registered with her how irritated I was.

I was relieved to have a moment of time where I didn't have to hear about Chase. There had to be something else I could get her to talk about. Skiing—that was it. I would mention how excited I was to learn how to snow ski. Man, I frickin' hated the snow. I hated being cold. I hated wearing beanies on my head and gloves on my hands. Without fail, my head would get unbearably itchy and I wouldn't be able to scratch it with gloves on. I could never really get a good scratch going, so it was inevitable that I would have to take the gloves off, making my hands cold and my hair frizzy. Besides, I was very tactile. I liked to feel surfaces around me, and when you wore gloves it screwed up the sensation.

When I came back from the restroom they were already pre-boarding our section. Cindy was bouncing up and down and acting like she had to pee.

"Sorry, I didn't think I took that long."

"Come on Wilson, I have to have an aisle seat. If I get stuck between you and some random person with B.O., I swear, I will *not* be a happy camper." She pointed to my duffel bag and turned toward the ticket agent.

What was I doing? I was leaving my best friend behind to spend the weekend with Cindy on the slight chance I would get to see Max Goldstein on a ski slope. *Oh, Max.* Okay, so I wasn't a gambler, but the *odds* of a slight chance were well worth the cost of a weekend with her. I texted Joanie, telling her we were getting on the plane and how much I wished she was with me. She didn't respond.

I couldn't blame her. In her eyes, I was going to Aspen to ski and hang out with our roommate. But in reality, I was stuck being Cindy's muse. Listening to all the things she wanted to say to Chumpy Chase. Something clicked in my head and it all made sense. I was the girl that made her look good. Shit, that was *it*. If she made me look like a total douche, then she looked good to Chase. Of course that was it. I had my work cut out for me.

"Great, the only seats in our section are window and middle. Well, guess you're next to B.O. man." She sent me a scathing glance.

"Fine, I don't mind."

I pushed my duffel bag up into the overhead storage and waited for her to squeeze in next to the window.

"Wait until he strikes up a conversation about his dead wife or his perfect children."

I pointed up to the open door of the storage above our heads. "Cindy, aren't you going to put your backpack up there?"

"Hell, no. I have my iPhone in here, all my make-up, and my wallet. It's going down at my feet." She shoved it under the seat in front of her.

"When we land in Denver, how are we getting to the cabin?"

"My dad has rented us a Toyota Sequoia. It will be there for us when we land."

"How far away is Aspen from Denver?"

"About four hours. We'll get there in time for a late dinner."

"Well, which type of burrito are you going to have?" I laughed. I thought it was funny—she didn't.

"My dad has a fully staffed kitchen at the cabin; we don't eat burritos." She turned toward the window, plugged her ears with her earphones, and started messing around with her iPhone.

Strike three. Now I understood why the big man upstairs didn't make me rich. He gave me the life I had to make me humble. I don't think Cindy knew what true struggles were. She grew up privileged—summers in Europe, winters skiing in Aspen. Her struggles were, like, which bracelet she was going to wear with which outfit. God forbid if she wore an outfit twice in the same month. In our dorm room, she took the entire closet *and* had an armoire imported from Italy to hold the rest of her clothes. I guess one of the benefits of having Cindy as a roommate was that, when we needed something to wear, she would pick out something from her closet and give it to us. Of course, she threw it up in your face when she needed a favor. *Remember when I gave you that cute lavender top from Christian Dior?* Those were the words of favors. She was never taught that people do things for you just because they were your friend. Pretty sad, huh? Maybe my reason for this trip was to show her that she didn't have to buy her friends. Wait—she bought my ticket to Denver. I'd better just stick to being her muse.

The plane took off and pressure raged heavy against my chest. The only thing I could relate it to was when you drop steeply on a rollercoaster. Luckily for me, the older gentleman next to me smelled like green apples mixed with caramel. He actually made me hungry. When I turned to him and inhaled through my nose, he looked at me and smiled.

"Sorry if I upset your friend. I am claustrophobic and can't sit confined with people on both sides of me."

"No problem, I understand." The space between us seemed to squeeze tighter.

He cleared his throat, "I'm John Samuel." He twisted and held out his hand.

"Wilson Mooney, nice to meet you." He had a nice, firm handshake.

His eyebrows scrunched together like two caterpillars kissing. "Wilson? Is that a family name?"

"No. More like a cruel joke; but definitely not a family name."

"You don't like it? I think it's pretty cool. It's different. How did your parents come up with that name?" *Oh come on, was he really interested in this story? Or was he trying to kill time in the air?*

"My mom played volleyball and loved the game; the day she found out she was pregnant, it was the big game against John

Muir High School, and the coaches didn't let her play. She named me after the ball. It was her homage to volleyball. She never played another day in her life."

"Really?"

"No, actually, I was named Wilson after the governor of California."

"Hum." He looked at me, almost believing until I cracked a smile.

"No, I wish I had a great story, but I don't." I turned and faced the seat in front of me. I didn't feel like telling him the truth about it. What person in their right mind would want to hear about my childhood? In particular, how I was named after a boy my mother wished was my father.

I glanced over to Cindy. Her eyes were closed, and she was bobbing her head back and forth; no doubt listening to some American Idol music she'd downloaded off iTunes. When it came to music, she and I were at two different ends of the spectrum. I listened to indie and alternative and she was into the more popular, commercialized, white-washed pop. Give me Ok Go, Vampire Weekend, or Death Cab for Cutie over Kelly Clarkson or Adam Lambert any day of the week. I needed music that provoked my mind and jump-started my intellect.

I pressed my head back in the seat and pushed the button to recline. Maybe the fact that Cindy was wrapped up in her music meant I was going to get a chance to sleep before we landed. It wasn't going to be long before I was stuck in a car with her for over four hours straight listening to her talk about Chase. I had just closed my eyes when the pilot's voice came over the speakers, informing us that we were about thirty minutes from landing in Denver. Well, at least I'll get to check my eyelids for holes for thirty minutes; better than nothing.

Heavy tapping on my shoulder jerked me from my deep slumber. It was Cindy.

"Wilson, we're in Denver. You need to wake up," she said as she stood waiting with her knee in her seat. Her earphones danced and tickled across my arm while she spoke and checked her text messages.

"Thanks," I turned to John, "Well, it was nice meeting you. Take care." I pushed to shake his hand.

"It's been my pleasure, Wilson." He grabbed my hand, shook it, then stood up to collect his carry-on. As the people thinned, I was able to bumble my way to the aisle and reach up to get my duffel bag. Cindy already had her backpack strapped across her shoulders and was ready to shuffle her way out of the plane. Man, it took forever to get off. Much longer than it took to get on. They needed to dismiss by rows and sections like they did when you boarded the plane. I guess it was much harder to control people once the plane stopped.

Organized chaos would be the only words to explain it—everyone vying for the perfect position; don't get stuck behind the shoe-removing stinky guy from seat 27C; but if you can, try and sandwich yourself between the two college-aged hot guys from row 24, seats A & B. God, that woman with the baby in seat 22C, please let her off first. If we were on *Survivor* she would be the first one voted off the island. I wouldn't hesitate to snuff out her fire.

Forty-five minutes later we were heading down the ramp and into the Denver terminal. My heart pounded heavy in my chest, chills rippled down my arms. I was just four hours away from being in the same town with Max Goldstein.

When we reached the open terminal there stood a guy with a sign, *Cindy and Wilson, I am your driver!*

"I thought your dad rented us a Sequoia to drive."

"Yeah, he did. Did you honestly think *I* was going to drive it there? It's snowing and cold. I don't drive in snow and cold weather." Cindy walked over to the driver dressed all in black with a white collared shirt and barked, "Grab my suitcase too."

She walked past him. I followed.

"Hi, I'm Wilson, thanks for picking us up." I reached my hand out.

He paused. "I'm Nick, you're welcome." He shook my hand and didn't let go before walking to the baggage claim.

"Wilson, please, he needs to pick up my suitcase." She pulled my arm and I lunged forward.

As long as I have known Cindy, I had never seen her outside of school functions. This was the first time, and I gotta say, I didn't like her. She was acting spoiled and rude, exactly like the girls Joanie and I would laugh at as they threw fits of rage and anger because they didn't get the grade they thought their daddies had bought for them. You know, the ones that didn't have to live by the rules because the rules were written for people like me, by people like them. I guess I saw her through different eyes at school; or maybe now that I didn't have Joanie as a buffer, I was seeing Cindy's true nature.

CHAPTER FOUR:

I turned to walk out to the checkpoint when I saw John, the man who sat next to me on the plane. He was smiling and shaking hands with some super hot guy. He noticed me and gave a little wave. I waved back. He pushed the guy's arm and they started walking over to me. He was breath-robbing, heart-stopping gorgeous. I pushed my hand to my mouth for a quick breath check. I didn't want to have skanky breath when he came over to me. My heart dropped into my stomach and my arms tingled with pins.

"Wilson, I hope you don't mind, I want to introduce you to my son, Wayne."

"Hi, nice to meet you." I stretched my hand out to him; my clammy, damp hand. It was so embarrassing.

"Likewise." My hand disappeared in his grasp. His contagious smile filled his face and overflowed his eyes.

"Your father likes my name," I blurted out, almost leaping toward him. *WHAT? Wait, what did I just say? Perfect, now he thinks I'm a complete idiot. Why am I such a disaster around guys?*

"I've never met anyone named Wilson before, great name. Are you vacationing in Denver?" He seemed interested in hearing what I was going to say.

"No. My roommate and I are going to Aspen to ski for a couple of days." I took my hand out of his and ran it through my dark blonde hair. I batted my eyelashes and cocked my head to the side. I balanced my feet on the outside edges of my tennis shoes, bending my ankles out and shoving my hands into the front pockets of my jeans.

"Wilson, come on we need to go!" Cindy yelled as she walked over to investigate who I was talking to.

"Okay, well I guess I gotta go, nice to meet you."
His blue eyes twinkled. "Yeah, it was... nice." I turned away waving as I started back to Cindy.

"Wait. Who. Was. That?" Cindy grabbed my arm and swung me around.

"John's son, Wayne."

"Who's John?"

"The guy who sat next to me in the plane. John Samuel." My chest tightened and I felt the blood rush to my face.

"Okay, well introduce me," she demanded as she pushed me toward him.

"Wayne?" I called before he turned, and that was when it happened. It was a total accident. It could have happened to anyone. It just so happened to be me. As Wayne turned to look at me his arm swung around and his hand brushed across my breasts. It didn't hurt; it was just so much more than embarrassing. My face blushed beet red, I didn't want to look him in the eyes.

"Oh I'm so sorry. I didn't know you were still standing there." His cheeks ran red.

"I wasn't. Anyway, this is Cindy, my roommate." I presented her using my hand to indicate a connection between them. "Cindy this is Wayne. Wayne...Cindy."

"It's my pleasure meeting you," Cindy whispered and pushed her hand to him.

"Nice to meet you, too." He looked at me widening his eyes. I couldn't help but signal back to him with a shrug. Embarrassed or not, I felt a connection with him. Wow, I just met him and we already have something in common, the distaste of Cindy's *I'm all that* attitude. I looked past him, and noticed his father calling him.

"Well, I'd better go; you know how parents with no patience can be." He turned to my roommate, "nice to meet you, Cindy." He turned back to me. "Hope to see you again, Wilson. I'm really sorry about knocking into your—you." His eyes narrowed, his face blushed and, for the first time, I felt a flutter for someone other than Max. He turned away and I watched his backside as he strutted over to his dad.

"Frickin' take a picture, it will last longer. The dude has to be gay. He didn't even make eye contact with me. He is definitely batting for the other team. All the straight guys *I* know make eye contact." She grabbed my arm and twisted me to walk the other way. I didn't answer her. I just smiled. That encounter would help me last four hours in the car with her.

Nick, our driver, led us to a midnight black Sequoia four-wheel-drive SUV. He seemed a little stressed out that he was driving us to Aspen. He loaded Cindy's suitcase into the back and ran around to her. She stood there waiting for him to open the door. Unbelievable. It was like she enjoyed making him her slave. If I hadn't seen it with my own eyes, I wouldn't have believed it. Somewhere between the Oakland airport and Denver, she had turned into one of those self-absorbed bitches you see on reality TV shows. You know the kind: they crash through the front door, making a grand entrance to a party and then start making out with your best friend's boyfriend. Or they throw a massive rag session because their friend bought the same shirt they bought and refused to take it back. Insignificant events in the realm of what normal people call the *real* world. She obviously didn't exist in the same reality that normal people did.

I knew how to deal with people like her. I have been dealing with them since I was eight years old and entered the boarding school milieu. You have to let what they say roll off your back; but stand up to them when you're backed into a corner. You walk a fine line when you're surrounded by self-absorbed, center-of-the-universe type people. Hang around them too much and you'd find yourself acting like they did; avoid them and you'd start wishing they would include you in their world; a very fine line.

Nick drove without saying a word. I thought it was weird. I wasn't the type of person to make small talk, but the trip to Aspen was over four hours and I didn't think I could take sitting in a car without hearing him say something. Not even a rumble from clearing his throat; nothing. So, being who I was, I took advantage of the actual gaps of time Cindy didn't fill with commentary about Chase, Aspen, or herself.

"Do you live in Aspen?" It was an innocent enough question. It wasn't like I was asking him out on a date or anything. His eyes went wide and his lips pulled across his teeth. His shoulders tightened. You'd think I just *hit* on him in front of his girlfriend. *Gosh, I was just making conversation that didn't have anything to do with Cindy.*

"No."

"Where do you live?" His eyes met mine in the rearview mirror, squinting to tell me to stop.

"Denver. I live in Denver," he mumbled.

"Excuse me, NICK—at what point did my father start paying you to talk? Wilson, he is here to get us to Aspen and that is it. He isn't being paid to tell you where he is from." She pushed her headphones in her ears and blared some music with a high-pitched, pre-pubescent girl's voice. She was going to damage her hearing turning those things up that high. Geez, I sounded just like Joanie telling me to turn the volume down on my iPod. My response was always the same, *okay, MOM.*

I think something went down between Cindy and Nick. *Yeah, I said it!* Someone had to. She was way too mean and vindictive to him. He was way too submissive. Maybe he didn't fall all over her when she tried to hit on him. Or maybe they dated and he did something to piss her off. My mind ran off with so many stories, in minutes I had her pregnant with twins and him running off with the butler's sixteen-year-old daughter, Mindy. When the relationship with Mindy went south, he came crawling back to Mr. Browler and asked to be Cindy's chauffeur. Self-inflicted torture for leaving her barefoot and pregnant.

"How did you start working for the Browler's?" I wanted to know. I needed to debunk the whole story line about Mindy. He looked back at me in the mirror, shifted to check Cindy, and then back to me.

"My mother and Cindy's father got married nine years ago. Her father is paying me to pick you up." A smile spread across his face. It looked like the blocks of humility shattered from his shoulders, and his whole demeanor shifted from burdened to liberated.

"Why do you let her treat you like dog shit?"

He shrugged his shoulders and leaned his head to the side. His eyes shifted between Cindy and me. I turned and noticed she had her eyes closed.

"She hates that her father married my mother." He kept shifting his eyes from the road to her.

"That's not your fault. Least she could do was see that you both are in the same boat," I preached.

"I know. But that's not going to happen anytime soon. I've been in her family for over ten years, and she still doesn't see me as more than a gold-digger's son."

"I'm sorry, that must really suck."

"No, I lived with her father and my mother while she was shipped off to boarding school. Now I'm a freshman at the University of Colorado."

"She never talked about her mom; is she still alive?"

"Yeah, I guess she lives in New York. Nobody ever sees her. She met a guy on the Internet and split. Left Cindy and nobody's heard from her since." His eyes grew, as he realized he might have shared too much information about Cindy's private life with me.

"Don't worry, I won't rat you out. Secret's safe with me." I winked at him and let him go back to driving.

"Thanks, I appreciate that."

I closed my eyes as the miles rolled by. I wanted to think about Wayne and Max, visualize them fighting each other over my affections. Instead, all I could think about was Cindy. Damn it! She was asleep and she *still* monopolized my mind. How she must've felt, knowing her mother left her for a guy off the Internet. Maybe that's why she acted the way she did. It was one thing to have someone take you away from your mother, but to have her just up and abandon you—wow, that was messed up.

There was a small part of me that believed my mother wanted me. Up until I turned twelve, I believed she was doing everything in her power to get me back. After that I gave up on believing. Cindy and I had more in common than I wanted to admit. We both had really screwed up life donors.

The Sequoia swerved to the right, enough to wake me up from my cat-nap.

"What the hell is going on?" Cindy screamed with her earphones still plugged into the sides of her head.

"Nothin'," Nick mumbled.

"It's so obvious I'm not talking about the space between your ears. I'm talking about your crazy driving." She pulled the earphones out and waited for his explanation.

"I need to take a break, go to the bathroom." His face blushed, I saw him glance at me in the mirror.

"Fine, I could use the break to stretch my legs. Next time, warn me." She leaned back and wrapped the earphone wires around her iPhone. She cursed him under her breath.

He swerved onto the exit and found the first gas station across the street. I was never one that liked to pee in a gas station bathroom, but when you gotta go, you have to deal with the filthy, oil-stained fixtures and urine-caked toilets.

I followed Cindy to the restroom. I looked at the door; just my luck, it was a unisex restroom. They were the worst. You didn't get a choice on which toilet to use. If someone didn't flush, you were S.O.L. The door behind me swung open and there stood Nick. He'd used the other restroom across the hall. I didn't feel like following him, but I had to go, so I slipped in behind him and into the restroom without touching the door.

Fifteen minutes later, we were back on the highway and heading to beautiful Aspen. I wanted to forget about Cindy's screwed up relationship with her mother. I didn't have room in my head to sort the memories of Max, Wayne, and the artificial memories I'd created of her mother slamming the door in her face at eight years old. All I wanted to do was close my eyes and see Wayne in the airport, to put him into social situations I projected in my mind—ski slopes and lodges with cozy fires filling huge stone fireplaces—to see myself laughing at his jokes as he rubbed my sore feet.

Then, just as Wayne was about to pull off my other sock, Max showed up in my fantasy. I don't even know how he got there. He just appeared in front of us.

"What is going on here?" Max asked Wayne. Those familiar fluttering butterflies decided to show up in my stomach.

"I'm rubbing my girlfriend's feet," Wayne told him. The butterflies burst from my gut and flew up and out to the open air.

"Who are you?" Wayne put my foot down on the cushion of the chair and stood up. They faced each other with barreled chests and eyes that stared each other down. Wow, I'd never imagined two hot guys fighting over me before.

"*I'm* her husband."

My eyes flew open and my heart pounded so hard it was about to come bursting from my chest. I sat up, pulling the seatbelt tight across my neck. I felt the pressure as it rose into the back of my throat, the excitement of a daydream that was too much.

"What's wrong? Are you okay?" Cindy blurted out. I couldn't answer her at first. My voice was caught in the huge bubble of shock that had wedged itself above my larynx. There was no way I was going to tell her what had just happened in my fantasy. I needed to come up with something else. I wished Joanie was there. I scanned my mind for some lame excuse for my jerking awake.

"I was falling, in my dream. Guess it's the motion of the car." *Good cover up. Way to think fast.* I took a deep breath and thought about what I had just witnessed in my dream.

"You need to drive better!" She stared Nick down. I waited for her to pop him upside the head, but she didn't.

"No, his driving is fine." The guilt for even mentioning his driving swelled in my gut.

"Sorry about that." He looked at me in the rearview mirror and flared his nostrils.

"Don't worry, it wasn't your fault," I answered his apology and looked away.

"Of course it was! Everything is his fault," Cindy said.
She must hate him. It wasn't his fault that her father chose to marry his mom. The more I thought about how wicked she was to him, the more I couldn't take it. I was done holding my tongue. This poor guy was taking the brunt of Cindy's anger at her father. Someone had to step in.

"You need to give him a break! You've been nothing but rude to him since we arrived in Denver."

"What? Why in the hell are you so interested in him or how I treat him? Please, if I didn't know any better I would think you'd want to hook up with him," she spat as she pushed her back into the door and faced me with a scathing look. Her lips drew tight across her teeth as her eyes closed to a squint.

"Come on, you've been on his case since you saw him at the airport. He hasn't done anything to you." Confidence surged through my body and I felt the need to fight this out until she saw what I was saying.

"Please—I see where you're going with this and, as honorable as you're trying to be, you have no idea what *this* is between him and me." She pushed her pointed finger back and forth between her chest and the front seat where Nick was sitting.

"Well, you might be surprised at what I know," the words flew from my mouth before I had a chance to look at Nick in the rearview mirror. His eyes narrowed. His face radiated a flash of red that rolled up from his jowls. I stopped, my lips pressed closed. I'd promised him I wouldn't rat him out.

"What? What do you know? What did you tell her?" She bounced her scowl between Nick and me.

Backpedal, I need to backpedal because of my big mouth. Think... come up with some brainless excuse for saying what I did. Before I got a chance, Nick covered me.

"Like I would even have a chance to talk to her." He turned around, glancing away from the road long enough to make eye contact with her. "You are so insecure. I had nothing to do with our parents getting married!" He pulled to the side of the highway and turned to her; he wasn't done spewing. Cindy must have seen red, because she just went off the hook.

"Shut up you frickin' gold-digging tool. You had everything to do with them getting married." She swung her arm up through the cab of the car and tried to hit him.

"Oh, no way, I am through taking your crap. I've felt guilty for long enough. I didn't have anything to do with *your* father shipping you off to boarding school. I fought for you. I'm done with feeling guilty because my parents got back together." He kept slapping her fists away from him. I just moved back into the farthest corner of the Sequoia.

"You're so full of bull crap, you didn't fight for me. I watched them the night they decided to send me away. They were concerned that I was going to hurt *you*. So instead of sending *you* away, they sent me—away. They wanted you more than me." She looked at me, tears rolling heavy down her cheeks. I'd never seen her cry before, not like this. These were real tears that trailed and marked her cheeks with evidence of her sincere anguish.

Nick was ruthless, "Paa-leese, just stop. You're so ridiculous. The self-pity has gotta go. It isn't going to work—I've known you too long." He was like a caged tiger that had been taunted for the last time. Three and a half hours in the car with her must have been the straw that broke the camel's back, because he didn't let up.

"You are such a self-centered bitch. Do you honestly think you have that much power over me? Everything I have EVER done for you was because *our* father asked me to. Not because I liked you or wanted anything from you." He pushed the driver's door open and got out onto the snow-plowed road. The chill of six degrees below zero flooded the SUV. The door slammed shut and Cindy pushed the switch of the automatic locks.

"I can't believe he's my half-brother," Cindy grumbled under her breath as she adjusted her iPhone on her lap and pulled her jacket up from by her feet. I had nothing to say. No comeback or snide remark.

CHAPTER FIVE:

Nick kept walking—I was still in shock that they were even blood-related. Cindy unbuckled her seat belt, jumped into the driver's seat, and started the engine. I could have sworn I saw a slight smile on her face.

"I better pick him up. I don't want to get blamed for his frostbitten stupidity."

"If he's your half-brother why do you talk about him that way? Do you really hate him that much?" I looked in the rearview mirror to catch her expression.

"I don't hate him. It's not like I wish him dead. I just don't like him. Come on, Wilson, he ended up with the perfect family; his mom and my dad hooked up in high school, she took off, and then ten years later she showed up on my dad's doorstep with Nick. Just goes to show you a one-night stand can work out." Her eyes filled the rearview mirror.

What's that supposed to mean? A one-night stand can work out. I felt myself boil inside. She knew I was born because of a one-night stand. I wanted to scream at her, tell her what a spoiled brat she was, but I didn't; instead, I swallowed and played along.

"I'm an outsider and all I can see is that you hate him enough to let him stand out there in sub-freezing temperatures." She put the Sequoia into gear and started toward him. He was walking at a pretty fast pace. His face was glossed bright red. The edges of his ears were the unfortunate victim of being hatless.

Cindy lowered the passenger's window and yelled across, telling him to get into the car before he froze to death. He kept walking.

"Come on, I'm sorry you're pissed off." Even when she apologized it was never her fault.

"I'll freeze before I get back into that car with you." His breath hung heavy before it crumbled and dissipated into the winter air.

The car rolled slowly, keeping pace with him. "Please. I can't drive in the snow. You're gonna make me kill innocent people." He shook his head back and forth and I knew why.

Cindy never took responsibility for anything. As long as I'd known her, she had always been that way. Nick didn't see her every day like I did. His skin wasn't as calloused as mine. If she broke a fingernail, it would be someone else's fault. That was Cindy.

Three years ago, we were collecting canned food for the Rumbling Tummies Food Bank and she volunteered to be one of the helpers who separated the food into categories. The day we were supposed to go, I got super sick with the flu and ended up staying at the dorm. They told her to stack the canned meats on the second shelf from the bottom. *Easy, right? Wrong.* She ended up stacking it on the third shelf with the canned soups.

She stacked fifty cans of Spam in three different pyramids and rearranged the soups in alphabetical order. When they asked her about it, she blamed her lack of following directions on me. *Can you believe that?* She told them she stacked the Spam with the soup because the cans of tuna fish packed in water reminded her of a very sick friend who had to stay back at the dorms. I still don't know how tuna packed in water reminded her of me. I assume it had to do with the boycott I started over 'dolphin safe' brands like Stark Tuna and the Ocean's Chicken. But you know what happens when you assume? You make an ASS out of U and ME. That was her in a nut shell…or a tuna fish can. At the end of the day, they thanked her and asked her to refrain from volunteering for their organization in the future suggesting that she might have a better fit with the OCD-anonymous group of Alameda County. Up until that day, I'd never heard of someone being fired from a volunteer position before.

At last, Cindy was able to get Nick into the SUV. She promised she wouldn't be rude and would try and give him the benefit of the doubt. I think it was the fact that she crashed the SUV into the side of a snow bank as she tried to cut him off from walking away. The last hour and fifteen minutes of the drive to Aspen was awkward and quiet.

I was glad when we pulled into a neighborhood that resembled Beverly Hills on steroids. It wasn't like I had ever seen a Beverly Hills house in real life, but having seen them on television, I could imagine how huge these places were. Nick pulled up at a massive entry to a gated community that had a booth as large as a small house. A security guard opened a window and asked a series of questions. I was waiting for the guy to ask for a copy of his birth certificate and a blood sample next. Instead, Nick pulled out his driver's license and a Starlingwood pass. After he proved he belonged there, he was able to enter the gated community of monstrous estates which only very few of the wealthy elite owned.

My heart was pounding. If Max's family owned a cabin here, I could only wonder where it was; and, if his family was wealthy enough to have a house up here, what was he doing working at Wesley? Maybe it was fate that he worked at my school. Maybe the universe wanted us to be together. Or kismet, or—destiny.

We drove for another twenty minutes through pimped-out cribs that only a few gazillionaires could afford. Finally, we turned down a long winding driveway and arrived at anything but a cabin; it was a mansion. This monster had a four-car garage. We could've driven the SUV right through the front doors. This manor was two stories high with humungous windows facing the snow-filled four acres that we'd passed as we drove in. The front porch was as big as a parking lot, with the largest chandelier I had ever seen. *Who had a chandelier out on their front porch?* I have to say, I was intimidated.

The only thing that went through my mind was how pretentious these people must be. I started to run tallies through my head as I got out and grabbed my duffel bag from the back. How many hungry refugees from Darfur could that chandelier feed? The Italian marble from the porch could rebuild a neighborhood in Louisiana. The front doors could build at least four schools in Mexico. I had to stop. This weekend would drive me crazy if I did that. I had to remember where I was. But, if just the front porch alone could help rebuild Haiti, I wondered what the inside could do?

"Come on, just leave your bag. We have staff to do that." Cindy grabbed my arm and pulled me to the steps. I held back and started to remove my shoes before I stepped on the marble.

Her face twisted. "What are you doing?"

My balance wasn't the greatest. "I'm taking my shoes off."

"You take your shoes off now your feet will freeze before you get to the front door." She swung her arm around to get me to follow her.

I turned to Nick who was still getting out of the SUV. I wanted to tell him to come in with us, but didn't want to stir up any more animosity between him and Cindy. I walked up the marble steps and across the massive front porch. Cindy pulled on the ginormous door and it swung open to soft, classical music welcoming us to the Chateau Browlers. It was a bit much. Cindy wasn't the least bit phased.

"Hello! We're finally here! Dad—Miranda—hello?" She passed under the oversized double staircase and around the colossal table holding a flower arrangement that would make any FTD franchise jealous. I was still at the front door trying to take off my scruffy, knock-off UGGs.

"Well, guess they must've gone out—will you stop it?" She tossed her hands in the air and spun them in circles, trying to get me to follow her. I shoved my foot back into my boot and followed her under the imperial staircase to the kitchen.

It wasn't your average kitchen; not even close. It was a restaurant kitchen. The stove looked like a contraption from outer space. The refrigerator and freezer were two separate appliances sprawled next to the bathtub-sized sink.

"Great, my dad and his wife won't be back until Sunday night!" She picked up a handwritten note from the counter and waved it above her head. Her face went deep red and her eyes glossed over.

"I frickin' knew it. I bet she took him away because I was coming this weekend. She is such a bitch!" She pulled her phone from her pocket.

I didn't know what to do, she was completely devastated. What kind of parent wasn't around when their kid came home from boarding school for the weekend? If there was one good thing that came out of my absent parents, it was my grandparents; they were always there for me. Anytime I came home from school, my grandma would have a package of my favorite cookies in the car when she picked me up. My bed was always turned down and Nemo, my teddy bear, would be waiting for me. Yeah, up until she died she always put Nemo on my bed when I came home.

I watched as Cindy paced across the kitchen to the dining room, her voice hurried and cracking. It was messed up that she came all that way from California to see her dad and he didn't have the decency to wait for her to show up. She looked like a lost little girl in a busy shopping center, utterly confused and desperate to be found. She hung up her phone, wiped her eyes with her arm.

"Forget him. He is such a frickin' A-hole! He said he had to fly out to New Mexico, problem with one of the stores. It's such bullshit—another excuse for being a screwed up parent."
I still didn't know what to say, so I told her what I thought might make her feel ok, maybe validate her frustration. I wanted to come up with something that would help her feel better. She wasn't the nicest person, but in the spirit of common courtesy the situation would warrant a couple of nice words. You would've thought.

"Sorry your dad's an A-hole."
Ok so it wasn't the best choice of words, but under the circumstances.

"Don't be sorry for something you have no control over. This is how my relationship has been with my dad my whole life. I'm the perfect example of a privileged, throw-away kid."

"Don't say that." It was so pathetic, I almost couldn't take it.

"It's the truth. Every major holiday, he's either gone or busy. Even when he's here, he's not really here. He's either on the phone or working on the computer in his office. He could never just hang out with me. On parent visiting days at school, everyone else had actual parents who came and saw them. You know what I got? A certified letter with some lame excuse about why he couldn't come and see me." She crumpled the letter and tossed it into the sink. "At least you can understand how I feel. Your family life is about as messed up as mine." She walked over and patted me across my back.

That, right there, was the difference between Cindy and me. I never considered my life any more messed up than the next person's. I was grateful that my grandparents made the choices they did when I was little. I wouldn't ask for *any* part of my life to be changed, because that would affect my life today; and I have to say, my life wasn't all that bad. Cause and effect—things I did created and fed what the outcome was going to be. For instance, if my mom and dad weren't so F'ed up, I wouldn't have ended up at Bethany School for Girls. I wouldn't have met Joanie and we wouldn't have been best friends. If I didn't go to Wesley, I wouldn't have had Max Goldstein for Government my senior year, and that just wasn't acceptable. I could've ended up in some jacked-up school, dating some tweaker who believed we were all put on this Earth to be farmed for food by aliens that worshiped the Hale-Bop comet, and that would've been worse than rotting in hell.

"This weekend is about fun right? I'm not going to let him screw it up." Cindy disappeared into a room off the kitchen. "What's your choice of drink?" her voice echoed from the other room.

"Um, how about a Diet Coke?" It didn't register with me, until she poked her head out and gave me the *'are you really that stupid?'* look.

"WTF, Wilson, I'm not talking about *that* type of drink. Get with it now." She rolled her eyes and disappeared again. I heard bottles clang together and shuffle against the shelving.

"Will you come in here and help me? I've only got two hands."

"Sorry." I rushed into the room. I expected it to be a pantry. Boy was I wrong. It was a mini liquor store. The only thing it was missing was the cash register. It was the size of a bedroom. The wall had shelves filled with all different types of alcohol. The back of the room had two huge glass-door refrigerators filled with different types of beers and wines. Between them, rack after rack of dark wine; and to my left, the hard liquor mixtures and potion bottles. Anything we wanted under the sun lived in that room. I wondered how many down-and-outers or alcoholics would have thought they had died and gone to heaven. I noticed Cindy already had tequila and vodka cradled in her arms. She wasn't just thinking of snagging a couple of beers and catching a slight buzz, she was determined to party hard tonight and worry about the leftovers later.

She poked her chin toward the other side of the room. "Grab the cranberry juice on the third shelf and the margarita mix below that. I like the strawberry one."

"Won't your dad notice it missing?" Maybe it was a naïve question, but one I felt obligated to ask.

"Hello-o, don't worry. He doesn't even come in here. Besides, we'll make sure the kitchen staff restocks the missing bottles before we leave. So when you're done playing the innocent goodie-two-shoes friend, put that down in the kitchen and grab some more. I've gotta make calls to all of my seasonal friends." She pulled a dark brown bottle off of the shelf.

Seasonal friends? What the hell was a seasonal friend? I didn't know such things existed. I was curious to know the definition. I could only imagine it would read something like this:

sea-son-al friend: [*see-zuh-nl frend*] A person who fulfills the needy voids of ostentatious people who travel to Aspen in the winter months for binge drinking and snow skiing.

It makes me wonder what adjective she put before my friendship.

I had pulled the last couple of bottles from the "liquor store" and was turning to walk out when I ran into Nick. The bottles squished my chest and his arms swung around me.

"Oh, Ouch! What the—" I stopped.

"Sorry. You okay? I didn't mean to stand in your way. I was coming in to find Cindy. This is usually her first stop when she gets here." He backed up and grabbed the bottles from my arms.

"She went to call some of her friends." I wrapped my arms around my chest and slid my hands into my armpits. I was hoping the sharp pains and numbness would subside.

He walked toward the boatload of booze we had piled on the counter. "Oh yeah, she wants to rage tonight. Let me guess, her dad left her a note, again."

"Yeah." I was always good at keeping conversations interesting.

"Seasonal friend calls right?" He put the bottles down.

"What's with that? Seasonal friends. It sounds so…detached."

"It's how she compartmentalizes her life. She doesn't have to invest in her seasonals. They all do it. It's different here."

"What's up with you then? You're so different from her."

"I don't know how different we really are. She has her agendas and I have mine." He walked over to the refrigerator and pulled it open, looking at the contents. It seemed ridiculous to stand there with the door wide open when the entire front was made of glass.

"You seem so much more down to earth than her. She always has reasons for what she does; never—just because." He handed me a Coke.

"We all have skeletons in our closets. Some of us are just better at hiding them behind the hangers filled with clothes."

"Yeah, right, you don't seem like the type of guy who has a pile of femur bones stuffed behind your collared shirts and navy blue blazers."

"How did you know I have navy blue blazers?" He smiled and, for the first time since I stepped foot in their "cabin," I was comfortable. I cracked the Coke open and took a swig. I actually found myself wishing I was hanging out with him instead of Cindy.

CHAPTER SIX:

Wish in one hand and spit in the other, see which one fills up faster. That was what my grandpa used to tell me. Even though the thought of it was grosser than gross, I understood what it meant. My grandpa always had little catchphrases like that. That was his way of teaching me life lessons. I could feel it in my bones, this weekend was going to be one of those life lessons.

Cindy strutted into the kitchen. I could tell she was determined and on a mission.

"There you are. Nick, would you call some of your more mature friends? Not that one that walks around hitting on all of my friends. Or the belching one." She stared through him.

"What about the one that—."

"What about that Calvin guy? He's cute and if my friends know he's coming with some of his friends," she interrupted him.

"Calvin? His family is in town this weekend. I'll give him a call but I doubt he'll come."

"Whatever; just make it work so we're balanced with guys." She went into the liquor room and started shuffling bottles.

"What's wrong with having more ladies than guys?"

I liked Nick; not in an *oh my God, he is so hot* way, but in a *wow, he's cool enough to hang out with for the weekend* way. Just knowing he was going to be around made the thought of hanging out with Cindy so much easier.

It wasn't long before the doorbell was ringing and Cindy was downing her second strawberry margarita. She was putting it on real thick for her seasonal friends. Treating Nick like crap, ignoring me, and acting like a total tease to the guys that showed up. I was pretty much done. It wasn't fun to hang out as wallpaper while she went on and on about how much her life sucked at Wesley. I grabbed my second can of Coke and went upstairs. I figured I could find a quiet room to call Joanie and tell her I arrived safely in Aspen.

It was around the fourth door on the right side when I found a room that wasn't occupied by people *hooking up*. I was beginning to think the life lesson for this weekend was "never help with a party where the hostess is a total lush." I'm not a square. I've partied, plenty of times. I just didn't want to let my guard down with Cindy. I didn't want to wake up tomorrow to the venomous poison that seemed to spew from her pie-hole so freely up here in Aspen. There you go—that lack of trust thing with me again.

I pushed the door shut and pulled my phone from my pocket. I had one more number to press and hit send when the door flew open and Nick came sauntering in.

"Oh, hey—looks like you found my room." He had two drinks in his hands.

"Sorry, I didn't know this was your room. Just wanted to escape the loud noise of American Idol and call my friend. All the other rooms appeared to be taken." I pushed my phone in my pocket and started to leave.

"You don't have to go. I know what you mean. I was on my way up here to chill out and escape too. Someone handed me this drink, told me it was a Skip and Go Naked. Would you like it?" He pushed it toward me.

"Skip and Go Naked? Almost sounds like a cheap pick-up line." I grabbed the drink and looked around the room.

"We could call it Walk Completely Clothed, but that's a crazy name for a drink. I guess they wouldn't sell as many if it was called that." He stood in the middle of the room watching me look at all the pictures of his friends on the wall.

I pointed to a picture thumb-tacked onto the bulletin board above his desk. "Is that you?"

His chest brushed across my shoulder as he pointed with the beer in his hand. "Yeah, and that's my buddy Calvin. He should be here tonight." The space between our bodies didn't exist. *Whoa—he was way too close.* I backed away from the desk and looked around the room to find something to change the subject.

"High school yearbook?" I pulled it off the shelf and sat on his bed. I figure if I buried my nose in the pages he would get the hint. He came and sat next to me, a completely awkward moment. I didn't want him to think I was leading him on. Totally not the vibe I was trying to send him.

He took a drink from his beer and set it down. "Yeah, my senior year." He snatched the book from my lap and thumbed through it then closed it. "Not much to see, just delinquents and punks. And that's just the girls. The guys are all much worse." I reached for it and he held it up high in the air.

"What are you afraid of? Scared to let me see the jacked haircut your mom gave you before your senior pictures?" I stood up and reached across him trying to get the book. I felt his hand go around my waist and heard a knock at the door before it swung open. We both froze, expecting to see Cindy in the doorway. It was a relief to see it was someone I didn't know. Nick twisted around and met him as he came into the room.

"Hey man, how are you? Didn't know if you were going to make it." Nick grabbed his hand and they did a guy shoulder-bump handshake. I could never get why guys did that. Maybe a hug was just too emotional for them.

"Well, I couldn't miss this one. Heard from the guys there were going to be hot chic—." The guy looked at me.

"Oh yeah Calvin, this is Wilson. She's a friend of Cindy's."

"Nice to meet you." He pushed his hand out to me. I shook it. There was something about his eyes.

"You look familiar to me. We've met before," I blurted out, pulling him closer to me. He flinched; I think I scared the life out of him.

"I don't think so, but it's nice to meet you." He let go of my hand and turned to Nick. "I hope you don't mind, I brought my brother. He's grabbing a beer."

"No problem. I didn't know your brother was in town." They continued like I wasn't even in the room. It was better for me anyway, perfect opportunity to escape. I grabbed my drink and headed to the door. I didn't make it half way there before I was stopped in my tracks.

"There you are bro. Nick, this is my brother Max. Max, this is Nick…and Wilson, right?" I shook my head up and down, my eyes glued on Max. My heart skipped and missed beats as our eyes met. Unbelievable, it was him. Mr. Goldstein, *my* Max. My mouth was dry as a desert and the pit of my stomach released all the butterflies that were waiting to greet him.

"Nick, nice to finally meet you," Max said as he shook his hand. Then our eyes met as he reached out and gently grabbed my hand. "My pleasure." I stared at him, and didn't say a word.

Calvin shrugged and interrupted, "I didn't grab a drink, so I'm going downstairs and getting something. Introduce me to the redhead hanging out by the kitchen." Calvin slapped Nick across the shoulder. Max watched them leave. He turned slowly as his earth green eyes traced the ground to me. I almost couldn't breathe.

"Wow, I can't believe you're here. I had no idea that Calvin was taking me to Cindy Browler's place." He looked at me, I still stood tongue-tied. What was I going to say? All the words I'd practiced evaporated in his eyes. He smelled so good, all I wanted to do was touch him.

"Hi, Mr. Goldstein." *Come on Wilson, hold it together. Do not lose it, not in front of him. I had that Naked, Go drink in my hand. Crap, I totally hope he will overlook the underage thing.*

"Wilson, please call me Max. We're not at school."

He smiled his half crooked smile and his eyes twinkled. "Besides, it makes me feel old. Are you going to drink that?" His hand reached for the long, slender glass filled with the Skip and Go Naked I hadn't even tasted yet. His fingers brushed and touched mine as they landed in between. He stared into my eyes.

"No, I wasn't, someone just handed it to me, I swear." I blinked and looked away.

I was such a baby. What a square. Busted from a government teacher I had the total hots for. Prepare for the lecture, it's coming. Wait, wait, here it comes.

"What's it called?" He took the glass from my hand.

"Skip and Go Naked." He looked at me, smiled, put it to his nose and inhaled.

"May I taste it?"

"Sure. I couldn't tell you what it tastes like. I haven't even put it to my mouth."

I watched him press the drink to his pouty, wet, inviting bottom lip and tilt the glass as the Naked went Skipping down his throat. Holy crap, for the sake of Pete, I wanted to be that drink. His shirt pulled at his bicep as he held the glass to his mouth, his neck exposed, I could swear he was inviting me to press my lips to his throat. I swallowed hard and smacked my lips.

"Not bad. Thanks." He handed it back to me. He took his hand and ran it through his hair. It fell perfect across his forehead. *Frickin' kill me now, hello, stimulus overload.*

"You're welcome."

He stared at me, and for a moment, time froze. An exchange of pure magnetism forced its way between us, enchanting me with the possibility of being with him beyond my fanciful thoughts.

"I'd better get back to my brother before I—before *he* gets into any trouble." He walked out of the room, leaving me with my half-swallowed Skippin' Naked.

I wasn't going to take a drink of the Going Naked Skippin' but, at this point, I needed something to cool the raging desires that kept catching my breath low in my throat and ripping it out. By the time I looked down at my glass, it was empty and I was feeling numb. I went downstairs to the kitchen and asked the person making the mixed drinks for another Naked Skipper. *Funny they seemed to know exactly what I was asking for.* Pretty quickly, I had another drink in my hand.

I couldn't help but look for him. God, he was so everything to me. I would give up food for him. If he told me that I couldn't eat pizza anymore, I would stop. He had no idea how much power he had over me. That was a scary thought. I was *never* one of *those* girls before him. You know the kind: they can't talk about anything but the guy they're crushing on. They become obsessed with getting close to them. Holy cow, now that was me! I was the freaky stalker girl. That was the one thing I *never* wanted to become—obsessed with a guy. I never wanted to let someone hold that type of power over me. Well, I've blown that deal. Good thing I didn't make it with the devil because he would have cashed in and I would be perspiring in hell right now.

"Oh My God Wilson, did you see who's here?" Cindy staggered over to me.

"Yeah, Mr. Goldstein."

"How did you know? And where have you been?" she slurred her words.

I hate to assume but I was going to do it anyway. She had to be on her third or fourth margarita.

"I went upstairs to call Joanie." *Which I got sidetracked from and didn't do.*

"I hope she's not too upset that you're here with me and she's not."

"I didn't get through to her. I'll try tomorrow." I looked past her, trying to find *him*.

"I can't wait to tell everyone back in Cali that Mr. Goldstein came to my house to party." She flipped her hair and swung around.

"Cindy! Wait, you can't do that." The pores of my skin opened and I began to perspire. Okay, I was sweating. If she told anyone he was here, then he would lose his job and I would lose my one good reason to stay at Wesley.

"What the hell? Why not? Don't you see the advantage I have now? No more B's in his class. I have to say, my "keeping quiet" should be worth a solid A in his class. Maybe even a letter of recommendation to Stanford. Whatcha think?"

I couldn't tell her what I really thought because, if I did, she would kick me to the snowy curb. But before I could stop myself the words came shooting from my mouth; and the couple of I'm Running Naked drinks didn't help.

"You're such a bitch." She leaned back, her face white as a ghost. "What the hell did you think I would say? Go for it. Nick was right, you are the most self-absorbed, conniving, heartless, demon of a person I have *ever* met. I don't think you're even capable of having a shred of common decency. The fact that you're willing to blackmail Mr. Goldstein is so frickin' twisted and pathetic. I can't stand here and look at your face any longer, I'm out." I walked away feeling pretty good that I'd released all the angst that had been bubbling in my gut the entire day. I glanced back and she hadn't moved. She stood there, struck by my words that were as sharp as daggers, and they'd sliced her down to the bone.

I had to find Max and tell him what Cindy was planning. I had to protect him. I couldn't lose him to her petty, stupid games. I scanned the living room, thinking maybe he was hanging with Nick; but no. I kept walking the entire main floor of the house. I couldn't find him anywhere; no sign of Nick or Calvin, either. I ended up at the bottom of the stairs. Upstairs was all just bedrooms and bathrooms. My heart fell into my gut. There were alot of really pretty girls here—I didn't want to think about it. I didn't want to think he was so shallow that he would hook up with a girl he just met. Nevertheless, my feet took my body up the stairs. My heart pounded loudly with each step. I could feel it aching while my mind kept recycling a forged vision of pushing open Nick's bedroom door and finding Max there with another girl who wasn't me. I didn't want to do this, but I had to find him. I reached for the first door knob, twisted it, and pushed the door open.

"Sorry, didn't know someone was in here." I looked to see it wasn't him, then shut the door. *One down, three more to go.* I twisted the knob on the second door, but it was locked. I knocked, but nobody answered. Great, that was easy and less embarrassing. The third door wasn't closed all the way and I could hear voices. They sounded like they were talking, so I pushed the door open. It was Calvin with the redhead he was trying to hook up with earlier. They were sitting on Cindy's bed looking at a photo album.

"Oh, sorry." I started to pull the door closed.

"HEY YOU, WAIT! It's Wilma right? Remember me, I'm Calvin, we met earlier—you were with Nick and my brother," he slurred his words and was way too loud. He'd obviously had too much to drink.

"Yeah, that's me, but it's Wilson." I kept pulling the door shut.

"No, hold on, wait, did you see what you did with my brother? Because I can't find him, anywhere." He stumbled forward and threw his hands in the air and looked around at the ground. What a shining example of the privileged elite of our society. I just hope he doesn't puke on my shoes.

"No, I didn't see where *I* put him. But if I stumble across him I'll tell him you're looking for him." I was losing my patience with this guy. He did the, *I'm totally wasted stagger dance* before he tried to open his eyes to look at me.

"Well, if you happen to remember where you hid him, tell him he's gonna need to find another ride home tonight. Okay, Wanda?" By this time the redheaded, one-night-stand girl was over grabbing him, helping him stand up.

"No problem, *Carson,* and my name is not Wilma, Wanda or any other lame W name you come up with. It's Wilson, W-I-L-S-O-N. Like the frickin' sports balls you play with." Calvin looked at me and stumbled back laughing. I slammed the door. If he was going to be my future brother-in-law he'd better learn my name, damn it. He was such a tool.

I'd struck out with the first three rooms. I was relieved and anxious at the same time. Relieved because I didn't find him in a room with another girl, but anxious because he was nowhere to be found. I stopped in front of Nick's bedroom door. It was shut but I could hear a group of people laughing and talking over each other. I would have knocked but they were so loud, I doubt they would've heard me anyway. So I invited myself in; nobody even noticed. There was a group of guys surrounding Nick's computer.

Holy Mary, Mother of God, there he was. Smiling and leaning back laughing. His black hair motioning for me to come closer with every movement he made. His hand owned the beer he held, his Levi's tight and snug exactly where I liked them to be. His shirt clung tight on his biceps and wrinkled at his waist. Yummy, my mouth watered. Endorphins crawled up my throat and waited to take him down. I felt like I was going to burst. *Breathe, breathe, inhale, now exhale.* I guess I was kinda loud catching my breath, because he turned and looked at me. His face went blank as he set down his beer. Now I don't know what was on that computer screen, and quite frankly I could give a rat's ass because, at that moment, I had the attention of the most gorgeous guy in the room.

CHAPTER SEVEN:

I inched toward the throng of guys hovering around the computer. I didn't want any of them to turn around, but I guess it was too late. They saw Max turn and every head spun to look at me. I froze, thinking if I didn't move they wouldn't see me, like I could really blend into the surroundings. I must've looked like a total jackass.

"Wilson! What's up? Lookin' for Cindy? 'Cuz she's not here." Nick intercepted me and turned me toward the door.

"No, actually I was coming up here to—" I stopped. *Did I really want to tell him who I came up to see? No, so I lied*, "I thought I left my drink up here." I looked around the room, haphazard as possible.

"I didn't see it. Why don't you head downstairs and get another one. It was a Skip and Go Naked, right?" Nick talked fast, trying to convince me to leave. He didn't want me to see what was on the computer screen. Funny, I didn't even look over at it. My eyes were focused on Max and the space that surrounded him. I turned toward the door to leave.

"Appreciate the beers, nice party, but I gotta go; getting up early to hit the slopes. Thanks, man." I heard Max tell Nick.

Their hands clasped into a firm handshake and Nick mumbled something back to him. I could feel Max's energy behind me as I walked down the hall. I wanted to look back so bad, see if he was following me. A ball of anticipation spiraled in the back of my throat. I felt him hurry to catch up.

"Wilson, wait up. Are you going home? I could give you a ride." He stopped me on the balcony between the staircases that circled down to the entry. He scratched at his head, pushed his hair away from his eyes, and shoved his hands in his pockets, glimpsing to see my reaction. *He can't do that to me. How am I supposed to concentrate on his question?* He continued talking, "I mean, I don't think it's a good idea, you driving after having some drinks." Out of the corner of my eye I saw Cindy below. I swallowed real hard, cleared my mind, and grabbed his arm.

"Mr. Gol—Max, there is something I've gotta tell you." I dragged him to the door across the hall. I didn't know if it was a closet or what; I didn't care. *Well, truthfully, I wouldn't have been able to handle being in a closet with him, being that close, smelling him. My head swam just thinking about it.* Fortunately, it was a super-humungous bathroom. I pushed him in and locked the door. Fifty people could hang out in this bathroom and there still would be room enough for a dance floor. Four sinks across the wall, each with its own heated towel rack. An oversized leather sofa like one you would normally find in a person's living room sat across from the sinks. There was a door separating us from a bathtub—one the size of a Smartcar—and the rest of the bathroom.

I paced back and forth, not knowing how to start. How was I going to tell him something that could potentially screw up the rest of my senior year with him at Wesley? The back of my head tingled with pins and needles and my hands were damp with perspiration. I could feel the blood drain from my face as I looked him in the eyes. Damn, this was going to be harder than I thought. What a disaster! Alone with him in a locked room, I could think of so many other things I wanted to do. Instead, I was stuck with being the killjoy.

"Mr. Mmm—Max,"

"Yeah? You okay? Something you wanna tell me?" he asked as he grabbed at my elbows and looked into my eyes. I couldn't breathe. He didn't look at me like a teacher checking on the well-being of his student. There was something more dynamic between us than that. He looked at me like he was waiting for me to say something he already knew. Urges swelled in my abdomen. Maybe I shouldn't tell him. Maybe I should see where this moment was going before I busted out with a total deal-breaker. But of course, being who I was, I just blurted it out.

"Cindy's going to blackmail you for an A in your class."

"Wait. What? Blackmail me for what?" His stare prodded past my menial thoughts.

"She's going to use tonight. She's going to say that you were drinking with some of your students." His hands dropped heavy from my elbows. He looked down.

"I'm sorry," I whispered to him.

"Me, too." I watched his hair cascade down toward the front of his expression. He seemed disappointed more than scared.

"I'm just glad she doesn't know." The words forced their way through my lips. I could have sworn I thought them in my head. But of course that wouldn't have been normal for me. The person who can't seem to keep her mouth shut. No, I said it out loud and he heard it.

"She doesn't know what?" His eyes narrowed when he looked at me. My heart fell into the pit of my stomach. What was I going to say? If I told him that I have a massive crush on him teetering on the edge of obsession, he could totally break my heart and laugh in my face. But if I didn't say anything, and later found out he felt the same way, I couldn't live with those consequences. I had to face the fact: I was like a deer caught in the headlights of a speeding car, ready to turn me into road kill. So I figured if I went down the middle of the road, following the solid yellow lines, there would be a chance he would swerve and I could see what his intentions were; just as long as I didn't trip over one of those damn yellow reflectors.

"Who—knows what?" I played completely confused; even went so far as to flip my hair back off my shoulders. It didn't work.

Or maybe it did...

He caught my chin between his thumb and index finger and guided my head to look up into his eyes. *Frickin' hit me with the speeding car, now. Take away my intense craving to force myself against him and taste his lips.* I was shuddering inside. This was it, he was touching my face and he smelled so delicious. I felt the gravitational pull between us and I could swear his face was moving closer to mine. Alright, the fact that our first kiss was going to happen in a bathroom wasn't too glamorous. That was a given. But I had to admit, it wouldn't matter to me if we were in a horse's stable surrounded by the stench of horse sweat. He was coming in to lay claim, and I couldn't wait. I wet my lips, anticipating in a matter of seconds we would be full-on making out. I closed my eyes, knowing that I was going to feel his kiss.

His hair brushed the edge of my lip and across my cheek. His nose pushed delicate against my hair as he exhaled; his breath tickled, heating the curves on my ear.

"Wilson," he whispered; I melted, "What is it that Cindy doesn't know?"

My eyes snapped open.

What the hell was this? This couldn't be happening. Here I was, jonesing to kiss him, and he was still concerned with who said what. Why couldn't I have kept my big mouth shut? My whole life, I've never possessed the ability to keep my inner monologue internal. Nothing new, but now the fallibility of keeping my private thoughts *private* screwed up my immediate future. Motivated by six little words that escaped my mouth, he teased me into playing a game. I was forced to call his bluff. I had to know if he was all in.

"Wouldn't you like to know?" I breathed softly, pushing my lips to his ear. Chills rampaged through my body as I felt him take a breath and exhale across my neck.

"I would."

As long as I didn't see his eyes, I could still play. Nerves wrapped around my insecurities and crushed them to dust.

"What are you willing to do to find out?" I heard the words float around his ear. It was like someone else said them, until I realized it was my lips that were moving.

He held his breath, I stopped moving. My heart sank down to my gut. I think I'd stepped over the invisible delicate line that was supposed to be drawn between us. His chest rose inhaling with what he was going to say. He pressed soft against my ear.

"I'd better go." He pulled away and never looked back at me as the door slammed shut behind him.

I flung my body down on the leather sofa. *I frickin' knew it.* That was me, couldn't ever seem to say the right thing at the perfect time. Abandoned in a bathroom and too bummed to leave, I closed my eyes and lay there for a long moment. I couldn't even bring myself to have a self-induced daydream about him. Why didn't I just throw my arms around him and plant a huge kiss on him? Maybe one more drink would have given me the confidence to do that.

Then again, with one more drink I could have done the walk of shame to the porcelain god and I haven't hugged *him* since my junior year when Joanie kept having me suck down martinis at her father's country club. I don't think I will ever drink another martini for as long as I live. Not only were we escorted out and asked never to return, but we were blacklisted at the ripe, young age of seventeen. It was totally stupid, and yet completely epic. Especially when Joanie's dad came home with the bar tab; who would've thought eight drinks would have cost over ninety-five dollars?

I felt my phone vibrate in my pocket and chime with a message. It was from Joanie.

WTF? U NEVR TXT ME! DID U GET THER SAF? MR. G THER?? CALL ME ASAP!

I texted her back, SORRY J- SAFE- WIL CAL 2MARO RELLY TIRED. C U. I didn't feel like going over what had just happened. I pushed the phone back into my pocket.

I felt a paper catch under my fingernail. I didn't remember putting anything in my pocket with my phone. I pulled it out. It was a yellow sticky note folded in half. There was nothing written on the outside of it. The sticky side was matched perfectly with the other, so it was hard to open. I pulled it apart and read what it said.

Matt Gladstone 925-555-2129

CALL ME TONIGHT 11:30

Holy Shit! WTF? My head spun so fast, I thought my eyes were actually moving in circles. *When did he put this in my pocket? I never felt him do it. I should have felt it if someone was trying to get into my pants.* I thought back to the bathroom at Wesley and how I'd flushed the last note he'd given me. I couldn't believe I didn't see it sooner. *Come on, Wilson, pull your head out and wake up to the world of forbidden love. He called himself Matt as a cover. I should've been able to figure that one out. Wait, this means…he likes me. He wants me to call him. What time is it?* I looked at the wall above the sofa; there was a huge clock above my head. Eleven twenty-eight; crazy, I didn't see it before. I had two minutes to think about how to start a conversation. I played with the words that danced in my head.

Hi, Mr. Goldstein. Hey, Max. Hi sexy, what's up? Skiing tomorrow? What do you think about all this snow? Want to kiss me? 'Cuz I want to kiss you. Sure, I'll meet you. What? You want to be my boyfriend?

I looked up to the clock, it was 11:30. My heart dropped into my stomach. It was time for me to call *him*. I pulled my phone from my pocket and dialed his number. I pressed send and sat on the sofa in the massive waiting area of the bathroom. One ring, two, then three…finally, on the fourth ring, he answered it.

"Hi, this is Max, please leave a message." Then there was a beep. I froze. What was I going to say? After a pretty significant pause, my phone chimed—call waiting; it was Max.

At least I get to say "hi" first; sometimes it was easier being the one to receive the call. Then the other person has to drive the conversation.

"Hello?"

"Hi, Wilson?" his voice filled my head and made a beeline to my heart.

"Yeah?"

"I just wanted to see if you were—okay. Are you?" His voice carried across my chest and down to feed the hungry butterflies filling my stomach.

"Yeah."

"I wanted to thank you about Cindy," his tone was so sexy on the phone. It caused the butterflies in my stomach to bounce low in my body.

"Okay."

I was doing it again. Not making conversation and sounding like a complete idiot.

"Well I guess I'll—"

"What are you doing tomorrow?" I interrupted. The butterflies were in full migration around my body. I already knew he was going skiing. So, what? I needed to keep the butterflies busy; I liked them being around. I heard him take a deep breath into the phone.

"I'm going skiing with a couple of buddies from college. Do you ski?" I could hear him shuffling things around.

"No. We were supposed to go tomorrow but that was before I told Cindy she was a bitch. Where are you?" I stood up and looked in the mirror above the sinks.

"I'm in my old room at my family's cabin. Where are you?" he asked back.

"I'm still at Cindy's."

"I figured that. Where are you in the cabin?" he said. His voice was low and growly.

"You wouldn't believe me if I told you," I snapped back.

"Well then let me guess. You're in Nick's room."

"No."

"Cindy's room?"

"Nope."

"You're not still in the bathroom are you?" his voice went up an octave.

"Yeah, as a matter of fact I am. That's where you left me." I was totally amazed at how much confidence I had over the phone.

"I left you? Mmmm. So you're not avoiding your friend?"

"Okay, maybe I am. But I don't have someone to protect me." I played the game.

"What about Nick? He's there. He looked like he wanted to protect you," his voice became low and I could tell he was setting a trap. He played his cards close to his chest, waiting for me to raise his bet or fold and go home. *Well, that's not the way I play.*

"What about him? He's a nice guy. But not the one I've been thinking about." My breath caught the quickened bubble that formed in the middle of my throat and escaped my body.

"Who were you thinking about? Because I could call him for you."

"I'm pretty sure you know who it is."

"Really, what does he look like?"

Damn it. How do I answer that? Too much information and he's going to win. Not enough, and he'll fold and walk away. Do I go with the ugly, yet cute, description to throw him off track or do I tell him the truth? Which one wouldn't scare him away? God, I wish Joanie was here. She is so much better at this then me. Okay, here it goes; on my own.

"He has these deep, green eyes that almost hypnotize you when you look into them. His shiny, black hair is off his collar but kinda long on top. He's taller than me and thoroughly buff. He looks really good in a T-shirt and jeans."

He was silent.

Maybe I should've gone with the ugly yet cute description. After a moment he cleared his throat.

"What do you know about this guy?"

"I know that he lives and works in California. He's not much older than me. His family has a cabin, and he's here this weekend. He came over tonight with his brother, but then had to leave for some reason. Left me in this bathroom and I never found out why."

I waited.

"Will you forgive him? He must have a lot to think about to leave you in that bathroom. But I bet he regrets not staying."

My heart sputtered and I caved in. This was so intense. *He likes me. Oh my God—he likes me. Don't give in yet.*

Now it was my turn to ask questions, "How do you know he regrets it?" I fished for answers.

"Because I know the guy, he's a good friend of mine. I know him better than I know myself."

"Has he ever talked about me?"

"Yeah."

"What has he said—about me?" *Okay, here we go.*

"He likes your humor. He thinks you're beautiful, smart, and he can't wait for weekends to roll by so he can get back to you."

Yeah, it was about time we both knew how we felt. This was the greatest day of my life.

"But—" he stopped.

"But, what?" I waited.

"But, I can't—he can't be with her." And with his words, in a matter of seconds, it had become my worst nightmare.

Fix it; I had to. This was not the way the game was supposed to go. My mind spun, trying to find anything that would pull him back. Make him see that our feelings were more important than numbers. Time was a continuum that we could twist and manipulate into gaps of experiences we could control and be patient with.

"Is it my age? I'll be eighteen in less than a month." My heart was pounding and crashing hard against my rib cage. I couldn't breathe. I felt like I was in the middle of a tightrope and someone jumped on the other end, causing it to bounce.

"Trust me, I know. But once you're eighteen there's still the fact that you're my student." his voice dropped low and almost went to a whisper.

I didn't say anything. I couldn't. There were no words that could explain the pain and despair I felt that raged throughout my body, mind, and soul. The tears fell fast. I tried not to sob but I couldn't help it. The back of my throat hurt from holding back the swell of anguish that struggled its way out. For the first time in my life, my heart was broken by a boy I loved.

CHAPTER EIGHT:

I didn't care how loud I cried. For the first time I knew what it felt like to have my heart broken. Really broken— ripped out, torn into a thousand pieces, and thrown on the floor. I fell back on the sofa in the huge bathroom and dropped my phone to the floor. *God, it was so painful.* My head throbbed with agony that circled around and poked at his words. *Why did he pull me in? What did he gain from doing that?* I didn't want to be this girl anymore. I didn't want to ache for the butterflies that had their wings torn off and lay suffering. I pulled my knees to my chest, curled up into a ball, and tried to save the last few butterflies that had a chance of surviving.

Leather was the worst type of sofa to cry into. My tears didn't soak in. They just sat there, motionless, waiting for me to wipe their existence clear. I couldn't. I had nothing left. My eyes swollen and burning, I closed them waiting for the pain to turn to anger. Lucid images of him standing in front of me flashed and stuck in my mind. His words filled my head and I couldn't get them to stop. All I wanted was to go home. Leave Aspen behind with the pain that struck me harder than the loss of my grandparents or the abandonment of my mother.

I heard a light knock at the bathroom door. I didn't want to open it. I didn't want to see anyone. I was a frickin' mess and I didn't need a couple of spoiled rich kids pointing it out to me. Another rap at the door echoed in the bathroom.

"Someone's in here," I said to the knocker on the other side.

"I know. Are you okay? Can I come in?" It was Nick. I could hear his hand slide across the door and jiggle the knob.

"I'm fine, thanks Nick," I choked the words out and started crying again.

"You don't sound fine. What's wrong?" he said louder.

"Please. I'll be fine. I just need a minute."

"Okay—if you need me, I'm right outside." He tapped on the door and then it was silent.

I looked at the massive clock that ticked away time, erasing the moments I'd lost crying. It was one o'clock in the morning. As much I wished it was a nightmare, I knew it was something real. I looked down at my phone, lying open on the floor. I picked it up and caught my reflection in the mirror above the sinks. Holy shit, I looked horrific. My eyes were bloodshot and my face was splotched red. My hair had twisted into fuzzy knots; I looked like I'd been hit by a speeding dump truck. Any attempt to fix my appearance was a total waste. I unlocked the door, shuffled back, and flopped on the sofa. I pulled my legs into a tight fold in front of my body, wrapped my arms around my knees, and closed my eyes as I dropped my chin to my chest. The latch clicked and I heard the door slide open across the expensive rock floor. My shoulders tightened with the thought of Nick seeing me in this state of mind. I didn't raise my head. Deep down I knew it was a bad idea to let him in. The door shut and I heard him push the lock. *At least he was thoughtful enough to keep other people out.* I could feel his presence standing in the middle of the room staring at me. But he didn't speak.

His shoes echoed as he cautiously walked toward me. I felt his hand stroke down across the top of my head. It felt so good. It reminded me of when I was a little girl and I would lie in my grandma's lap while she rubbed my hair. The hypnotic rhythm she kept with the light pressure of her hand made me feel calm and protected. I could have sworn I smelled butterscotch, her favorite candy. She must be here with me, telling me to get up and pull it together. An ache welled in my heart, for losses she'd never know. I turned my head to feel his hand sweep across the side of my cheek. Tears formed a lake, cradled in the corner of my eye.

"I'm sorry," he apologized. The tip of his fingers tickled across and pushed my hair back off my face. The butterflies that were desecrated in the pit of my stomach fluttered back to life. It took my brain a couple of seconds to register what my eyes recognized at once.

It was *him*.

I stared, unable to formulate words to express the mix of emotions that raged in my body. He came back.

"You're here," I said as he bent down in front of me. He was the smell of familiar butterscotch, and the taste of raw heart break.

"Hi," Max whispered. His eyes were red and his lips were pulled straight across his expression. I knew he had his own set of demons he was fighting.

"You came back?"

"I needed to know you were okay." He rested his hands on my knees. Desperation surged in my body. *What was he doing? He told me that we couldn't be together. Did he change his mind? I couldn't let him hurt me. I wasn't that type of girl.*

"I'm okay. I'll be fine." I pushed his hands off my knees and stood up. I left him standing at the sofa as I washed my hands and splashed water on my face.

"Wilson, it's complicated." I caught his reflection in the mirror.

"I get it."

I was so emotionally twisted; right could've been wrong, up could've been down, and I wouldn't have known the difference.

"I didn't plan on this. I never anticipated the feelings I have for you." He started toward me. Passion raged hot in my body, weakening my glacial anger. I tried to hold tight.

"Stop, please. I can't do this. I'm not one of those girls you can tease and walk away from. I don't have the luxury of a family to pick me off the floor. It's only me, that's all I have." I turned and faced him. I felt the tears roll down my cheeks. I didn't want to cry. He stood close to me; too close to keep my pain personal.

"I'm not one of those guys. There are a ton of reasons why I shouldn't be with you, but none are convincing enough to keep me from being here, tonight." He pushed his hand to my face, drying my tears with his fingers. I felt my knees bend. I leaned back against the bathroom counter for support. His other hand pushed my hair away from my neck and slid up, cradling my ear. His touch was so warm and soft. Every movement he made was in slow motion. I felt his fingers press strongly against the back of my head. The muscles in his arms flexed, and I watched his eyes dance from my eyes to my mouth and back. My lips damp, I parted them and closed my eyes.

"You have me," he whispered across my lips before I felt him press delicately against my mouth. His lips tasted sweet, better than I ever imagined. He pulled away. I tangled my hands in his hair and brought him back to me. I didn't want him to stop kissing me. I opened my mouth and, with his tongue, a whole new world was exposed to me. Uncontrollable urges flooded my body and I was scared. Not of him French kissing me, but of what could happen next.

He dragged his hands down, pressing them firm against my back, locking my body against his chest. His mouth left mine and he mapped his way down my neck. I didn't want him to stop, but I needed to tell him I wasn't that experienced. In fact, I had no experience at all. Something I'd failed to mention before. Not out of embarrassment; I just never had a reason to talk about it. It wasn't like I hadn't had opportunities—I'd never met anyone I thought was worth sharing that part of my body with—until now. Physically, I was a woman, and my body was more than ready. Problem was, my mind was still wading in the pool of inexperience and the innocence of my first real kiss.

"I've never, you know...with anyone before." I felt my face flush red. I'd never visualized telling him anything like that before. He stopped kissing me. His lucent green eyes studied my expression, looking to fill in the blank.

"You're a virgin," he whispered as he pressed his lips on my forehead. I could feel his smile.

"Yeah." I pulled away from him and looked down at the floor.

"Hey, wait, where you going? You think that changes how I feel about you?" He grabbed my chin and looked me in the eyes. "It doesn't. I can wait." He locked his hands behind my waist. I felt a huge brick of fear crumble under the reassurance he created about sex. I stretched up and kissed him.

"Not all guys are about one thing." He pushed my hair off my face and tucked it behind my ear. "Look, it's really late. I should probably go." He opened the bathroom door and waited to follow me out.

I didn't expect to see Nick passed out in the hall. His room was just down and across from the bathroom. I guess it was too far to go when you drank way too many beers on a Friday night. Max turned him over and tried to wake him up. He was out. We were able to anchor him enough to get him to stand up. I pulled his arm around my neck and helped Max take him to his room. Nick woke up and wasn't making any sense.

"Well, what do you know—it's the screaming, crying Wilma that wouldn't let me in to help her."

"Yeah, it's me. I want to get you to your room. You need to go to bed." He pulled his left arm tight and I twisted close to him. I could smell the tequila and beer mix on his breath.

"You're ready to take me to bed? Wow, I just met you today, too." Nick pulled me to his face, trying to kiss me. Max adjusted his weight to lean toward him.

"Who the hell is this guy? Do I know him? Do I know you?" Nick was sloppy and slurring his words.

"No, I don't think we've met before. I'm Max, a friend of Wilson's." Max curled his hand around to give an awkward handshake.

"Okay, well—yeah, I need to get to my room. I think you're in the second bedroom over there, WAN-DUH." He laughed and pointed down the hall. He was getting really heavy and I was already done carrying him.

"Thanks. Here you go… let me take off your shoes." He plopped down on the edge of his bed. Max got one shoe off and I got the other. I wrapped the comforter around his body so he wouldn't get cold. *I frickin' hate taking care of drunk people.* I clicked his lamp, and closed his door.

Max headed down to the second bedroom. He turned the knob and it opened right up. The maids must have locked it during the party. He checked it and the room was empty. The bed was turned down and inviting. I closed the door behind me and pressed the lock. Max furrowed his eyebrows.

"I don't want you to leave, it's too late. Just sleep here tonight." I swallowed the huge, anxious ball of nerves. I just hope we'll be able to fall asleep.

"I don't know if that's the best idea with Cindy in the next room."

I pointed across the room to an oversized floral-patterned sofa.

"Sleep on the sofa, then. We'll keep everything innocent enough."

He paused for a moment, then reached across the bed and grabbed one of the pillows. I took the wool throw at the foot and handed it to him. My hands tangled in the blanket, he pulled me close. I lost my breath. Endorphins electrified my body and I wanted him to kiss me again. He let out a low growl as his lips found the space below my ear.

"I don't know if I can stay on the couch," he whispered, tickling my neck. Chills chased each other rapidly down my spine. He was making it hard to justify my need to wait.

"I'll wake you up early so you can leave without being seen." I wanted him to stay so bad I could come up with any plan better than his excuses.

"It's not that. I don't know if I can stay on this couch with you in that bed." He pressed his lips to mine and tasted my desires, which spoke louder than words.

I felt his hands slide up my back and pull me closer to him; my hands released the blanket and wrapped up around his head. I felt my feet leave the ground as he kissed me and carried me across the room. Like a feather, he set me tenderly on the bed and pulled away. I didn't want him to stop. All sense of self preservation, moral values, and fears of the unknown disappeared in the flash of his eyes. I wanted him forever. I caught him around the neck and pulled him down on top of me. He was comfortably heavy in all the right places. I pulled his shirt from his pants and slid my hands up under across the skin on his back. He was scorching hot. Urges stronger than any addiction rushed my body. I tried to pull his shirt over his head. I wanted to see him. The hair on his chest, the muscles forced under his tight skin, the trail below his navel—I wanted to see all of it. He pulled away from my lips and lifted his body off mine.

"I think I'd better go to the couch." He bounced up off the bed. His shirt fell back over his stomach. I didn't argue. I was steaming, and if I didn't cool down, I wasn't going to be able to sleep. Odds were already stacked against me that I wasn't going to wake up early tomorrow to go skiing. He grabbed the blanket from the floor and shook it out before falling onto the enormous floral sofa. I lifted my head from the bed and watched him curl up, by himself, before I got up to change into my pajamas.

"Where are you going?"

"To get my PJ's out of my bag and change."

"You can change here. I'll close my eyes." He adjusted his body under the blanket and squeezed his eyes shut.

"I want to brush my teeth, too. I'll be right back." I grabbed my stuff and snuck out the door.

Before he could miss me, I was back—with fresh breath and comfortable flannel pajamas. Not the most attractive outfit, but I really hadn't planned on sleeping in the same room with him when I packed. I shut the door, ran, and jumped onto the bed. I turned to say goodnight and my heart dropped into my stomach. He wasn't on the sofa. His blanket was pushed toward the end and his pillow was on the floor. He was gone. I felt a rush of panic flood my mind. There had to be a logical explanation for him not being here. I had to keep it together; I could do this. I slid off the bed and sauntered to the door. Maybe he had to go to the bathroom. Or he needed to get a drink. But what if Cindy saw him? Or he got spooked and left? What if he decided I wasn't worth it? All the insecurities embedded by my mother flooded over me.

I was only six years old when I woke up at three-thirty in the morning, terrorized by a nightmare and my mom was nowhere to be found. Seven hours later, at ten forty-five, she stumbled into the apartment smelling of burnt cigarettes and cheap booze. When I tried to tell her I was scared, she wouldn't listen; instead she lectured me about her long night and how selfish I was for not letting her sleep.

The door swung open and Max was carrying two glasses of water.

"Nice PJ's. I thought you might be thirsty. Besides after you drink alcohol, you should hydrate." He pushed one of the waters at me.

Tears welled in my eyes. *Damn it! I didn't want to be one of those girls.*

"What's wrong? You okay?" He held me, searching for answers.

"Nothing. It's just I guess I'm not use to things like this." I held the water glass up to him.

"A glass of water?" He looked at me crazily, I smiled.

"Yeah, that's it."

"Well, maybe you should—get used to it." He pulled me closer and gave me a delicate kiss on my forehead before he turned and went to the sofa. I crawled into bed.

"Max?"

"Yeah?"

"Will you sleep next to me?" My hands tingled and my feet went cold. He looked so inviting. I wanted his arms around me and his body against me.

"I thought you'd never ask. Yes, please." He flipped his blanket off, hopped over me and crawled into bed behind me. I felt his hand slide up my thigh, across my hip, and tuck around my waist. His face planted into the curve of my neck and the space between our bodies lessened. I could really get used to this.

CHAPTER NINE:

"Wilson, get up! We gotta go," Cindy yelled and pounded on my door.

Good thing the door was locked. Last thing I needed was Cindy jumping to all these crazy conclusions about Max and me.

She kept on pounding and yelling, "Come on, let me in." I would have thought she was still bent out of shape about me telling her off last night.

"Okay, hold on," I yelled back. Hopefully I was loud enough to shut her up.

I turned to look at Max and noticed he wasn't there. I pushed my hand around the sheets. His side of the bed was still warm. I popped up and looked around the room. He was sitting on the sofa frantically tying his shoes.

"What are you doing?" I whispered.

"I can't take the chance of her finding me with you," he whispered. He snuck his belt and his jacket from the sofa.

"Who are you talking to?" Cindy hit the door again and Max jumped behind the arm of the sofa. He was like a spooked cat that had found a dead snake. He was so worried about her, it almost ruined my morning.

"Nobody, I am trying to get dressed. I'll meet you downstairs. Give me five minutes okay?" I walked over to the door and waited to hear what she would grumble under her breath.

"Fine, but hurry up. I want to get there before the Vaughns. They are so last season." I listened for her footsteps to disappear down the hall.

"That was a close call." I turned and he was right in front of me.

"Yeah, it was. What are we going to do?"

"About what?"

"About getting out of here without being seen?" his voice strained.

"I don't know. That jump you did over the arm of the sofa was pretty impressive. Maybe you'll have to climb out the window?" I teased him. I am so glad I did, because he grabbed me around my thighs, hoisted me up on his shoulder and tossed me on the bed.

I totally screamed—loudly—when he let go of me. He stood there, his finger across his pursed lips. I couldn't stop laughing. Next thing I knew, he was laying on top of me. His legs straddled mine and his hand was cupped across my mouth.

"Shhhhh. You don't want Cindy back up here, do you?" His eyes blazed wickedly and I liked it.

I shook my head; he was still covering my mouth.

"I'm going to let go, don't laugh." He pulled his hand from my mouth. "Don't laugh," he teased.

I didn't know how I was going to keep my feelings for him a secret. He looks at me and I melt. How was I going to keep that from Cindy? How was I ever going sit in another room with him and not totally broadcast how I felt? How were we supposed to act when people were around? Couldn't I just stay in this room with him forever? I could just live in his eyes all day; breathing in his scent for the rest of my life. I loved that idea.

"Hello? Where are you?" He rested his forehead on mine.

"Right here, with you." He lowered his mouth to mine, teasing me, barely touching his lips to mine. *So, not fair.* Then he kissed me and I didn't care about the sounds we made. He was on top of me and I wasn't able to get up. I could feel him wanting more than we had time for. He pulled his lips from mine and trailed down my neck to my collarbone. I leaned my head back and I wanted him to go further.

"Aaahhh, I can't—wait. You're so impossible to resist," he sighed. "I gotta wait. I gotta wait," he chanted, reminding himself of his self-imposed limits. I guess they were my limits, too. But at the rate we were going, they were going to be impossible to keep much longer. He crawled back off me. I laid there for a minute to regroup the butterflies that had decided to fly south, bring them back to the cage in my gut.

I had to get up; get ready to go skiing. I had to leave Max all day so I could put long skinny planks on my feet, sticks in my hands, and slide down a hill covered in cement-hard, freezing snow. It's not like I had anything better to do. I *so* did not want to go. The only thing I looked forward to was trying to find time to sneak away with Max.

I dragged myself off the bed and rummaged through my bag. I found a pair of fashionably ripped-up jeans and a long sleeve scoop-neck T-shirt. Perfect: today it had to be about the outfit I wore, not the functionality of it.

"I'm going to change and go downstairs. I'll keep Cindy busy while you find your way out," I told him. Not because I wanted him to leave; I needed to remind myself that I didn't want Cindy to know anything about Max and me.

"Thanks." He grabbed my hand, pulled me into a hug and kissed my forehead.

"You're welcome. I'll text you when we get to the ski lodge."

"Bye." He pecked me on the lips. Good self-control. Not too long, lingering on the lips. I left and glanced back for a split second while I shut the door.

That was so hard. I took a deep breath and tried to shake off the disappointment that crept into my mind. I didn't want to leave him, I didn't want to ski, and I didn't want to hang with Cindy for the day knowing that Max was going to be near but unobtainable.

"There you are! How're you feeling?" Nick caught me coming down the stairs.

"I'm fine. A little tired. How 'bout you? You were pretty wasted last night." I twisted the jeans I was carrying into a ball, adjusting them from one hand to the other. I had to keep busy and look interested.

"My head is throbbing, but other than that, I'm up." He rubbed his head, messing up his hair.

"I guess that's the best you can ask for. I'd better find Cindy, she's already pissed that I wasn't up earlier. See you later." I started down the stairs.

"Oh, hey Wilson, don't worry about the thing with Max Goldstein." He started back up the stairs.

What? Wait, what the hell was that? What did he mean, 'thing with Max?' My heart dropped clear down to my toes. *What does he know about us?* I turned back to him.

"Max?" I played it as naïvely as I could. I had to cover any trace of anything between Max and me.

"Come on, Wilson, I know what's going on between you guys."

"What's going on? There's nothing going on." I pushed the words hard. I needed make him believe nothing was going on.

"I heard you last night. But look, I talked to Cindy this morning and everything is cool. She understands." He stepped down a couple of stairs to be eye level with me.

It's over. That's it, we are so caught. Max's career is over. He'll have to resign from Wesley. I won't see him anymore and, since I caused him to lose his job, he'll hate me. I don't think I can handle him hating me. Every feeling I felt last night was tainted with guilt and my memory of us together last night was totally ruined. *I just can't let that happen.*

"Nothing happened. It would be her word against mine, because nothing happened." Desperate words flew from my mouth, trying to find a way to convince Nick to believe me. My hands wrapped tight in the clothes I was holding. I felt the edges of my ears burn red. My stomach twisted and I could feel the urge to get sick bubbling to the back of my throat.

"I heard differently. I guess you ripped Cindy another hole and she just stood there, shocked." He acted out what he thought she would look like. "I would've paid money to see that." He started to laugh. I was totally confused.

"What are you talking about?" I shifted my weight across to my other leg and felt the fuzz of confusion cloud my head.

"The fight you and Cindy got into last night? About Goldstein—because he happened to show up to a jailbait drinking fest. Why? What are you talking about?" He cocked his head, waiting for an answer.

"Oh, yeah. Okay, that's what I thought you were talking about. I got a little confused. I guess I drank more than I thought last night. It takes a little time for words to catch up to my brain." Relief splashed over my body. I'd dodged a pretty big bullet. *Thank you, God, or whoever is watching over me.* I turned to continue down the stairs.

"Hey, Wilson, is he still sleeping?" He looked me dead in the eyes. My heart sank. I couldn't even act like I didn't know who he was talking about. I wanted to ask who he was referring to, but it would be a waste of my breath. He knew that Max was with me last night. It must have been because we'd carried him to bed.

"No," I answered automatically. Huge beads of sweat pushed through my pores. My throat went dry and my heart pounded at marathon speed.

"I won't tell. Your secret's safe with me." He winked, and his eyes glistened.

The need to explain swamped me in total guilt. There was nothing I could do to change the facts—Nick knew about Max spending the night.

"Nothing happened. He fell asleep on the sofa. That's it." I stepped up toward him.

He pushed his hands against his chest. "You don't have to convince me. I'm not a snitch." Maybe it was out of desperation or the fact that there was nothing I could do to change his mind. But somehow, I believed him.

"Thanks." I made sure to look at him square in the eyes before I started back downstairs.

I had to believe he was being truthful with me. What other choice did I have? He had me by the short hairs (another one of my grandpa's sayings). He'd seen us together last night and, whether he could prove it or not, rumors tend to spread like wildfire around our school. The truth always gets twisted into a lie and people always get hurt.

I turned the corner, still not dressed in the clothes I was holding. Cindy stared at me. I thought she was going to blow a gasket, daggers flew from her eyes.

"Wilson. Why aren't you dressed? We've gotta go." She paced over to me. I didn't even realize I still had my PJ's on and my clothes twisted in my hands. I had to think fast with some lame excuse of why I still wasn't dressed.

"I didn't know if these were okay to wear skiing?" I held up the pants and shirt.

"They're completely hideous and totally wrong. You can't ski in those." She grabbed them and tossed them on a chair that looked like it belonged in a museum. "Let me get you one of last year's outfits." She climbed the stairs and yelled back, "Go eat the breakfast Lupita made."

This was bad. Not where I needed Cindy to go right now. Tongue-tied, I couldn't think of anything to get her to come back downstairs.

"Wait! I'll come with you," I screamed, and booked up the stairs after her.

"Whatever; hurry up. We don't have all day." She passed the closed door I stayed behind last night with Max. She didn't even give it a second look. Good sign, she must not have thought there was anything there she needed to investigate. She pulled open the door across from Nick's room. It was a walk-in closet filled with ski gear. Everything you needed, from the skis down to the thermal underwear people layer with when they're cold. The entire back wall was a shelving unit of wire baskets overflowing with all types of sunglasses, boots, goggles, gloves, and miscellaneous hats. I guess that was the type of closet people had when you lived at the base of a ski resort. She spun around, looked at me, then started rummaging through the baskets.

"You'll need sunglasses, gloves, and a headband. Socks are a must," she stated, going over a checklist in her head. Cindy flung items at me as she named them off. She shuffled her way to the clothes rack, pushing and pulling outfit after outfit—all hung perfectly on hangers, all sorted by brand and color.

"You'll definitely need an outfit. Let's see—yeah, that one won't fit. That's the one I'm wearing. I wore that one last month. This is SO not you. Hmm, let's see...here it is. This is the one you should wear." She held up a one-piece baby blue suit that had a zipper from the crotch to the chin and a built-in hood. It looked like something you'd wear as you stepped out of the space shuttle onto the moon. *Hell, no!*

One small step forward for fashion and one huge step back for me wearing that! I couldn't believe she pulled that thing out for me.

"Is there something a little less—blue?"

"Christ, Wilson, this is a five hundred dollar Shugga suit by North Face. Get with the times! Just go try it on." She flung it across the pile of things I already had in my hands and stared at me. I turned and walked to my room.

"Come out and show me," she howled as I heard the hangers scrape across the bar. It was as if we were shopping and she was throwing me the clothes she didn't want to waste time trying on.

I know why she chose that snowsuit for me. Less attention on me meant more for her. Who in their right mind would wear something so hideous? I was reaching for the knob when the door flew open. It was Nick. My heart dropped.

"What are you doing in my bedroom?"

"I was helping Max—out." He shoved his hands into his pockets as he rocked back and forth.

"Out?"

"How else was he going to get out with Cindy coming upstairs?" He pulled his hands from his pockets and pointed to the open window.

"Holy shit, isn't that pretty far down?" I tossed the crap in my hands onto the floor and ran to the window. He wasn't out there.

"Relax, he only fell down the last ten feet." He pushed the window closed and smiled. I could only hope he was kidding.

"Thanks."

"You're welcome." He turned and walked out, closing the door. I still couldn't believe he and Cindy had the same dad.

I opened the window and looked down. I saw the impression of his body where he'd fallen, but no other sign of him. He was gone. I knew that the faster I could get ready to go, the sooner we'd be together. I hurried to the powder blue baby vomit of a spacesuit, unzipped it, and threw it on the bed. I pulled off my top and slid off my pajama bottoms. As ugly as that thing looked lying there, I hoped it would cling and hang in all the right places. If I was going to be looking like I belonged in a seventies space movie, I wanted to make sure I was the sexiest seventies space babe around. I grabbed the suit and slid one leg in, then the next. It actually felt silky-smooth against my skin. I pulled it up over my hips—it was really comfortable—pushed one arm through, then the next; I grabbed the zipper and pulled it up to my navel. That's when I caught myself in the reflection of the window. The suit was actually really cute. I pulled the zipper up to just cover my bra. *Hello, cleavage!* I turned and spun to see how I looked from all angles. I pushed my arms against my body making my breasts to look bigger than they really were.

"Wow, wouldn't Max like to see that," I mumbled to myself. I bent down, grabbed the white fluffy headband out of the pile of stuff Cindy had given me, and flipped my hair back, pulling it onto my head.

"Yeah, I would."

I spun around quickly. Max was crouched on the windowsill, holding onto the glass for balance.

"Oh my God! You scared me. What are you doing here?"

"I'm sorry. I got down to my car and realized my keys were still here. I thought you would have left already." He hopped into the room. His nose wrinkled and he winced as he landed.

"Are you okay?"

He was still bent low.

"I'm fine, just landed wrong when I left the first time." He stood up, his eyes traveling across my body as he smiled and bit his lower lip. I grabbed the zipper on the snowsuit and pulled it up to the bottom of my chin.

"How long were you there in the window?" I pulled the headband off. My face burned red, I totally couldn't believe he saw what I'd been doing.

"I wasn't there long; just long enough to hear you say something about *me*—liking *this*." He shook his head. His hands pushed up and down through the air pointing at the moon suit I had on. He couldn't stop staring at me. I had to feel good about that. I guess it clung and hung exactly where it should. My body temperature rose I was getting real hot.

"You really like it?" I grabbed the zipper and lowered it without thinking, just enough to make his mouth open.

"Absolutely," he said losing his breath. He nudged super-close. His eyes fixed, his aroma swarmed my body as his hand slid around to the small of my back and his other caught the handle of the zipper. I lost my breath.

"You see this spot," he said as his lips kissed low on my neck. "And this spot here." He kissed low enough on my chest to send shivers down my body.

"You have to keep them protected from the cold." He tenderly pulled up on the zipper until I was completely covered.

"That's better," he exhaled.

"Thanks," I could barely talk. My bones were shaking. I really liked him kissing my exposed skin. He slid his other arm around me and pulled me to his chest.

"You might have to change out of this outfit. I don't know if I can keep away from you."

"Really? Baby blue and all?" I couldn't believe he liked the outfit that much.

"It isn't the color; it's the woman wearing it. And she is irresistibly sexy in it." His words brushed across my ear while his lips found their way to the curve where my jaw met my neck. Mmm, he was so good at that. He navigated across my cheek to my mouth. He caught my lower lip and gently pushed my mouth open for our last kiss before we had to go our separate ways today. I didn't want to pull away, but if I didn't get back in that hallway, Cindy would come looking for me. I pulled my lower body away from him, hoping my lips would follow.

"I gotta get back to Cindy," I spoke softly to him.

"I know. I'll see you later," he said as I pulled away.

I walked away, only glancing back to see him still standing, waiting for me to come back. I walked out the door.

CHAPTER TEN:

It was good I left Max when I did; Cindy was heading to my room with her arms full of more ski gear.

"Oh, you've decided to come back. What the hell took you so long? I don't know if I like that suit on you. It's a bit too blue." Cindy would always make up an excuse why she didn't like something; especially if she thought it made you look better than her.

"I'm fine with it. Blue is okay, I guess. Let's get going so we can make sure you get there before the Vaughns. Hey, what's going on with Chase Romero?" I had to get her mind off me wearing the baby blue suit.

"Nothing, he's not in town this weekend. He's made the football team and he's tied up with some practice squad thing. But you're right; I gotta beat the Vaughns. They are such douches. Total mouth breathers. I swear, something is wrong with that entire family." She rummaged through the pile she'd tossed in the hall and pulled out a couple of things she needed.

"I need to go grab the stuff you gave me and I'll meet you downstairs," I told her, waiting to see her roll her eyes at me.

"Fine, hurry up." She walked down the hall, leaving the pile of ski stuff in the middle of the floor. As she bounced down the stairs, I watched until her head sank below the top step. I heard her gripe something about cleaning up the pile in the hall and making something to eat.

I turned and ran to my room. I took a deep breath before I opened the door. I had a feeling he might not be there, but what if he didn't sneak out yet? What a bonus. Bad for me, there lay my pile of ski paraphernalia in the middle of the room, but no Max. I swiped it up, shut the door and left behind some of the best memories in my entire life.

"Nick, you promised you would drive me around this weekend. You know how I hate to drive in the snow." Cindy was slamming things around the kitchen.

"Something came up. I can't take you," Nick told her. His eyes followed me walking in.

"I'll drive," I spoke up, piling the stuff in my hands onto the stool next to me.

"You're not driving. Nick's going to drive us. That's why my dad is *paying* him this weekend." She poured a glass of orange juice and slid it across the slippery rock counter to me.

"I don't mind." I took a swig.

"I do! He's going to drop us off on the way to wherever he's going. Right, Nick?" She picked up a glass of orange juice and sipped without making any slurping noises. Her eyes fixed on his, almost like she was holding something over his head. A personal conversation I wasn't privy to. It must've been something real bad because he shook his head and started for the front door.

"I'm leaving in five minutes. You better be ready," he grumbled and walked out. I turned and looked at Cindy to see what she might say—nothing. She just looked at me, shrugged her shoulders and grabbed an apple from the gigantic fruit bowl on the counter.

I couldn't live that way. It was so awful. Their relationship was so tumultuous. The handful of times I'd seen them together, it was hell. If she wasn't demanding something from him, she was degrading him and making him feel worthless. I think they thrived on chaos. They were attracted to it, because it gave them something to feel. It justified their anger for the lack of personal relationships with their parents. There, that's my psychoanalysis of their interpersonal relations. Take it for what it's worth, a ski lift up the hill.

We threw our stuff in a designer duffel bag and let the hired help load it into the back of the Sequoia. I sat in the backseat behind Nick. My stomach twisted tight—a familiar spot I wasn't comfortable with, but I couldn't get my mind to convince my body to change sides with Cindy. There was the fact that if she sat right behind him she'd rack-a-pop him across the back of the head. What's a rack-a-pop? Again, a word my grandfather taught me. It's when someone gives you a whack across the back of the head with the palm of their hand, causing a popping sound and making your hair poof. That's a rack-a-pop. Seeing their volatile relationship first hand, I didn't want to be anywhere near when the rack-a-pops turned into fisticuffs.

Cindy hopped into the seat next to me. She already had her earphones plugging her ears. I wondered if she did it to avoid fighting with Nick. Shut herself out of the world around her. No skin off my teeth, I figured it gave me a moment to text Joanie. I pulled my phone from the itsy-bitsy pocket at the waist of my retro blue snowsuit. I swear the pocket had to be for looks.

HEY J- MISS U! LOTS 2 TELL. STRUCK GOLD! 2M2T (too much to text). HED'N 2 SKI RESORT. TXT L8R. BYE

I sent it, then thought about the words I'd put in the text. That was going to torture her, and if I didn't get cell service up at the resort, she was going to keep trying until I'd either have a gazillion messages on my phone or she got through. I couldn't blame her; I would do the same thing. After all, she has been on the Goldstein carnival ride with me from the beginning. She was the only person in the entire world that knew how I felt about him and the only one I trusted with my secret.

It was a forced trust I had with Nick, not by choice. Even though I never came out and admitted anything to him, he knew something was up between Max and me.

"So, how'd you sleep last night? You look a little tired." Nick looked at me through the rearview mirror. I couldn't breathe deeply enough. My heart flopped to my feet. I stared at him in the mirror, then glanced at Cindy. The muscles in my jaw clenched so tight, it felt like my teeth were cracking under the tension.

"Fine, probably shouldn't have had that second drink. But I didn't have any problems falling asleep." My eyes burned from staring into the rearview mirror. I heard Cindy's volume increase in her ears, to the point where I could make out that she was listening to a female singer belting out high notes about love gone wrong.

He'd better not go there with me.

"You were warm enough, right?" He looked at Cindy then looked back at me in the mirror.

"Sure," I mumbled and looked out the window. *What was he doing? Why was he pulling this now?* I looked back at him in the mirror.

"I just want to make sure you're comfortable with the *blanket* you're sleeping with. Sometimes you might have to *change* blankets to get cozy and comfortable."

Did he really want to do this with Cindy in the car? I'm not a vindictive person, but I will pull out the big guns and go down swinging if he wants to brawl.

"I was *very* happy to have the blanket I had wrapped around me last night."

"Just checking to see if you might want to try a different one; maybe one that hasn't been around so long. You could try it tonight." A crooked smile covered his face.

"Thanks for the offer, but I think I'll stick with the one I have. It was exactly what I needed." Glancing at Cindy, she was still taken in by the world of commercial rock that screamed from her iPhone.

"Alright, your loss." He looked at me in the mirror for the last time.

"I can only imagine." As I looked out the window, my eyes stung from the shining stars glistening off the white frosted mountains. I pushed the window down. I was getting uncomfortably warm in the baby blue sauna suit from Cindy. But there was no way I was going to take it off. Max liked it and that was enough to keep me in it. The crisp, chilly air burned dry and refreshing down my throat. The freezing breeze swirled around my hair and down the front of my suit. Goosebumps rippled on my skin, down my arms and up through the back of my neck.

"Jesus Christ, Wilson, roll up your window! I really don't want to have to fix my hair again," Cindy barked, pulling out her earphones.

"Sorry, just needed some air." I didn't feel like caving to her demand, but I was feeling a bit chilly.

"There'll be plenty of air later. We're almost there and you can breathe all the air you want. Nick, remember to pull up to the front so I don't have to carry the skis that far." Her finger pointed toward the two chartered buses waiting in the loading zone.

Nick pulled up behind them, blocking the entry for anyone else. He jumped out of the SUV, pulled open the back, and started to unload our ski stuff, piling it on the gothic marble bench welcoming us. He put our skis in a rack and walked around to my side of the SUV. His breath, heavy with smoke, warned me I was going to freeze. He yanked my door open. The rush of the Colorado air was shocking at first. My nose stung, and my lips glossed a frost-tingling chill. I guess it was dumb of me to lick my lips before I got out of the car. At least the rest of my body was warm.

Nick held out his hand to help me out onto the snow-covered ground.

"Thanks," I said grabbing him to make sure I didn't fall. The asphalt was more slippery than it appeared.

"You're welcome, anytime." As he helped me out, his other hand clutched at my elbow.

"Hello—I need some help over here." Cindy held her iPhone and earbuds in the air so he could see her hands were full. Nick completely ignored her, didn't even look her way.

"I think I can get it from here." The last thing I needed was to be stuck at this overpriced snow park with a pissed off rich girl holding a grudge.

"Are you sure?"

"Totally sure, I'm fine. Cindy looks likes she needs you." I nodded toward her still sitting in the Sequoia, waiting for Nick to open the door.

"Okay, and what I said earlier about your blanket—well, if you're happy with it, then I'll leave it alone."

"I appreciate it. I'm very happy with my blanket."

"Nick! I'm waiting," Cindy demanded, staring at him.

"That's my cue." He shuffled his way to her door and opened it.

"Did you call ahead requesting the instructor for Wilson?"

"No, I thought you would have called. I mean, she is your friend and all," he snapped at her.

"No. When I talked to you on Thursday I told you to call Shane and book a lesson for Wilson with *him*. He's the best, and I wanted *him* to teach her." She flipped her hair away from her neck. She was splotchy red and steaming mad. "Now it's too late and she'll get stuck with one of those "I'm just here for a month" flunky people who can't ski their way down a bunny slope let alone a beginner run." She slammed the car door.

"I'm sorry." He looked like the same brow-beaten Nick I'd met at the airport.

"Sorry doesn't make up for your lack of common sense. You need to schedule a lesson for her. We'll be waiting inside. Come on, Wilson." She grabbed the designer bag and trudged to the big rock and brick building I assumed was the lodge. I shrugged my shoulders and gave him a glance as I slipped past him.

She grumbled the entire way to the lodge. How incompetent he was, how if she wants anything done she's gotta do it herself.

"I'm sorry. I really wanted this to be a good experience for you."

"Don't worry about it. I'm fine. I think I'll be okay learning from whoever teaches me."

The door swung open, inviting me to a whole new world of designer people, foreign opulence, and limitless possibilities. Everything looked like it was from a movie. Beautiful people with hair styles and diamond rings were encapsulated in narcissistic conversations about their travels and money. Enormous rock fireplaces raged with bonfire-sized flames. Notebook computers and iPads littered the tables. Songs in different languages blasted from cell phones people couldn't wait to answer. I was *way* out of my league. I was a seventies space girl in a borrowed powder blue zip-up suit.

Cindy grabbed my hand and pulled me to the bar. She perched on a tall stool and waved to the bartender at the other end. He came over immediately, and leaned over to her. Before I had myself planted on the stool, she was already whispering something into his ear. She leaned back and looked him in the eyes. She was totally flirting with him. He shook his head and turned to grab two clear mugs.

"You're thirsty right?" Cindy eyed me up and down. I didn't get a chance to answer her before the drinks appeared before us. "I ordered you an Irish Coffee—something to warm you up."

"Thanks." I guess I should've been grateful.

"You're welcome."

I didn't like coffee. Never have. I tried my grandfather's once when I was about seven. He was the type of person who believed if you wanted to drink coffee, you had to drink it black. I was the type who hated bitter, dark drinks that made your mouth feel like it had just swallowed hot dirt. I hoped the Irish made it better. I watched Cindy grab hers up and take a sip.

"Mmm, so good. Thanks, Jeremy." She held the mug between her hands. He waved at her as he helped the next person leaning over the bar to talk to him.

"Try it, Wilson. It will warm you up and get you ready to ski." She pushed her mug toward me.

"Cheers." I didn't want to drink it, but I didn't want to be rude either. I took a small sip and was pleasantly surprised when it didn't taste half bad. It was sweet enough to take away the aftertaste of the coffee and warm enough to heat my core.

"Pretty good, huh?" Cindy sipped hers again.

"Yeah, it's good." It wasn't long before my mug was half empty and I was feeling relaxed.

The little idiosyncrasies of Cindy that would normally piss me off disappeared with every sip I took of the Irish coffee. I don't know what was in it, but I had to be grateful to Jeremy, the bartender, for making it.

"Okay, good news, I got a private lesson for you. But the deal is it starts in fifteen minutes." Nick hustled over out of breath.

"That's great. Thank you."

"Is it with Shane?" Cindy insisted.

"No, but I've been assured he's a really good instructor," Nick countered.

"I don't mind who teaches me. Was there alcohol in that drink?" I interrupted.

"What in the hell did you order her, Cindy?"

"Just an Irish Coffee; no biggie!" She told him.

Nick grabbed the mug from my hands. "Geez, do you have a death wish for her? She's never skied before," he barked at her before sliding the mug toward the back of the counter.

"No, she's fine. Don't be such a dweeb. She'll be just fine." She slid off the stool and picked up the bag. "Let's get going before Nick melts the snow with all his hot air."

"You need to meet your instructor out the back door and to the left. You'll see a sign that says private instruction. You can't miss it. I'll be back around four." He left without waiting for any response from us.

I followed Cindy to a waiting area. Soft leather benches lined the walls. She pulled the bag off her shoulder and sat down. She fished out gloves, hats, sunglasses, and boots and tossed them toward me. It didn't take long to get ready to go. The boots were the most uncomfortable things I've ever put on my feet before. *How in the hell do you walk in boots that don't bend where your feet normally do? Heel to toe, clomp, clomp, clomp. Wow what a sexy walk. Now I really looked like I belonged on the moon.*

We went out the back door and down the metal steps. Sure enough, to the left side was a carved wooden sign telling me that was where I belonged. My cheeks were already freezing and my cold nose hurt. Cindy grabbed her skis from the rack next to the deck.

"I'm going to get a couple runs in. I'll meet you back here in an hour, okay?" She looked at me, assuming I understood what a couple of runs meant. I nodded my head and started over to the area where I was going to let some person strap boards to my feet and instruct me on how to go down the side of a mountain without getting hurt.

"You need to grab your skis, those ones there." She pointed to the rack. I grabbed the blue and white Rossignol skis I assumed were mine and clunked my way to the lesson area.

By the time I'd walked twenty feet, my thighs were burning and I could feel the onset of Charley horses in my calves. I had to stop walking every couple of feet to adjust and shuffle the skis from one hand to the other. It wasn't like they were super heavy, just awkward to hold, and carrying them while trying to walk in the ski boots was a chore. I could only assume the more practice I had dealing with skis and boots, the better I would get at handling them. Except I had another ten feet to go when the skis fell into the snow; they somehow hooked against each other in a weird cross pattern and I couldn't get them to go back together. I was completely confused how to fix them. I looked like a total rookie.

"Here, let me help you, Wilson," a guy's voice floated through the air. I'd heard it before but it wasn't familiar. As I turned and looked up to see who was coming to help me, my heart dropped in my gut. It was Wayne Samuel, John's son, the man from the airplane ride.

"Oh my God! Wow, hi, Wayne. Thanks. It's my first time skiing."

"Well don't worry. I won't have you do anything crazy." He smiled, picking up my crossed skis and fixing them. "I'm your instructor today." He handed me back the skis perfectly organized. His eyes smiled, matching his lips.

"Really?" I nodded my head and swallowed hard. He was really good looking—crystal clear blue eyes that you could dive into and naughty blond hair with just enough curl to catch your fingers. I could tell I was going to have a major problem focusing today. Between him and Max, I didn't know how I was ever going to learn how to ski.

CHAPTER ELEVEN:

Forty-five minutes was how long it took me to understand how to clear my boot of snow and click in and out of the skis, toe then heel. It was really hard to focus. I wanted to pay attention, but my thoughts would get all tangled up in where Max was. It was even harder when Wayne snapped out of his skis, wrapped his hands around my waist, and showed me how to bend at the knees and lean to turn.

"When you feel me press on your side I want you to lean that way." He pressed my left side. I leaned. He pressed on my waist to the right. Of course I leaned that way too.

"That's good. Now bend more at your knees." I guess I didn't do it the way I was supposed to because he grabbed my waist and stood right in front of me. His hands slid across my hips and down to the front of my thighs. He looked me in the eyes, his hands stayed on my legs.

"Do you feel the muscles working right through here?" His hands rubbed the outsides of my thighs.

"Yeah, they burn." *Wow, how cute is he? He's grabbing my legs. Focus, Wilson.*

"That's just how I want you when we get on the ski lift and go down the beginner run."

"Whoa, wait; ski lift? We're not doing that today, are we? I mean, that's like the next time I'm here." Every feeling of insecurity twisted and knotted in my stomach.

Who would have thought that barreling down the side of a mountain would happen forty-five minutes after I put the skis on my feet?

"You'll do just fine. I'm going to be right there with you. I won't let anything happen to you. Trust me?" his voice lowered and he pulled off his gloves.

"I don't know, this seems way too soon. I think—"

"Wilson, trust me." He grabbed my chin, just like Max did. My head swam, and electricity surged throughout my body. My heart wanted Max but my endorphins raged for the guy touching me.

"I'll trust you." The words hardly made it out of my mouth. My legs trembled with waves of fear.

"You're shaking." He grabbed my shoulders. "Don't be afraid."

"I'm cold," I lied.

I was so frickin' scared.

"Well, let's get you moving then." He dropped his skis next to me, clipped them on his boots, and grabbed his poles.

We worked our way down to the ski lift. It was actually only about fifteen feet away from where we were. We had to wait in a line for beginning skiers. This was the time instructors were giving their pep talks. At least Wayne kept me thinking I could do it. Time passed so quickly, I didn't realize we were up. I watched Wayne signal the operator in the booth. The guy's voice echoed across the walkie-talkie he held to his mouth.

"High nest, first-timer entering lift. Slowing the lift. Repeat, beginner approaching the chair; turtle speed."

He might as well have frickin' announced it across the loudspeakers in the lodge, too. I could feel the blood flooding to my cheeks. There must have been fifty people on the open-air death trap ahead of me and about the same number waiting behind in line. I shuffled out with Wayne holding one arm and the lift operator holding my other. My skis crossed and the chair caught me right at mid-thigh. Wayne pulled me close to him and held his arm around me. Adrenaline thrashed and filled every cell of my body. I didn't want to fall seventy feet to my death, so I held really still and barely breathed. He was so relaxed.

"You can open your eyes now." Wayne leaned toward me, making the chair sway.

"What are you doing? Don't make it move—oh my God." I tried to breathe shallow. My muscles burned.

"It's okay; you're not going to fall. I will make sure of it." He locked his poles across my lap. "You're safe, see? How long are you in Aspen for?" he asked low.

"Just until Sunday, then we head back home," I answered quietly. I didn't want to make the chair move.

"Where's home?"

"Northern California, the Bay Area. You?" I looked up at him, still shaking inside. We were really high up now.

He smiled. "Wherever there's snow."

"Well that's totally vague and mysterious. So I can assume you lived in Russia?"

"In 2006; for eight months."

"How long are you living here?"

"I'm here until February." He adjusted his legs, his skis bounced in the air so chunks of snow fell to their deaths.

110

"Then where are you going?" I tried not to look down.

"I haven't decided yet." He looked out.

"Have you ever lived in Northern California? Tahoe area? I hear some of the best skiing is up there—that's just what I've heard." I followed his eyes to where he was looking.

"Never lived there. Always thought about it, just haven't made it yet. Now listen, when we come up to the top, you'll want to hold your ski tips up so they catch the hill. As the chair swings around, you will need to slide off." He held his skis up, causing the chair to move again. I truly didn't know I was that afraid of heights before I was on this ski lift.

"Are they going to slow it down? Because right now I feel like we are flying super fast," My hands hurt from clenching the metal arm of the chair.

"Yeah, they will. And I'll follow right behind you." He pulled his poles off my lap and pulled his sunglasses across his eyes. He nodded to the guy in the booth running the top end. So, of course, the chair lift slowed to a crawl and I heard the guy tell the lower operator about the same slow turtle; newbie skier coming off now. I inched my back away from the chair and sat on the edge. I felt the chair drop lower and I was pizza-plowing down the embankment. I felt Wayne behind me; his skis slid up between my feet and his hands caught my waist as I slid forward toward the beginner trail.

"Not too bad, Wilson. Now, I'll go down first. I want you to follow my motions. Remember: make sure you plow, keeping the tips of your skis together in a V shape. Stay parallel with the mountain." He pointed to my sunglasses on the top of my head. I pulled them down and tried to get my heart to stop thumping so hard.

I can do this. I chanted to myself over and over in my head until I had a tiny spark of confidence in my body. *Wait a minute.*

This hill didn't look that steep from the chair. Stop being a baby, Wilson, you can do this. I watched him ski down the hill far enough away to give me the space to either succeed at getting down to him or completely kill myself trying.

Out of the corner of my eye I saw a beautiful woman skiing across the slope behind me to someone waiting for her. I heard her tell him to wait. Not usually a big deal in the scheme of people skiing up and down hills; however, it was the words she yelled that caused me to look. I almost fell over.

"Max, you better wait for me!" She skied over, snapped her skis off, and clomped over to hug him. She wrapped around him and he locked his arms around her. I couldn't tell if she kissed him because I couldn't see his face through her thick curly brown hair. He had a beanie that covered his head and sunglasses that hid his expression. That couldn't be my Max. I twisted to see what was happening between them. As he lowered her to the ground, she grabbed his beanie off, messed up his hair, and stepped back. He smiled and pulled off his sunglasses. My heart shattered. Chills radiated from the inside out. It was my Max. He was staring at her.

Who was that girl? She was unbelievably perfect— something I wasn't. Her smile, her hair…she looked worldly and very comfortable with him. You might as well crush me into a billion pieces. Broken wishes and jagged dreams: cargo I thought only needy girls owned. I wasn't supposed to be one of them. I *wasn't* one of them. I'd always considered myself independent, personable, and emotionally strong before this weekend. I glanced back and saw the pretty girl laughing and pushing her fingers to move Max's hair out of his eyes. She was touching him and he looked like he was right at home. I guess I was wrong. I was a self conscious, emotionally broken and disenchanted, needy girl.

"What's the holdup? You can do this. Don't think about it," Wayne yelled up to me.

I turned back to face down the mountain. He was hard to see through the tears that stung so cold in my eyes. My cheeks wet, frozen with icy lines of complete devastation, I held my breath and leaned forward. I needed to get away from them. I didn't need to see anymore, I was tortured enough.

I felt my balance teeter too far in front of me. My knees stretched, my calves pulled, and my stomach coiled. I was heading straight to Wayne with full force. I couldn't get my skis to pitch into a V, and I was going too fast to stop. I couldn't see through the tear-heavy lashes that clogged my vision. Fear and exhilaration spun out of control through my body. Was it because I was skiing down the hill, or because this heartbreak was the worst ever? I couldn't answer, I just felt my body somersault forward. White and blue swirled around me—sun then snow, sky then pain. I swore I heard my name being screamed like a parent trying to stop a child from running across a busy street.

When my body stopped tumbling and sliding, I heard the sound of snow cutting across like paper when it's ripped into long strips. Wayne snapped off his skis and hopped down to me.

"Wilson, are you okay? Answer me." He bent down to me, pulling off his gloves to clear the snow-drenched hair from my face.

"I'm sorry. Maybe I'm not cut out to be a skier." My pride was bruised and my heart was wounded. My body was fine; it was my soul that hurt all over.

"Wow that was quite a tumble you took." His thumb pulled down on my lower lid as he stared into my eyes. "Can you feel your feet? Move your fingers?" He pulled off my gloves. I moved my fingers.

"Can you feel that?" He stroked my fingertips.

"Yeah, I'm fine. I just want to sit up." I raised my head from the snow.

"Wait. Let me help you." He adjusted my head and I felt his hands slide under my neck. He pressed his fingertips into my spine. "Does that hurt?"

"No, I really am fine. Just feel a little stupid," I told him as I tried to sit up.

He slid under my back and pulled me against his chest.

"Just sit here a minute. Give yourself a moment before you try to stand up." I felt his hands slide up the sides of my neck. I could feel his heart beat against my back. I rested against him. He was so comforting, like a down blanket that warmed me on a blustery day. I closed my eyes and tried to stop the ache from consuming the rest of my body. Wrong solution—all I could see was Max and that girl together. How she was touching him, and how he was smiling at her. His hands held her tight against his body. *NO, I can't take this.* I opened my eyes to stop the visions. Stop the swell of devastation trying to take over every part of my body. Wayne's arm wrapped across my chest, his hands pulled my hair away from my left temple, and he pressed hard.

"Ouch." I flinched, pain shooting through my head. He scooped up some snow and pressed it against the side of my head.

"You've got a pretty sizable gash. The ski must've hit you." He pulled his hand back and I saw the blood. Behind it, I caught someone standing there. My eyes focused on the figure—it was Max. Wayne pressed his hand back onto my head.

"Hey buddy, could you ski down and get medic? I don't have a walkie-talkie," Wayne asked Max, a total stranger to him. Max's face was ghostly white. His eyes showed me just how bad it must have looked. He stared into my eyes for a second, I looked away, and he skied down past us.

"Lucky that guy stopped. I think you'll be fine, but I want a medic to take a look at it. What were you thinking?" His other hand slid against my forehead and across to my temple. His hand had to be freezing from holding the snow against my cut.

"Nothing; just trying to make it down to you." There was no way I was really going to tell him what was clouding my thoughts.

"Well, next time you need to think about something else, like coming to dinner with me tonight." I could feel his body tighten and adjust to my weight.

My heart thumped strong in my chest. Oh my frickin' God, he was amazingly gorgeous. It was so tempting to accept his invitation. I took a deep breath to tell him I didn't think it was the best idea when I heard the engine of a snowmobile winding high and the slosh of the blades cutting through the snow. *Again!* First the slowing of the ski lift, and now I was going to be taken down the hill in a basket behind a snowmobile. I was two for two in strikeouts. This was definitely not my sport.

The driver and Wayne got me into the basket. Wayne sat at the front with my head in his lap. It was a short ride down, considering it was just the bunny slope I'd wrecked on. They dragged me to the first aid station where, outside the door, I saw Max and Cindy waiting. My eyes met Max's as I was lifted to stand up. I was light headed and the blood gushed into my sight. I fell back into Wayne's chest and he held me as he helped me into the small room.

"I need to go in there—that's my friend," Cindy told them. Max grabbed her arm and kept her back.

"I'm sorry, Miss, we don't have room for more than the injured party and the medical staff. But we will get her taken care of as fast as we can." I saw Max looking in at me as the door closed.

"Okay, what happened here?" the medic asked Wayne.

"Well, I was about fifteen feet below her, waiting for her to start down the slope. This being her first run, I didn't want to go too far ahead. From what I could tell, her skis crossed and she flipped several times in the air. I think her ski must've busted her across her left temple. She slid past me and stopped. I skied down to her…" He shuffled his body back and forth. His hands spun and tangled up with each other, showing a reenactment of what had happened.

"Miss Mooney, do you remember what happened?" the medic asked as he patted the side of my head with gauze. I swallowed hard and answered as best I could. But I was preoccupied with worrying about Max and Cindy together waiting for me. If she pressed him, he might crack.

"Kinda. I remember leaning forward, then my skis crossed and I rolled. But it was almost like a feeling instead of a memory. By the time I opened my eyes, he was down next to me." I pointed to Wayne, who stood up and held the gauze on my temple while the medic grabbed a roll of tape and cross-stuck it on my head. The medic continued to check me for brain damage, asking me all these ambiguous questions I couldn't answer without asking him something back.

"So Miss Mooney, is this your first time skiing?" The guy pulled down my lower eyelid to shine a little flashlight across my pupils.

Did he not hear Wayne explain to him this was my first time skiing? Is this guy serious? Even if I didn't just fall down the side of an ice covered bunny slope, could he not tell it was my first time?

"Yeah, it's my first time. If you want to call it skiing." I touched the bandage taped across the side of my head; it stung and burned deep.

"Do you remember hitting your head?" the medic asked.

"No."

"Double vision?" he asked.

"Nope," I breathed.

"Dizzy? Sick to your stomach?"

"Not really." I was getting frustrated.

"What is this guy's name?" He pointed to Wayne.

"He's Wayne Samuel, my ski instructor."

"Well, make sure he gives you another lesson. Or get your money back." He popped Wayne in the chest. "You're going to be fine. Are you here with someone?"

"Yeah, she's right outside." I pointed toward the door.

"Okay, good. Let me go talk to her." He opened the door. Cindy was talking on her iPhone.

"I gotta go, the doctor just came out. I'll call you right back." She pulled her phone from her ear. "Is she okay? What happened?" She pressed for answers. It was a good thing he left the door open, because I was able to see exactly what was being said.

"She's fine. She hit her head on her ski and suffered a gash. My suggestion is to keep an eye on her. I don't see any signs of a concussion or anything more serious. But that doesn't mean it can't occur."

"So she's okay? Can she continue skiing today?"

"Well, I think she should go to the lodge, warm up, and see how she feels a little later."

"I'll take her over there. No problem," Wayne interrupted, almost leaping between the medic and Cindy.

"Oh, and who are you again?" Cindy snapped.

"Wayne Samuel, her ski instructor. I don't mind staying with her while you take some more runs with your boyfriend." He pointed over to Max.

"Number one, he is not my boyfriend and number two, I know you from somewhere." She tapped her finger across her lips.

"I met you at the airport. My father sat next to you guys on the plane—John Samuel."

"Oh, yeah, your father was the man who took my seat. I met you in the Denver airport where you picked him up, right? Okay, well that makes me feel better that you'll sit with her. We just got here and I *would* like to take a couple more runs. You're okay with that, right, Wilson?" She looked into the room and saw that I was sitting up. I waved my hand and looked past her to find Max. He was pacing back and forth. I could tell he wanted to come over and check on me but couldn't with Cindy hovering so close.

"Go. I'll be fine. Go ski." I fanned my hands, shooing her away.

"Okay, I'll meet you in the lodge in an hour." She put on her skis and slid away.

"What do you say, my best pupil, are you ready to get up and make it to the lodge?" Wayne wrapped his arm around my back and locked his hand under my arm.

"I can take her," a voice broke my focus, "How are you?" Max stood in the doorway. I wanted to be angry with him. I really wanted him to feel the pain I felt watching him hold another girl.

"I've been better," I was short of breath.

"I'm Max, a friend of Wilson's." He held out his hand.

"Wayne. Nice to meet you." He shook it.

I watched the guys size each other up and down before Wayne broke the tension.

"Would you mind grabbing her skis?" Max took my skis and flung them over his left shoulder, then picked up his and rested them on his right.

Wayne walked with me to the lodge, keeping his arm around my back and his other hand supporting me in case I became too weak. I was fine. I actually felt pretty good and was able to walk on my own. All the way to the lodge I leaned into Wayne, while Max followed behind carrying my skis—a small payback for breaking my heart.

CHAPTER TWELVE:

The door to the lodge swung open and Wayne helped me through. I was fine and he really didn't need to hold me so tightly. It was because of the ski boots that I wobbled and lost my balance. When I looked behind us to Max, he was staring a hole through Wayne's back as he put the skis into the rack. But his face softened and his eyes rounded when he noticed I was looking at him. He can't do that to me. *I* was the one that was hurt. I was the one that should have been so mad I could've spit nails. He was the one that started this game. It was his hands that locked around that girl, his smile that kept her interested, and his eyes that welcomed her attention.

There was something about Max that made butterflies come to life in my stomach. The same ones he had tamed to flutter when I thought about him. The ones that now lay dying in my gut. He had spilled the nectar that kept them vibrant and alive, leaving them with nothing to feed on but the leftover residue of betrayal. *Yeah, you could say I was hurt.*

I let Wayne take me to a quiet corner of the lodge. He made sure I was comfortable before he went to the bar. I kept staring at the door, waiting for Max to come in. *Didn't he feel the same way about me? Wasn't he going to at least put up a fight to get me back?* I shouldn't even feel this way. I should have been pissed. I should try to find him and confront him about his new girlfriend. *Damn-it, where was he?*

"Here you go." Wayne balanced a hot cocoa in his grip and pushed it toward me.

"Thank you. Is there alcohol in this?" I asked before I took a drink. He looked at me with his eyebrows scrunched and his lips tightened across his mouth.

"No, just hot cocoa, that's all."

I took a small swig. It scorched down my throat, clearing the pain Max created by not coming in to fight for me.

"Thanks," I croaked.

"No problem. Have you thought about my offer?" He sat across from me, his back to the door.

"What offer was that?" I teased.

"You don't remember? I asked if you'd like to go to dinner with me tonight." He kept his hands busy spinning his mug of hot cocoa.

"Oh, yeah, I remember. Thanks, but I think I'd better stick close to Cindy tonight." I drank my cocoa.

"Why don't you bring her? Purely friends, okay?"

"I didn't hit my head that hard. I really don't feel comfortable subjecting you to her." I tapped his hand and laughed. He didn't laugh back.

"Well, I still have some time to convince you to go to dinner with me." He picked up his chair and slid it in front of me without the table between us.

I was a little surprised when Wayne grabbed my feet and pulled off my boots. Cool air washed across my socks and my feet could actually feel the temperature on the outside. They had been held captive long enough. He snatched my ankle, ran his cool hands down my foot, and began to press his fingers into the bottom between my arch and toes. It felt so good. My head fell back to rest on the top of the chair, *heavenly*.

"Wayne Samuel, your next client is here. Please report to lessons. Wayne Samuel," a voice came over the loud speaker.

"Son of a bit—Wilson, I'm so sorry. But I have to take this lesson. I cancelled on her last week and she is a regular client. If I cancel again…" He laid my feet on the chair after he stood up.

"Wayne, don't worry about it. I've got a hot cocoa and I can walk if I need anything. Go." I shooed him away with my hands.

"I'll make it up to you, I promise, dinner tonight." He rubbed my ankle.

"Nice try. I really need to go home with Cindy. Thanks for helping me." He smiled and walked straight out the back door.

I sat at the big table alone. Time surrounded me, clicking by in slow motion. Every time the door flew open my heart dropped wanting to see Max walk through it. Every time, I was sadly disappointed. I figured I'd just be better off watching people around the lodge because waiting for him was worse than throwing up in my mouth and not having a place to spit it out.

I noticed that the people sitting around me were totally consumed by their laptops, phones, and iPads. Next to me was a dad on his netbook, clicking away while his son was glued to his iPod. His little brother poked his DS with a stylus, cheering out loud when he passed another level. *Why weren't they out skiing? What was so important they couldn't go out and spend time together on the slopes? Why even come?* My eyes scanned to the next table—another family that sat together and didn't talk. I wondered if they even realized how they are shutting each other out. Did they even know what they had? Sometimes I wondered what it would be like to have a brother or a sister. To live in a normal family with a mom and dad. What it would feel like to have people around who loved you, because that was what they were supposed to do? A chill ran down my spine; I took a deep breath, clearing the stale air that clung to my lungs.

I felt my phone vibrate in my tiny blue pocket. It was Joanie, my best friend in the entire world. I must have been sitting in a spot that gets cell reception because it also vibrated with five text messages and four voicemails.

I answered her call, "Hi, J."

"Wilson, what is going on? I'm freaking out over here. You can't leave me texts like that. I need clear, spelled-out, detailed information," she paused to take a breath.

"Sorry, I know. The minute I sent it I knew I should've just called you."

"Well? Details. And don't leave anything out. Did you see Mr. Goldstein? What happened?" her voice jumped over itself.

"Yeah, I saw him. Joanie, he spent the night with me." The words tumbled out of my mouth.

"GET OUT, you're such a liar! How did it happen? I want every detail. Was he any good?"

"J, we didn't do anything like that. He came over to Cindy's with his brother Calvin."

"He has a brother? How old is he?" I could hear her smiling.

"I think he's a little older than us. Anyway, we got to talking and one thing led to another and he kissed me in a bathroom."

"Oh my God, you're killing me, I can't believe this. He kissed you—in a bathroom. Was it wet? Did he stick his tongue in your mouth? Was he any good? I can't frickin' believe it. Mr. Goldstein." She wouldn't stop talking.

"He was better than good. It was so unbelievable. He was really, really good—like he knew what he was doing—good." I felt pressure rise in my chest and my face burst into a smile I couldn't contain.

"What about Cindy? Does she know? Because if she knows, we're so screwed." That was what I loved about Joanie, she dove right in and lived experiences with me. I could feel her excitement for me, her protective presence, and I knew it was real. She was real. So I knew when she found out he was with someone else, she would feel as betrayed as I did.

"Cindy doesn't know. But I think her brother does."

"Wait, Cindy has a brother? She never told us she had a brother."

"Yeah, a half brother, Nick. A real down-to-earth guy, you would really like him. Anyway, I was supposed to meet Max here at the ski resort."

"MAX, you call him by his first name?" she choked.

"He told me to. It would sound too weird if he finished French kissing me and I called him Mr. Goldstein."

"Yeah, you're right. So what are you doing now?"

"Well, I'm sitting here in the lodge waiting for Cindy to finish skiing. I kinda fell going down the hill."

"Kinda fell? Are you okay? Why is Cindy still skiing? That is so—her!" I could hear the protective side of her search for the answers to what was happening.

"I was going to go down the bunny slope when I saw Max hugging another girl. J, she was really, really pretty. And she looked older than me, closer to his age, completely out of my league." I stopped talking. She could hear in my voice that I was going to cry.

"Wilson, don't cry. Now stop. Wait. Don't ever think someone is better than you. I don't care what they look like.

You are so beautiful and smart, there is no reason to feel that way. Did he grab her or did she grab him?"

"What does that matter?"

"Because, if she grabbed him, it wasn't his fault. Girls can be very overbearing. You know that. Did he kiss her?" her voice was low and monotone.

"She grabbed him, but he held her in his arms. Then she pulled off his beanie and he smiled. I didn't see him kiss her." I was still mad.

"Well there you go, Wilson, she grabbed him, he didn't kiss her, and so what if he smiled at her. None of this tells me how you got hurt."

"I decided to get away from seeing them together. I leaned too far forward and stacked down the hill."

"Who stopped you?"

"Max?" I said as I looked up from the hot cocoa I was swirling as I talked to Joanie. He was standing in front of me, waiting for me to finish my phone conversation.

"Max stopped you?" I heard Joanie ask me.

"No, Joanie, I need to call you back," my voice was low. I closed the phone and slipped it into my little pocket.

I was so confused. When I thought about him with another girl I could feel the hurt seep into every corner of my body. But when I stared into his eyes, he captured my heart and filled me with such want, I ached. I didn't want to give into him. He stood there waiting for me to invite him to sit. I didn't.

"Are you okay? I saw you fall down the hill, it looked really bad." He dropped his hand, bouncing it on the chair in front of him.

"I couldn't focus. I became distracted when I leaned forward and started going down the slope. I lost my balance and fell forward." I waited for him to talk again.

"Good thing that guy Wayne was there to help you," he mumbled.

"I guess," I spat.

"You seemed really comfortable with him." He looked into my eyes.

"Not really. He was the only guy that wasn't preoccupied with a girl clamped on his body." I looked down at my drink.

The wheels spun in his head as he tried to figure out where I was going with this.

"I don't understand what you're saying. I'm really lost because, last night," his voice rose. He cleared his throat and started whispering, "Last night meant something to you, right? Because I can't do this with you." He stepped back.

"You know, I thought last night was great…better than great. It was amazing…even unmatchable. But today I watched you hold a beautiful girl against your chest, looking at her like she was the only one you wanted. You're right, you can't do this with me. I can't be a weekend girl for you." I stomped to the women's bathroom. The door slammed shut. I cranked the knob on the sink and held my hands under the water until I had a puddle I could splash across my face. It was so hard to tell him that. I kept splashing water against my face, careful to keep my bandage dry, yet trying to cool the fire that raged.

The door swung open, it was Max. My jaw hit the floor. I couldn't believe he was in the women's restroom, the one place any girl knew was untouchable for a guy. He leaned against the door, keeping space between us.

"Wilson, don't play this game with me. I didn't risk everything to be with you only to waste it on a misunderstanding."

"I saw everything. How she jumped into your arms and you held her tight to your body. The way you looked at her when she...touched...you"

A toilet flushed, causing both of us to wait. He stood rigid, apologizing with his body language to the older woman who acted like she didn't see us together in the bathroom. She washed her hands and slid out. Max pushed the door shut and twisted the lock

A smile opened across his face. "You have nothing to worry about." He walked closer to me.

"I know, because I'm just a naïve high schooler who was given a chance to experience what it felt like to kiss her government teacher."

I turned away from him. He stood unmoved.

I know what I did. I stabbed him through the heart with my words, drenched in taboo.

"Is that how you see me—as your government teacher? Because if I saw you as a student I wouldn't be here right now. When I look at you I see the girl I want to be with. Have since the first day you walked into my room." He stared at me through the huge mirror above the sink; pain was etched in the stress lines of his face.

There was something safe about the mirror; I didn't crumble in his pain.

"I know where I've drawn my line. There's nobody I've felt this way about in my entire life and I'm scared. Scared of what you might think, how it all feels, and I'm scared of being hurt. Max, seeing you with that girl—hurt." Tears sped down my cheeks, "Why do you want to be with me?" I whispered. *I was seventeen and inexperienced; she was his age and worldly.*

"You really don't see it? When I am with you I can't keep my head from swimming and my heart from pounding so hard it feels like it's going to burst from my chest. You are the most beautiful girl I've ever seen in my life. You are so smart; I finally feel alive when I am with you. I want to be with you because nobody has ever made me feel the way you do." He stood behind me, his body pressed against my back; he slid his hands around my waist and dropped his mouth to my ear. "She's a family friend. I've known her since we were little. Her parents and my parents are good friends. I swear to you, she is nothing more than a friend. Wilson...I'm so sorry." He turned me around. I felt his hand sweep the tears off my cheeks.

"I'm not used to this. It's so intense. I feel like such an idiot." I buried my face in his chest and tried to apologize. "I'm sorry for jumping to conclusions." He elevated my head to look at him.

"It's okay. Don't apologize, I understand." He pushed me to his chest and wrapped his arms tight around. His hand stroked across my hair and I felt the same, hypnotic rhythm that tamed the worry in my body when I was little. He pressed his lips to the top of my head. I found home in his arms; I was convinced she was nothing more than a friend to him.

I heard a key enter the lock and twist to open. I'd forgotten we were in a public restroom. How embarrassing was this going to be? Max pulled me into one of the stalls. I heard the resort employee tell the person it shouldn't have been locked.

"Shhh. Don't make any noise," he whispered so low I almost couldn't hear him.

It was a good thing the stall was enclosed all the way to the floor and there was some soothing music playing to camouflage our conversation. I tried to keep quiet, but it was really hard looking at him and seeing the faces he kept making at me. I had to clear my throat.

"Shhh," he covered my mouth with his lips. He tasted scrumptious—cinnamon with a hint of sugar. Low tingling in my body demanded my hands to tangle in his hair. The stall was so small, our bodies pressed firmly against each other. My body was teeming in the baby blue man-magnet ski outfit. He dropped his lips from mine following the line of my jaw; I pulled my head back. He reached his hands to my zipper and pulled it down to my navel. The flush of cool air raged across my uncovered skin. His lips followed the open space inviting him in. His hands drifted up under the suit, peeling it off my shoulders, dragging it back off my skin. He stopped and his eyes tracked mine.

"Are you okay?" he asked. I nodded a slight bounce, yes.

I had a myriad of different emotions flooding my body. I wanted him to touch me, kiss me, and press against me so hard I could feel our bodies melt, but I was scared. Frightened of the emotional responsibility it created. He was so experienced and I wasn't. How far were we going to let this go? He kissed the top of my shoulder, dragging his lips up across to my neck, right below my earlobe. He pulled away when he noticed I froze.

"Did I do something wrong?" he asked in a hushed voice.

I didn't say anything, just shook my head. There was nothing he did wrong. He knew exactly how to make me quake and shiver deep inside with just his kiss. Overwhelming urges surged through my body and I didn't know how to stop them. My eyes glossed with tears of relief. He wanted only me and I wanted him in a way the stall wouldn't allow.

"Let's get out of here. Take me somewhere. I want to go with you," I whispered and wiped my eyes. Even though I didn't know if I was ready for him, I didn't care. I wanted to get away with him, alone.

"What about Cindy? You can't leave her here."

"I can take care of Cindy but Nick's going to pick us up at four. Can you get me back here by four?" He pulled up the collar on my suit, sliding it back over my shoulders.

"Yeah, I think I can do that." He pulled the zipper on my space suit; his eyes danced with mine.

"I guess I should have asked you if you wanted to take me…?" I whispered.

"In more ways than you know." He smiled, "I have the perfect place." He reached across, his hand brushing my waist, and turned the lock on the stall. "Meet me out front in ten minutes at the big marble bench," he murmured into my ear.

My heart bounced as I kissed him in the space below his jaw. I snuck out of the stall, washed my hands, and entered into the reality of a secret love.

CHAPTER THIRTEEN:

There has always been something private about bathrooms. Usually you were in them alone and you would get out as fast as you went in. So I couldn't figure out what it meant that, the two times Max and I really started to make out, we were in bathrooms. There had to be some correlation between him and private spaces. Maybe it was because it was the one place where people wouldn't barge in on you. At least now we were going to get some time alone away from vanities and toilets. All I needed to do was get out before Cindy saw me and find my way to the big marble bench; easy enough. My heart was in my throat and my butterflies were hovering somewhere below my stomach.

I had just put my imitation UGGS on my feet when Cindy came and plopped down on the bench where we left all our stuff.

"Oh, I gotta tell you, it's a total bummer you're hurt. There are some real gorgeous guys hanging around the slopes today." She pulled her headband off and shook her head.

"Yeah, kinda a bummer." I watched her, waiting to see where she was going with her conversation.

"I met these two guys, total eye candy. Look, see if I have cavities, they are so sweet." She held her mouth open. I laughed.

"Wow, yeah, I see a couple. Well, did you talk to them?" I asked while Cindy put her headband back on.

"Hello, of course. That's why I wanted to ask you if you would be pissed if I kept skiing with them? 'Cuz I could totally tell them to come hang out here with us," she offered.

"NO, I don't mind if you go skiing with them. I'm good. You should go. Don't worry about me." I could feel the pressure lift from my chest. If she was going to be preoccupied with her eye candy, I could go with Max and she wouldn't even miss me.

"Are you sure?" She leaned against me, shoving her elbow into my side.

"Totally sure." I couldn't get her to leave soon enough.

"Okay, so we'll meet back here about a quarter to four. Sound good?" She hugged me and didn't wait for my answer before she clomped off. I stood there for a second. I couldn't believe it was that easy. I was ready for the beat-down, drag-out fight.

I hustled through the busy lodge. It was lunch time and everyone was coming in to rest and eat—the perfect time to get lost in the droves of people waiting in line to order.

"Wilson?" I heard someone call me. My heart dropped like a pinball, down into my stomach. It was Wayne. Why? What in the universe was stopping me from getting to Max? I smiled and turned back to him.

"Hi, Wayne." As bothered as I was by him finding me, he was so gorgeous I couldn't find the words to leave.

"Well, you look better. Are you ready to hit the slopes again? I'm done with lessons," he said holding his hands out.

"Um, well actually, Wayne, I was just going to go home." I pointed to the front doors of the lodge.

"Well, I could take you home," he said pointing to the back door. "I'm parked right out back."

"Oh, no, you don't have to do that. Besides, my friend is already here...probably waiting outside already. But I appreciate the offer." I gave him a small peck on the cheek. "And thanks for teaching me how to ski today." I broke for the front door.

"Wait, can I call you?" He stopped me from leaving.

Just the situation I didn't want to happen. I shouldn't have used him to make Max jealous. What was I going to say? *No, you can't call me; I'm dating my government teacher.* How was I going to get out of this without hurting his feelings? Another time when I needed Joanie's insightful wisdom on guys.

"Wayne. I'm sorry if I did anything to make you think I was available. I—,"

"You have a boyfriend?" he cut me off. He looked like a puppy that got punished for chewing up my best pair of shoes.

"Yeah, something like that." I looked down at my feet. "But if I didn't, I wouldn't hesitate to give you my phone number," I said looking up into his eyes.

"Well, he's one lucky guy. I hope he knows how lucky he is." He leaned over and kissed me on the cheek.

"Thanks. I'll see you around." I turned and opened the huge door.

It was cold outside. I wasn't used to it. My breath was white as it hung then scattered in the air. The cold reached down my throat and plastered my lungs with chills. My eyes stung from the sun beating down on the bright, snow-covered ground. I had to find Max fast. I didn't want Cindy to see me leave with him, and the fact that I'd just turned Wayne down really weighed heavy on my mind. He was such a nice guy.

"Wilson?"

I turned and saw Max standing outside of a small, shiny black sports car. He pulled the handle and held the door for me. He made sure I was in and buckled before he closed it. I watched him strut in front of the car, speeding to get in because it was so cold. He slipped in and fit perfectly behind the wheel. The butterflies came back strong and low. His aroma filled the car and flicked a switch on in my body. He had taken off his jacket and was wearing a gray zip-up hoodie, just small enough to encourage me.

He reached his hand across the space between us and pushed my hair back from my temple.

"Are you really okay? Does it hurt?" he asked, his eyes filled with concern.

My body shivered when he touched me. "I'm okay," I whispered.

"I really am sorry I upset you," he apologized, brushing his fingers down my arm, clutching my hand.

"I know." I took a deep breath, "So what kind of car is this?" *I wasn't stupid, I knew what kind of car it was. I just didn't want the focus to be on me.*

"I don't know, a BMW Z-something," he answered, narrowing his eyes.

"Really? Is it yours? Or did you rent it to impress girls?"

"It's mine and, no, I wouldn't rent it to impress girls— unless it's working?" He looked over at me and smiled.

"Yeah, it's working," I said real low.

"I guess my plan is falling into place."

"Plan? Something I must hear about." I shifted my body to slightly face him.

"Eventually, you'll see it. What was your favorite color again?" He was smooth.

"Green—yours is blue." He stared at me and his cheeks rose above his smile.

"What else do you know about me?" His eyes squinted.

"Well, I know you drive a BMW Z4. I know your favorite color is blue and you really like Italian food. I know you're honorable and sensitive and you're really passionate about your job." I looked out the window.

"Wow, you figured all that out by getting in my car? What else do you know?" He slid his hand to my thigh. My butterflies noticed.

"I know you like to stay after work to plan your next day. I know you smell good and your family has a cabin here. I know you like to listen to new bands that nobody has ever heard of." I took a breath. He looked at me and shook his head.

"What?"

"You're collecting data on me." He laughed, amused.

"Well, what do you know about me?" I watched his face. His smile dropped and his lips pulled tight.

"I know enough about you. Your favorite color is green. You look really good in powder blue ski suits." He stopped.

"That's it? Really? Wow you're so misinformed. Quite sad," I played.

"Okay fine, I know you're an only child. You've been in boarding schools since you were eight years old. Your grandparents raised you and, sadly, you lost your grandfather a few weeks ago. I know your best friend is Joanie Emerson, and that you're here in this car with me because you find me completely irresistible. That's what I know." He smiled.

I didn't say anything. I pushed my window down and felt the freeze swirl around my hair like the hands of God, trying to clasp a necklace without looking. He had me pegged. I was a person who didn't have a family. I guess the wounds didn't heal as quickly as I had thought.

"It's your turn—tell me what else you know about me." He glanced over. I cleared my throat and started to tell him what I knew.

"I know you also drive a Champagne-colored Lexus. I know this is your first year teaching on your own. I know you hate sweaters but you have to wear them to work. I know you immediately go and change your clothes once classes are over. You *are* irresistible in a flannel button-down with a cotton T-shirt and jeans. You like to stay after to watch me erase your boards," I said, trying to keep my family life away from this conversation.

"That's the best part. Watching you drag those huge erasers across my boards. When did you know...you had feelings for me?"

"Pretty much the first time I saw you. Last year you came into my history class to cover for Mr. Kringer." I felt the car swerve.

"You knew then? That long ago?"

"Yeah, you were trying to explain the significance of comparing the Industrial Revolution to modern times. You were so passionate." I stared out the window lost in a moment.

"Well the first time I knew it was something more for me was the day you walked into my government class. You were so confident. You sauntered past me and looked right into my eyes. You had your hair pulled back off your face. You sat right in the front row. It was such torture but I took it, because even that little bit of you was worth it." His forehead creased and his eyelids dropped as he told me this. Wow, he was pulling me into his world and I wanted to feel it.

"Where are you taking me?" I asked as he turned down a long driveway.

"You'll see." He glanced at me.

"What if I want to know now?"

"That depends on how badly you want to know," he played back to me.

What was going to be the best way to get him to talk? I grabbed the zipper on my moon suit and lowered it just enough to torture him.

"I wonder where we're going." I mumbled. His eyes caressed my body and hovered at my chest.

"My house," he answered, biting his lower lip. "I hope you don't mind. Nobody's there. We can have the place to ourselves."

He drove down to an exceptionally breathtaking contemporary mansion. Huge pillars invited me to the rippled glass double doors. Earth-toned multicolored slate sheathed the porch and walls. Statues of partially nude angels pouring water from huge vases fit flawlessly on either side. The whole top story of the house appeared to be one big window separated by the roof of the gigantic porch. With the huge parking area and no cars around, it seemed vacant. He pushed a button and pulled the car into one of the four garages.

"Well, here we are." He took a deep breath.

He slipped out and tracked to my side, pulling my door open. His chivalry was so romantic, something guys my age didn't have. He held his hand out to me, inviting me to him. I took hold and he pulled me from the car. He curved his arm around my waist and shut the door. His hand pressed delicately across my hip and I could feel his warmth through my suit.

"Right this way." He held his other hand out, pointing the way to a plain white door. He leaned across me and pushed it open. I stepped in and stopped short. His body pressed against me. I don't think he expected me to stop. My breath was robbed. We were in the most beautiful kitchen I'd ever seen.

"It's okay to keep walking." His hands wrapped around me. His warm breath steamed across my neck.

I noticed a massive basket loaded with boots and shoes next to me on the floor. I leaned against him and pulled my boots off.

"You don't have to do that." He anchored himself against the door frame.

"Do *you* usually do it?"

"Yeah, but—"

"But nothing, I want to honor your parents' wishes." I dropped my boots into the basket. He pulled off his and stacked them next to it.

He caught my hand and pulled me through the kitchen of my dreams. Huge white cabinets with brushed chrome handles, glossy black countertops with gray lines that glistened as the sun from the huge skylights bounced off them. On the butcher block island, a delicate arrangement of orchids warmed the room. Brushed stainless steel appliances punctuated the space.

"Max, this is beautiful."

"The kitchen? Wait until you see my favorite room."

He pulled me into the equally gorgeous modern dining room. Warm, deep red walls and dark mahogany crown molding encased the room. A table fit for twelve sat centered under a gigantic glass light that sent bright stars of crystal dancing against the walls. I couldn't keep from getting dizzy as he pulled me into his favorite room.

"This is your favorite room? This is not a room." I spun to take it in.

"It's called a great room. This is where I spend most of my time when I'm here." He guided me around, pointing out what he liked about it. One whole side of the room was filled from floor to ceiling with books. The other side held an enormous pool table with a stained glass light over it. The fireplace was made from giant river rocks partnered with an old stressed chunk of wood protruding out above the opening. A soft leather sofa facing the gigantic plasma screen T.V. above the fireplace separated one side from the other. Sunlight shone down from six massive skylights peppered throughout the open-beamed ceiling. I could see why he loved it in here. It was warm, functional, and fun.

"Play you a game of pool," I offered, grabbing a pool stick and spinning it in my hands. I didn't know how to play.

"Really? I'm pretty good at it. You'll have to prepare to be spanked." He grabbed a pool stick and rubbed a small block on the tip.

"Spanked, huh? Well, let's just see how much you know," I teased.

He grabbed a triangle and set it down on the green. He pulled a bunch of balls from the pockets and dropped them into the shape. Then he mixed them up and slid it across, gently pulling the triangle off.

"Stripes or solids?"

"Excuse me?"

"Do you want to be solids or stripes? The balls you're trying to hit into the pockets." He looked at me, astonished I didn't understand the question.

"Stripes."

"Ladies first." He backed away from the table and rested his pool stick on the ground, his hands stacked near the top of it.

"Okay, thanks." I held the stick up. I could figure this out; all I needed to do was break up the pyramid of balls.

"Wait, you need to hit the white cue ball into the group of balls to break them up." He grabbed it from the other side of the table.

"I knew that." I smiled and held the stick across my chest, resting it in one hand while I clutched it in the other. I felt the muscles in my arms get tight.

"Wait, you need to rest your aiming hand on the table. Here, let me help you." He put his stick against the wall and pulled mine from my hands, demonstrating how I was supposed to hold and aim it. I tried; I guess I didn't get it because, in a flash, his body was up against mine. His smell invaded me, marching its way down to feed my butterflies. His arm wrapped around and held my aiming hand. His other arm followed mine, resting his hand on my pool stick. His head tight against me, his breath warmed my ear with words of encouragement.

"Do you feel the motion? Forward and back." He moved the pool stick. His chest pressed heavy across my body.

I nodded.

"One, two, three." He tangled the words in my hair and helped me push the stick, hitting the white ball. The crack of the break echoed through the room.

"Nice break," he breathed into my ear. I shivered as he slid his hands up my arms.

"Thanks; couldn't have done it without your help."

"Looks like you're solids. You get to shoot again." He pointed to the ball in the little basket at the corner.

I held the stick wrong again. This time on purpose. He noticed and slid up behind me, holding his hands against my hips.

"You need to bend more at the waist, like this." He pushed down on my back with his chest. He was teasing me. I could barely focus.

"Let me see you do it by yourself." He pulled away and I tapped the white ball straight into the pocket.

"No fair, you did that on purpose," I straightened to tell him.

"Of course I did. That's my strategy. Now step aside and watch." He grabbed his pool stick and made it look easy.

He bent level with the table. His hair fell to his eyes; his arms stretched tight across the table. The curve of his back and the bend of his knees were so incredibly tasty looking. He snapped the pool stick forward and knocked two striped balls into the side pockets. In one shot he was beating me.

He circled the table, studying his next move. I leaned against it and blocked him.

"Excuse me—I need that spot to score." He pointed to me. Without saying a word I refused to move. He put his pool stick on the table and came next to me. His hands pressed at my waist, browsed up my sides, and across my ribs to under my arms. He brought his face close. I inhaled the scent of his breath.

"I need to score here." He pulled back, making eye contact with me. I knew he was going to score—maybe not all the way, but far enough.

"Okay, let's see what you can do." I kissed him and fireworks exploded low in my groin. He pressed hard against my mouth. I pushed my hands through his hair and around his ears. Down past his jaw line my hands found the perfect spot. His hands slid down to my hips and across to the back of my thighs. I felt his arm tighten when his hands caught and lifted me to his waist. I wrapped my legs around him as he set me on the table. He kissed me before his lips drifted, tracing the line of my jaw down to my collar bone and across the top of my chest. He stopped and looked into my eyes. My skin ran cold as he pulled on the zipper of my suit. Watching my reaction the entire time, his eyes asked for permission. He stopped at my navel. My hands pulled at the zipper of his hoodie. Waiting for the right to touch, he helped me take his sweatshirt off. I pulled up at the bottom of his shirt and he lifted his hands in the air. I pulled it off, too. His chest was exquisite—muscular and tight with just the perfect amount of hair. I pushed my lips to the space between his collar bone and neck. He pushed to clear my shoulders of my space suit. I pulled my arms out of the sleeves and wrapped my bare arms around him, feeling the exchange of our body heat. He kissed my neck, pressing light; it sent goose bumps through to my chest. I felt his hands caress their way up to the clasp of my bra and work to release the tension. My heart leapt high into my throat. I guess this was it—this was going to be the moment I let him see me, exposed.

"Wait." I pushed against him. His hands pressed hard into my back.

"Yeah?" he whispered into my ear.

"I don't want to do this—" I swallowed, trying to lose the extra bubble in my throat before I continued "here. Take me to your bedroom," I whispered back to him.

"Nobody's home," he breathed.

"I just don't feel comfortable doing this here." He bent down, grabbed his hoodie from the floor, and wrapped it around me. I slid my arms through the sleeves and zipped it up. He lifted me off the pool table and slipped his hand into mine. He kissed me so softly and led me up to his room.

CHAPTER FOURTEEN:

I waited for him to let me in. He slid his body against my back and opened the door. He pressed his chest against me. I entered, looked around, and glanced back to him. He seemed a little shy about having me in his space. He shrugged his shoulders and forced his hands in his pockets as he followed me.

"This is my room."

His room was masculine and clean. A black, four-post, queen-sized bed was draped with a burgundy and dark green comforter. A huge stack of pillows at the head and a folded brown wool blanket at the foot made his bed look super cozy. Framed black and white blown-up photos of mountains covered in snow splashed the walls. A plasma TV hung over the slate fireplace.

"It's very comfortable. I really like these pictures of the mountains." I stopped in front of an aerial photo of a construction site.

"Yeah, that one is this place here. That's when my family was having it built." He pointed to the picture. "See this tree here? That's the tree out front to the left. That's the garage...and that is my room, there."

I watched as he got lost in the picture of his family history. Desires bridged across my mind to my heart, and I couldn't stop myself from picking up where we'd left off in the great room. I pulled the zipper down on my sweatshirt. His eyes intensified and fixed on mine; he reached up to stop me when the zipper reached my bra.

"Are you sure you want to do this?"

"Yes, I am." My voice caught in a shiver and wavered slightly. *I couldn't say I wasn't scared or nervous, but who wouldn't be? This was the first time anyone other than Joanie and Cindy was going to see me naked from the waist up.*

"Because I can wait for you."

"I know you can," I nodded and let him finish pulling the zipper open. His head tilted to one side and his eyes strained.

He slipped his sizable hands up the sides of my sweatshirt. I could tell he was waiting for an okay, so I grasped his hands and spread them apart; my sweatshirt opened. He gently took it off my arms, leaving my bra resting loosely across my chest; his fingers slinked under the straps at my shoulders. He wet his lips with the tip of his tongue, swallowed, and pulled. I stood there—naked. It wasn't so bad. He liked what he saw; it felt good. I pushed my hands past his chest and down around his torso, into the curve of his lower back. Our bodies fit together perfectly, and I swam in his warmth.

He kissed me wildly with his tongue; I could tell he was letting go of caution. His lips deserted mine, wandering along my neck and down to right above my chest. I ran my hands through his soft, black hair. Tangling any fears into knots, I let them fly away with the wind.

He plucked his mouth from my skin, paused—I was taken by his ability to make me feel so much more emotion than I ever thought possible—and looked at me. I nodded, afraid to say anything; I didn't know what would come out. I could tell him to take me all the way, that was how strongly my feelings were raging for him.

His hands dropped to my waist as he continued to kiss me above my chest. I pushed my hands around his neck and bent to get him to come back to my lips. His hands caressing my back, chills rippled down my spine. He lifted me to his bed.

Cool air wafted over my naked skin before he slinked up across my body and kissed me. His knee slid up between my legs and pressed against me; I was so hot from the waist down. The damn space suit was suffocating me and retaining the heat he'd created down low.

I wanted to take it off, but didn't want to imply that I was ready to go *that* far. His lips pressed lower on my chest and brushed across the front. Chills thrashed through my body. While he lingered there, he looked up at me. His mouth was so delicate, his tongue so warm, I felt the intense connection lower in my body. The way his hand traced my side and all around me, his experience was almost frightening.

I'd wondered what it might feel like to have him explore my body, entirely. I had no idea that it would be so passionate. Everything he did felt so natural. It made me wonder if it was a sign that I should go all the way with him. His mouth traipsed between my breasts and down above my navel.

"Max?"

"Yeah, did I go too far?" He narrowed his eyes.

"No, I'm just really hot in this ski suit."

"Okay…"

"But I don't want to give you the wrong impression."

"And what impression would that be?" He dragged his finger across my stomach, piquing my arousal.

"That I was ready to…sleep with you." I could feel the blood flush fast to my cheeks.

"Well, you've already done that."

"Max, you know what I mean."

He took a deep breath.

"We won't do anything you aren't ready to do." He stared into my eyes, sincere.

I reached down to my blue suit's zipper; he took over and unzipped it down below my panties. Clutching the sides of my suit, he started to tug as I lifted my hips. My panties rolled down just enough to make him stop. Correcting them while he pulled, he flung the skin tight suit off my body.

Dragging his hands on my leg, and across my stomach, he eventually arrived at my neck.

"Are you cold?"

My fingers automatically worked the waist of his jeans, unbuttoning them and tugging slow on the zipper.

What was I doing? Was I really ready to go all the way with him?

"I'm okay. I just think it's only fair that, if I'm almost naked, you should be too." I pushed up, kissing him as my fingers caught his belt loops and yanked down.

"Wait, wait. Hold on," he held his pants on and hopped off the bed. "Oh man, Wilson, you don't know what you do to me." He snapped his top button, went to his dresser, grabbed out a pair of sweats and a T-shirt, and held them out to me.

I felt like I'd been kicked in the stomach. I couldn't stop my insides from twisting, even when I wrapped my arms around my chest.

"Did I do something wrong? Because if I did—."

"No, you've done nothing wrong. Everything you did was more than right." He sat next to me and caressed my cheeks. "I want to be with you so bad, I lose my breath, and I can't breathe. But I want to make sure you're ready—really ready. I don't want you to regret your first time...with me." He gingerly pressed his mouth below my temple and unfolded the white T-shirt before he slid it over my head. It smelled like him. He pulled it down over my torso, brushing the back of his hand against my naked skin, then slipped me into his sweats one leg at a time, dragging them skillfully up past my waist. I was drowning in them. He crept onto the bed and wrapped his arms around me.

I guess I had to be grateful that one of us was looking out for our best interests, because I sure wasn't. He had me so worked up, I could've sold my soul to the devil and wouldn't have discovered it until it was too late.

Damn, his honorable intentions made me want to be with him even more.

"What if I don't want to wait? What if I told you I was ready right now?" I rubbed my hand across his bare stomach and pressed his chest. The mountain of pillows was wedged firmly behind him.

"I know you're not." He caught my hair and pushed it behind my ear.

"No, I mean, what if I changed my mind and am saying that I've decided I wanted you to make love to me right now? Just take me—right here, right now." I felt the butterflies agree with my decision. I swung my leg across him and sat low on his lap. He clasped his hands quickly around my waist, and I could feel how much he wanted me.

I smoothed my hands against his and grabbed them from my waist. I locked my fingers with his and pinned them down above his head as he pretended to try and break free. My lips tickled his, soft and warm.

"Wilson, you know you're making it really hard for me to do the right thing." He thrust his mouth open against mine when I pressed downward against his lap. My lips trailed his chin, then his neck, and the span of his chest. When I let go of his hands, he grabbed around my waist. I was expecting him to lift me off but, instead, he drove me down against him. His hands sped up under my shirt, caressing my back, weighing me solid on his chest. Our mouths locked, tasting the sweet flavor of ecstasy. Rolling me over, his body pressed heavy against mine; at the same moment his breath caught a low growl, deep in his throat, as he pulled away.

"Don't stop." My body shivered.

With the tips of his fingers, he brushed my skin and pushed the hair back from my face. Our eyes met.

"I have to wait. I have to. It's important to me. I need to wait for both our sakes," he tried to convince me. *Yeah, like I should believe in fairytales or the Easter Bunny, too.* I didn't need anything to persuade me. I knew what he wanted, and I was supposed to respect that.

"How long?" My heart thrashed.

His brows crumpled unevenly. "A month."

"Thirty days!"

"Once you're eighteen." He stared at me.

I sat up on my elbows, causing him to back off me. Those weren't the words I'd expected to come bolting from his mouth. I thought he wanted to wait because it was going to be my first time and he wanted to make sure I was ready for all the emotional baggage it carried. I could feel the pressure in my chest explode and roar to life, a blaze that burnt deep to my core. I sat up and pushed my hands to my eyes.

"Wilson, when I look at you—when I am with you—I don't see a seventeen-year-old girl. I see a beautiful woman I want to spend time with. But that doesn't erase the fact that you're seventeen and I am twenty-two." He seized my wrists and pulled my hands off my eyes.

"I wish it wasn't so complicated." I twisted off his bed and swiped up the ski suit that brought me there. "I'd better change so you can take me back." I headed to the door, stretching; he caught me at my waist, "Hold on." He pulled me back onto the bed, his expression plastered with burdens I'd never considered. He struggled with what to say.

"There is this part of me that keeps battling with these thoughts of you resenting me—for being *the guy* that took your virginity. I don't want to be that guy. The last twenty-four hours have been incredible—spectacular—but, in less than another twenty-four hours, we'll be back at Wesley. You will still be seventeen and considered under-aged. I will still be twenty-two. You'll still be my student and I'll still be your teacher." His eyes tightened as he searched for my reaction.

As ridiculous as it was, I could see his point. After all, he was the one who had the most at stake. He could lose his job and be thrown in jail for sex with a minor; his life would be ruined. Me, I would most likely be treated like a victim.

"I understand. I wish it didn't matter. But what's a month?" I leaned back between his legs against his chest. He wrapped his arms around me.

"Thirty days."

"We can wait four weeks."

"Seven hundred twenty hours, but who's counting?" He pressed his face to my ear, his smile caught my hair, and swells of contentment flooded my body. "I'd better get you back before Cindy starts wondering where you went," he tried to push me up off his chest. I didn't budge.

My heart fell into my stomach. I wanted to spend my last night in Aspen with him. Who knew what it was going to be like when we were back at Wesley on Monday.

"I wish I could stay with you." I pushed harder against him, I wasn't going to let go until I absolutely had to. He felt so soothing.

I heard a soft knock at the door.

"Maxi?" a silky warm voice swam through the air.

He pushed me up and grabbed a shirt from on top of his dresser. "Yeah, mom."

"You decent?" her voice was soft and comforting. He pulled the T-shirt over his body and opened the door just enough to peek out.

"Yeah." He made sure she saw him.

"You coming...downstairs? I have the Vaughns coming over for dinner tonight; your sister and Dan are coming too. I was hoping you could help me with dinner." He tried to say something. She continued to talk. "Have you seen your brother? He mentioned something about bringing a friend tonight." She reached up and pulled a little at his bangs. "You need another haircut." He took a breath to respond and she sustained the one way conversation. She slid her hand around his waist. "What are you eating down in California? You're getting too thin."

"Ma! I'm fine." He shifted and shrugged without letting go of the door handle or the door jam. She released his waist and walked down the hall. "Hey I'm bringing someone to dinner tonight, too, okay?" he told her, trying to ask without looking like he was asking. He leaned out into the hall and tapped his foot on the floor waiting for her to say something.

"That's fine," she echoed down the hall.

"*She's* from California," he volunteered. I felt my heart leap in my chest. Her voice grew closer. I wish I could see her but I didn't want to intrude on their family moment.

"*She?* A girl? Well, she must be someone pretty special if you're bringing her here tonight," her tone was expectant.

I couldn't breathe. Her desire for his happiness took every bitter memory I had stored about my mother and shattered it to powdery dust. She was his mother; he was her son. My memory bank of a perfect family held a zero balance.

"Yeah, she is," he said. I heard her kiss him.

"Well, honey, then I can't wait to meet her," she told him and walked back down the hall.

I took a deep, burning breath. I wanted to be a part of her so bad. I wanted what he had—to own it, live it. Let it pour over me and fill every hole my birth parents had torn into my heart. My body trembled and my muscles cramped; I tried not to cry. I heard his feet land on the floor fast. His hands pushed my hair back from my face and held me tight to his chest. I wept.

"Hey, shhh. It's okay. Sweetie, what's wrong?" His voice was reassuring, his body swayed with soothing intentions. It was all-consuming to acknowledge there were people in this world worth crying for.

"You don't know how lucky you are to have normal," I choked.

He had everyday interactions—mundane, plain experiences with his mother—something more priceless than gold. Something so rare to me, I could've killed for a tiny drop of it, but to him it was as common as grains of sand on a beach.

"I know I'm lucky; my mom is a very special woman. Wilson, please say you'll come to dinner with me tonight."

Wedged underneath his chin, I nodded against his chest.

"Good, now how am I going to get you all to myself tonight?" He held his lips to the top of my head. The warmth from his breath sent chills down through my body. I was where I belonged.

CHAPTER FIFTEEN:

The ride back to the ski resort was anything but silent. We were busy trying to figure out how to steal me away from Cindy's to be with him and his family for dinner. Everything we came up with seemed impossible—I'd been kidnapped, held for ransom, or even that I ran away with a guy I met on the ski slope—they were all too totally creepy to consider. Then it hit me: the fact that Nick knows about us and he hasn't said anything to Cindy shows me he might be our best option. Now I just had to come up with a way to convince him to help us.

"I could try and get Nick to cover for me," I said.

"I don't know about that. I think there's more to him than you think," Max snapped back, "I've seen the way he looks at you."

"He's grateful to me for standing up to Cindy. That's all," I played down his concerns.

I wasn't blind. I knew Nick liked me as more than a friend. But I wasn't going to worry Max with that, or give Nick the opportunity.

"I can tell when guys are checking out my girlfriend. He's got something for you." He glanced at me and back to the road. His eyes widened, trying to assure me he was right. I was too busy replaying the word *girlfriend* in my head. He called me his girlfriend. My butterflies cheered. My heart overflowed with so much excitement I had to keep reminding myself to breathe.

"Maximillian Goldstein, you're not jealous are you?" Watching his profile as he drove, I got my answer.

"Jealous? No. Fully aware of other guys checking you out? Absolutely. And he's one I gotta watch out for." He glanced at my reaction, his hand glided through the air between us and landed on my thigh. "And to have my girlfriend dressed in this curve-catching, body-hugging suit just makes my job that much harder."

Oh my God. Okay, if I could climb over and start making out with him I would. He was so good at nurturing my butterflies. They loved it when he touched me and used words that feed their insatiable appetite. I was silent for a delectable moment.

"I've noticed you've used that word quite a few times," I said looking down at his hand rub across the baby blue satin fabric of my ski suit.

"What word?" he was confused.

"Girlfriend." I took in his expression as I looked at him. His face ran warm, his lips curled to catch my excitement, and his eyes danced glimpses with mine.

"Is it okay to call you that?" He pulled over.

"I guess that depends on your definition." I followed his eyes tracing up my body. His jaw flexed and he pitched a growl low in his throat.

"Well, how would you like the definition to read?" he asked.

Now that wasn't fair. I know exactly how I wanted it to read and it included words like relationship, exclusive, and monogamous. The problem was, I didn't know what his definition was going to be. What if I go and blurt out what I want it to be and it doesn't match his ideas? I will be the fastest ex-girlfriend of a relationship that never developed beyond a misinterpreted definition.

"Tell me one word that represents your definition." *I got him now.* I watched his face as he thought about it. If he came up with a word, then I could just build on that one with a meaning that satisfied both our interpretations.

"One word? It would have to be—what if I can't come up with one word?" he teased. I reached over and tried to push him, he grabbed my hands.

"Wilson." He looked me in the eyes. I was still trying to battle past his hands to his chest.

"Yeah?" I stopped pushing.

"That's my one-word definition of my girlfriend," he said. I froze. He did it again. He never stopped making me want him entirely way too much.

"Your turn. What one word would define being my girlfriend?" He leaned toward me as he asked.

"Okay, it would have to be—yes." His eyes smoldered, stirring a desire that was automatic within me. I captured his neck and pulled him across to kiss me.

I didn't care really what words defined the feelings, emotions, and events that had taken place this weekend. What I had right now was so much more than I truly ever thought was going to happen. Name it, define it, and even own it; I loved the fact that he was with me, calling me his girlfriend, and wanted me to meet his family.

"Magnificently sensual," he breathed as he pulled away. His eyes slowly opened to look at my lips.

"Only one word at a time, that was the challenge. You lose and I win." I grabbed his shirt and pulled him closer to me.

"What do you win?" he spoke against my lips.

"Any question I want to ask. Nothing's off limits."

"Nothing's off limits?"

"Nothing," I answered. He pulled away; I watched his mind tilt off to another world, one I wondered if he was ready to share with me. *Maybe I should've thought this through before I decided to put it out there. There I went again, my mouth speaking before my mind was ready.*

"What do you want to know?" he interrupted the dialogue in my head.

Great. Was I ready to ask what was racing through my mind? Or would it be better to pretend I wanted to know some safe answer to some random question? Of course I pulled the "same old, same old" and decided to put it out there.

"How many—'Wilsons' have you had?" I felt the question scratch out of my throat and fill the car. He looked out the front window. His cheek caved slightly into the side of his face and I watched the muscles through his jaw tense up past his temples. He turned to me, indicating he wanted some clarification on the question. I nodded.

"When you say *had*, does that mean serious ones? Ones who I've been…intimate with?" His eyes tightened and his eyebrows curved to a serious expression.

"Yeah, that's exactly what I mean." I swallowed, waiting for him to think carefully about his answer. His eyes rounded, reminisced by the bridged memories I shouldn't have asked him to remember. His mouth broke to a slight smile that flooded his eyes.

I've changed my mind. It wasn't too late, was it? I've decided I don't want to know. I don't care how many girls he's slept with. My question became the perfect excuse to relive his life before me.

"Wilson, do you really want to know the answer to this question?" He tapped the heel of his hand onto the steering wheel. His attempt to give me the time I needed to decide.

"Because once it's out there, I can't take it back. I can't make it okay or change my history before I met you." He stared at me. I could tell he wasn't comfortable telling me.

"You don't have to tell me if you don't want to," my voice broke.

"Three—I've been intimate with three people." I stared at him; he grabbed the wheel looking at his hands.

A silence filled the car. There was the irrational part of me that was worried he was going to tell me double digits. Three wasn't horrible. Ideal, for me, would have been one; but if you think about it, three is actually a pretty reasonable number. He was twenty-two—with high school and college alone he could've easily had a lot more. I'm okay with that.

"Were any of them serious girlfriends?"

What was I doing? It was like I wanted to be tortured. Who owned the car before I bought it, right? Not even close. This was so much more emotional. At least you can get a car detailed and remove evidence of personal ownership. You can't remove the evidence of an emotional memory imprinted onto the soul of a person. Each experience with every one of those women had left a part of his essence changed forever.

"At the time I was with them, at that particular point, they all held some type of significance in my life. Can I say I was *serious* with all of them? I would be lying if I said I yes." He shifted his body to face me, bouncing his fist on his knee.

"Thank you."

"For what?" He looked around the car scowling.

"For being honest enough to share that with me. As hard as it was to hear you say it, it had to be even harder to tell me."

"Well then, you're welcome." He took a deep breath and ran his fingers through his hair, causing it to curl back off his face and down around his ears. "We'd better get you back. It's already twenty to four." He started the car, pulled down into the parking lot of the ski resort, and found a place to park away from the front curb.

"I think this is the best spot so we aren't seen," he said as he hopped out of the car, raced around, and held open my door. He grabbed my hand to help me out. He pushed the door shut and leaned against it. I noticed his eyes glistening as he pulled me close to him. His hands tracked around my waist and rested across my back. I lost my hands in his hair. I felt him take a deep breath and exhale it across my neck as he leaned into me.

"Dinner's at 6;30. I was hoping you could be there around 5:30." His hands pulled out from around my waist and anchored up around the sides of my head, pressing against my ears. I heard the echo of his lips as he dragged them across my cheek to my mouth. A primal deep moan in his throat vibrated to my center. He was deliciously warm, creating in my body a flash of hope that he wasn't kissing me goodbye. I didn't want him to leave.

"Max? Your parents...what are you going to tell them?" My heart thumped sturdily in my chest. He pulled me closer.

"About what?" he asked against my skin.

"About us."

"What about us?"

"They're going to want to know how we met. What are you ready to tell them?" I pulled back. I wanted to look at him and see what he was going to say. He curved his lips to one side of his face and shook his head. His eyes squinted tight. He took a deep breath and I watched as his words mingled with the condensation that swirled around our taboo.

"I'm not. They don't need to know." He stood straight, his muscles turned firm and cold.

"They're gonna want to know how we met. We'd better get our stories straight. How about a video store?...a library...a grocery store? Oh, I got it, how about a stripper bar?" I tried to lighten his mood. I felt his body pull back from mine.

I didn't like the distance creeping between us. I'd found the *one* subject he wasn't willing to share with anyone, including me.

"Nobody needs to know how we met. It's better that way. Trust me." He stared at the ground. Lingering time filled the space where his eyes should have blinked. He was captivated by the pictures in his head—evidence he must have kept filed and locked somewhere safe away from anyone trying to break in.

I crouched down, trying to knock him free from the impervious hold the thoughts had on him.

"Okay, nobody will know. But we have to decide what our story will be. Just in case someone asks." I pushed his head up to look at me. I could tell he was unsettled. He must have buried it deep in his soul to pretend there wasn't an unwritten rule about our circumstances.

"We met at a coffee shop," I told him. He smiled, I continued, "You ordered the same drink as I did; a double mocha with whip cream and those tiny chocolate sprinkles. We sat and talked for hours about politics, religion, and sports."

He laughed.

"Sports, huh? Really?" His eyebrows creased, lightening the weight in his expression. He pulled at the little pockets of my blue suit, bringing me to lie against him.

"I guess there's some stuff you'll need to learn about me. Like my extensive knowledge of professional sports teams in the Bay Area." I cuddled my face into his chest.

"Really." He laughed, tilting his head back.

"Really! Ask me something." I pushed my elbows up onto his chest so he could see I was serious.

"Okay. Let's see—what two teams played in the eighty-nine World Series?"

"Oh, please, this is no challenge at all. It was the Oakland A's and the San Francisco Giants. Oakland swept them in four games. First two games were in Oakland, the third was rescheduled because of the Loma Prieta earthquake, then the other two were in San Francisco." I faked a yawn and stretched my arms into the air.

He grabbed around my back, chills rushed my skin as he spun me against his car. He pushed strong against me, he explored my neck, kissing his way up to behind my ear.

"God, you make me so crazy. How am I going to exist for the next couple of hours without being next to you?" He pushed his forehead to mine. Our arms knotted around each other, keeping me heated to the perfect temperature of arousal. He didn't know how hard it was for me not to just get back into his car and go to his place.

I shivered at the thought of walking away from him. He noticed and unzipped his jacket. I slid my hands up under his shirt, around his waist, and up his back. His fiery-hot skin burned across my frosted hands. He wrapped the front of his jacket around us, swaddling me in his comfortable embrace.

"Do I have to leave? Because I could live right here, forever." I pushed my nose to his aroma and drowned in his heartbeat.

"It's 4:15. You better go find Nick and Cindy." He waited until I pulled away to let me go.

He gave me a gentle kiss, tugging away until I anchored my hands into his hair, hauling him back to my lips. I needed the feeling of this kiss to radiate and last me for the next couple of hours. Like the first sweet taste of a forbidden fruit before it is ripped out of your hands. I didn't want to be the one to walk away. He pushed his hands to my cheeks and I felt him back away from our kiss.

"You really better go before they come looking for you." He kissed my forehead. I trembled. His hand, tender to the touch, encouraged me to walk away from him. I looked back, at him standing there, vacant of me in his arms; he looked empty. I felt the wings of my butterflies become motionless. It would be one hour and fifteen minutes before they'd fly again. But who was counting?

CHAPTER SIXTEEN:

It was the longest walk from where I had left Max in the parking lot to the front of the ski lodge. Even though it was less than a hundred feet, it felt like universes away. Only now I noticed the chill that wrapped and bound me tight into a battle between the emotional intensity that burned in my core and the bone-freezing resentment trying to snuff it out. I belonged with Max. When I was with him, nothing else mattered; nothing else existed. Was it altogether healthy of me to get lost in his existence? Probably not. But when you're handed a weekend with someone you've dreamt about for so long, you live in that moment until it doesn't exist anymore.

My moment evaporated in seconds when I saw the black Sequoia parked in the loading zone. The back hatch was up and Nick was loading our duffel bags. Cindy was hanging on some random guy. The regret hiccupped into my throat. *Would they really miss me if I just decided to turn back?* I slipped in next to the chartered buses and came up behind Cindy. Nick grabbed the skis and spotted me.

"Hey, Wilson, whoa, what happened to you?" He pointed to the side of my head. I pressed my hand to it and felt the bandage that I had forgotten was even there.

"She fell down the bunny slope. Wonder if it was because she didn't have Shane to teach her?" Cindy leaned away from the guy she was wrapped around and pointed at Nick. She started in right away with bashing him. It was as if I hadn't left. Gosh, why didn't I just stay with Max?

Nick ignored Cindy's digs, as usual. It was nothing new to him. Her inability to keep her opinions to herself was as common as Aspen snow in the winter.

"Are you okay?" he asked turning to load Cindy's skis into the SUV.

"Yeah. I don't think I'm cut out to be a skier. I spent most of the day hanging out in the lodge," I bold-face lied. A surge of anticipation crawled up the back of my neck. Blood rushed to my cheeks, and the muscles around my mouth uncontrollably tightened to a smirk.

"You should've called me. I'd have come and picked you up." I handed him my skis, which he must have collected from in front of the lodge.

"Nah, I was fine. They have tons of books and a TV. I was fine," as each word came out of my mouth I could feel the excitement build trying to wake up the dormant butterflies in my gut.

I glanced at Cindy only to find that she was completely taken in by the ski stud she'd been with all day. She was so involved with him, she didn't see that we were sitting in the car waiting for her to say goodbye.

"I can't believe this guy likes her. She is so full of herself," Nick said, looking at me in the rearview mirror.

"Maybe some guys like a confident girl." I met his eyes then looked away.

"Or maybe this guy sees her as an easy target." He shuffled his eyes between Cindy and me.

"What?" I choked. Cindy was not an easy target. She knew what she wanted and how to get it. If anything, she was targeting that guy. I wouldn't be surprised if she'd marked him when we first arrived. She was anything but an easy target.

"If she keeps acting like she's *easy*, she will keep attracting these guys that only want one thing from her. And it isn't her phone number." He looked at her kissing him goodbye. "See…right there…why is she doing that? She's just reconfirming to him that she's easy." He held his hand out toward Cindy.

I tried not to take offense to what he was saying. It wasn't like he was talking about me. He was a guy and that was what he thought. That could have been how most guys thought. *Give her some attention and she'll fall into your lap.* But it was my roommate—and his half sister—he was talking about. I had to say something.

"Most girls are hopeless romantic creatures when it comes to guys that only exist in their heads. Cindy's no different. So when someone shows up that even comes marginally close to her *perfect* guy, she gets hooked. Just like most girls." I clicked on my seatbelt and waited for Cindy to get in. Nick looked at me in the mirror, waiting for my eyes to catch him.

"Are you one of those girls, Wilson?"

"What, a hopeless romantic that is after a guy that really doesn't exist?" He shook his head as I asked.

"No. I'm not." *My guy really does exist.*

He twisted to look out the window. He tapped the horn a couple of times to get Cindy's attention. Nick held his arm in the air and pointed to his wrist. It was getting late and I still needed to ask Nick if he would cover for me.

"Cindy, I've gotta go. I have dinner plans tonight," Nick yelled as he swirled his hand in the air, indicating for her to wrap up her goodbye.

She gave her ski stud a quick peck on the cheek and ran over to us. She glanced back waving at him. He waved and watched her get into the car.

"Geez, Nick, you don't have to be such a rude-ass clown. I was just saying goodbye to him." She pulled her door closed and ran the seatbelt across her chest before she turned to me.

"And where were *you* Wilson?" She stared at me. Her eyes widened when I didn't answer right away. My throat sped dry. My skin rushed with panic, abandoning any sense of security. Her expression told me she knew more than she was asking. Maybe it was my own conscience drawing that look from her. Maybe she didn't expect anything and I'm just thinking she knows something. Nick glanced back at me in the mirror.

Appear innocent, profess nothing and deny everything.

"I was here." I pushed my hand through my hair catching my fingers in a knot behind my ear. I bent and pulled my fingers apart trying to untangle the twisted, intricate mess created by the environment.

"Funny, I went to where you were sitting around a quarter to four, and you weren't there. I waited 'til four o'clock, and you still didn't come back. So I packed our bags." She bounced her back against her seat and lowered her chin looking at me. Her eyes shrank and her brows dropped with her familiar Cindy'ism likeness. It was the same look she'd given me when she thought I was the one who broke her favorite pair of Vera Wang heels.

I tried not to swallow hard. I wasn't caught by any means. I just had to make sure I came up with a plausible excuse, that's all.

"Yeah, thanks for doing that."

"So where were you?"

"I was probably in the restroom," I told her. It was my attempt to throw her a bone and come up with the easiest place she might have found me, if she'd been looking.

"No, nope, I looked in the restrooms, restaurant, and ski shops. I even went down to the rental area. You weren't anywhere." She held her fingers in the air, pushing them down as she named the places she'd nosed around to find me.

"Well, I don't know what to tell you. I was hanging out with Wayne in the lodge. When he got called for a lesson, I walked around the shops, ate lunch, and went to the restroom. Then I met up with you guys here. Maybe we just missed each other." Nick and I met eyes in the rearview mirror. He was nodding so slightly I almost didn't catch it.

"Maybe—Nick, who are you going to dinner with?" She switched her attention to him, a small reprieve from her accusations.

"A friend." He turned and looked back across to her.

"Where are you and a friend going?" She dropped her eyes and looked at the tips of her fingernails. I could see she was trying to come across like she really didn't care; far from it. She always needed to know everything everyone else was doing. Especially if it meant she was going to be alone.

"We're going to his family's cabin. I guess his mom's making this huge spread and is having a dinner party for some friends. He has to be there, but at least we'll eat before we hit the clubs," he told her like it was no big deal. My heart was racing.

"Where are you guys gonna go?"

"Studio Works first, then I don't know from there," he said.

"Studio is so weak. You guys should go to Polaris, that's the place to be. Anyone who's anybody goes there." She leaned forward and slapped his shoulder.

I wanted to go back to the part of the conversation where he talked about whose cabin he was going to.

"Polaris, isn't that the one that lets eighteen-year-olds in?"

"Yeah," Cindy said.

"No, thanks. We want to hit the clubs where the youngest person is twenty-one. Too much jailbait at Polaris." He turned down the road to their cabin.

"Your loss. Everyone who's anybody goes there," she rubbed her words in. (Just a little dig.)

He turned down the driveway and had to slam on his brakes. Stopped in front of the gate was a black BMW Z4. I leaned forward toward the center of the car with the wind knocked out of me. I was twisting and knotting up inside. *What was he doing here? Had he lost his mind?* Different excuses crowded my head. How was I going to explain that nothing was going on between Max and me? I couldn't catch my breath. My heart thumped, heavy and quick. I started feeling light-headed.

Please, please, please just stay in the car, I requested in my head as the door to the Z4 swung open.

Don't get out, stay in the car. One leg stretched out then the other. He paused before I saw the tilt of his hair peek out from behind the shadow of his door. I tried to squeeze my eyes shut as he leaned out, but I couldn't. I wanted to see him. I had fireworks going off in my body, and it was because of him.

As he leaned out of the car, a mix of pure relief and clouded disappointment splashed down my body. It was Calvin, Max's younger brother. He walked back to us and Nick lowered his window.

"Hey, Calvin. How long you been waiting?" Nick asked as he shook his hand.

"Not long, just thought I would pick you up early." Calvin grabbed the door and leaned in. He shifted to make eye contact with Cindy and me.

"Hi, ladies." He smiled—amazing how much he looked like his brother.

"So you're the one taking Nick out tonight, huh?" Cindy asked him. He shifted his stance, locking his hands to the roof.

"I'm not taking him out. We're going to go to the clubs together." He turned a little red. His eyes glistened with the same heart-robbing appeal as his brother.

"Let me open the gate so you can come down to the house," Nick told him. Calvin strutted over to his car and slipped in.

I watched the Z4 as it turned and sped down to the cabin. It was a very sexy car, especially when I thought of Max driving it.

He parked; we pulled up next to him. I looked into the passenger's seat and shivers paced through my body: *I was sitting in that seat less than an hour ago.*

Nick hopped out of the Sequoia and opened my door. I got out and stretched. He shuffled over to Cindy's door and opened it. She monopolized him in a conversation about where he was going tonight. Calvin had already slipped out of the BMW and walked over.

"Wilson, right?" he asked, holding out his hand to me.

"Yes, that's me. Thanks for remembering." He snatched my hand, drowning it in his.

"Nice to see you again." His eyes clung to mine; I felt a small piece of paper drop and rest in the palm of my hand. As he pulled away he formed his lips to mouth his brother's name. I closed my hand and shoved it into my pocket. My heart leapt into my throat. What I really wanted to do was run into the guest bedroom, lock the door, and read what Max had written.

"You too, thanks," I said with my fingers around the note, never wanting to let it go.

"Calvin, I'm gonna get ready, then we can take off," Nick told him. We shuffled through the grand entry and past the kitchen. Nick broke off and climbed upstairs.

Cindy was following us, glued to her iPhone. I was surprised she didn't trip over the steps coming into the house. She tossed her head back and laughed loud, sending echoes through the whole house.

"Oh my God, Chase is actually in town and he's going to Polaris with Mike and Drew."

Now I know Chase. Cindy has been crushin' on him since the ninth grade, but I had no idea who Mike and Drew were. I guess it really didn't matter, though, because Cindy knew. As she texted back whoever was sending her the information, her smile was almost contagious.

"Wilson, you are going to Polaris tonight with me. You would really like Drew. He is really cute and, well, just your type." She grabbed my arm and yanked me upstairs. I glanced back at Calvin. His eyes narrowed and he pulled his phone from his pocket as he watched me disappear upstairs. I wasn't ready for this. I needed time to think. I already had a date—to spend the evening with Max and his family.

Hanging out with Cindy while she tried to hook up with Chase was not on my agenda. And what was this 'he's just your type' comment? Like she really knows my 'type;' I can tell her a lot about my type, and he doesn't hang out with guys like Chase Romero. My 'type' actually has brains. He isn't selfish and really cares about my feelings. He's sensitive, kind, and gentle. He oozes chivalry when most guys these days couldn't even tell you what it was. He is drop-dead gorgeous and makes my heart stop when he walks into the room.

My phone rang loudly in the little pocket of my blue ski suit. All I wanted to do was change and get to Max's house. Cindy was still pulling me along.

"Cindy, I need to take this call." I slipped my arm out from her grip and went into my guest room.

"Fine, get ready while you're in there," she yelled as I shut the door.

I pulled the phone from my pocket and noticed it was a 970 area code. My skin rushed cold.

"Hello?" I paced the room waiting to hear the voice on the other end.

"Wilson?" My heart dropped. "Do you miss me?" his voice caressed its way down my body and got my butterflies to move.

"Yeah," my mouth watered and I choked on my words, "I really do."

"Calvin gave you a folded piece of paper right?" his voice tickled me.

"Yeah, I haven't had a chance to read it yet," I hesitated telling him. I heard him take a deep breath and slowly exhale a low guttural moan through his nose. I could almost picture his eyes low and disappointed. His mouth curved to a slight smile, playing with my emotions, pulling me in.

"Well that just won't do…Do you have it right now?" he asked. I pushed my hand into my pocket and caught it between my fingers.

"Yeah, I do." I pulled it out. My hand was shaking. I didn't want to disappoint him.

"In your hand?" I could hear him speak through his smile.

"Um-hum," I answered down in my throat. I held the note tight in my fingers, almost until they ached.

"Open it real slow." His voice was so incredibly hot.

I visualized him grabbing my hand and holding it shut, his eyes grazing across mine just enough to make me want to kiss him. I wish he was here.

"Right now?" I whispered.

"Yes, right now," he told me. I wedged the phone between my shoulder and ear.

It was folded to the size of a pack of matches like the ones you'd get at a restaurant. I pulled at the small piece of tape holding it shut. The paper released its pinned tension and I could feel something shift inside. I pulled up the top fold and then the others. Words in his writing spoke to me on the page.

"Read it out loud, so I can hear what you're thinking," his voice stroked the hopeless romantic deep within me.

"You hold the key. Keep it close to your heart." Words circled the small piece of cotton covering up the middle of the page. His words, his handwriting, dissolved me into a place I've never been. I pulled the soft, thin cotton cover from the middle of the paper. My breath left me. A pile of delicate gold-linked chain circled intricately around a daintily thin, open gold heart pendant with a tiny key dangling in the middle. It was so beautiful, I couldn't breathe.

"It's beautiful," I gasped. "Max, you shouldn't—." I couldn't continue.

"I had to. I just wish I was there to put it on you," he whispered.

"Me too," I answered him, holding it in the air. It sparkled in the sunlight.

"I wanted to give it to you in person, but I didn't want to make you wait," his words were deliberate, low and precise.

"Thank you. I'll wait for you to put it on me tonight—at dinner."

"So you're not going out with Cindy?" his voice rose.

"What? No. I thought you wanted me to go to dinner at your parent's place. Why would you think I was going out with Cindy?" For a moment I felt kicked in the stomach.

"Calvin heard her pressuring you—."

"And, of course, he called you," I finished his sentence, "Because he's got your back, right?" I teased.

"Something like that. He just thought you might crack and choose to go out with her," his voice broke a little.

"Max, this is my last night in Aspen. I sure don't want to spend it in a dance club. I want to be with you. Wherever you are."

"Me, too," he sounded like a little boy, reassured.

Cindy pounded on the door. I jumped.

"Wilson, are you ready?" She sounded like she had her mouth against the door. She was so loud.

"No, almost." I pulled the phone from my head and yelled. I pulled the zipper down on the baby blue space suit and pulled my arms out. The top hung at my waist when I stuck the phone back to my ear.

"Max? Sorry about that. I need to get dressed for tonight." The chill of the room draped my exposed skin.

"Well hurry up, Wilson. I just got off the phone with Jillian and she wants us to pick her up and go to dinner," Cindy spoke loudly through the door. She always did that; invited other people without seeing if the person she was with from the beginning wanted to have another person with them.

"Hold on, Max," I whispered into the phone. "Okay I'll be right out," I yelled toward the door. I heard Cindy shuffle down the stairs.

"Are you still there?" I asked Max.

"Yeah, I'm here," he whispered.

"God she can stress me out. I've gotta come up with a reason why I can't go with her tonight." I struggled to pull my legs out of the light blue moon suit.

"What are you doing?" he asked real quiet and low.

"Changing my clothes." The moon suit was finally on the floor.

"Changing? So, what are you wearing right now?" I could swear I heard him bite his lower lip.

"Nothing," I teased him.

"Nothing," he growled. I could hear him shift the phone.

"Well, my bra and panties," I mentioned.

"Mmmm, what I wouldn't give to be there helping you right now," he breathed. Goosebumps rose with his words.

"What are you willing to give?" I whispered.

"What do you want?" he breathed.

"An evening alone with you," I said as I took my time.

He didn't answer. I could tell he was thinking. He exhaled slowly.

"What are you thinking about?" I broke his train of thought.

"You. What you look like with the blue suit down around your waist," he said as he swallowed and tangled his words in his breath.

His words tickled me. I wanted to play with him—tease him a little—and make him feel the same way I was feeling. So I took a deep breath and started the game.

"Did you hear that?" I urged.

"What?" he asked fast.

"The clasp on my bra," I tempted him.

"Mmm, I want to hear it slide off your skin," his voice pulled low in my body.

I put the phone against my skin and dragged my bra across it.

"Did you hear that?"

"Yeah," he answered in a low growl. "Are you cold?"

"Freezing," I played. My body core was burning hot.

"Would I be able to *see* that you were cold if I was looking at you?" he pushed back.

"Definitely," I taunted him.

"If I was there, would you let me warm your skin?" he inquired.

"Depends," I was really getting into this.

"Depends on what?" he prodded for an answer.

"On how you would do it," I laughed a little.

"A blanket?" he mumbled.

"No."

"My hands?" he spoke a little clearer.

"Possibly," I teased.

"My lips?" he asked.

"Definitely," I craved, deep in my body, the warmth of his lips against my skin.

"You'd let me taste your skin?" he asked gently.

"Yes," my breath caught on the word.

"All of your skin?" he said softly.

"*All* of my skin," I provoked him.

I put the phone next to me on the bed. I grabbed my panties and dragged them off across my legs.

"What was that?"

"My panties," I whispered.

"Where are they?" he wanted to know.

"In my hand."

"I'm on my way," he said fast and then there was silence.

"Max? Hello?"

Silence.

CHAPTER SEVENTEEN:

What was I going to do? Cindy was expecting me to go to dinner and clubs with her tonight (I'd much rather stay back and pluck my eyebrows), and Max was on his way to pick me up. I guess my tease had been a little too much for him. One major problem: how would I get Cindy out of here before Max showed up?

I slipped into the clothes Cindy told me were hideous earlier today and hurried downstairs. She had Calvin cornered in the kitchen.

"So, Cal, what's the age gap between you and your brother?" She leaned across the counter.

"He's fourteen months older than me. I'm twenty-one and he's twenty-two."

"He dating anyone?" She dropped her hand to his forearm.

Calvin looked back at me. I gave him a quick nod, hoping he realized that he needed to keep us private.

"Ahh, not that I know of. That's one thing he's always real quiet about." He pulled back from the counter, sliding his arm out from under her hand.

175

"How about you, is there someone special?" She looked up and saw me. "Hey, Wilson—you're going to wear that?" She crinkled her nose.

"Actually, Cindy, my head really hurts. I think I'm just going to hang back tonight," I mumbled and looked at Calvin.

"Wilson, come on. You're killing me. It was supposed to be you, me, and Jillian; three guys and two girls? It doesn't work. Come on, you have to go." She walked over to me, grabbed my hand, and held it out, looking at my outfit. "We'll have to do something about what you're wearing."

"Cindy, really, I'm not going. You and your friend can handle it," I forced the air out of my lungs.

Nick interrupted me as he came into the room, "Hey, Calvin, ready to go? See you later Wilson, Cindy." He grabbed an apple from the gigantic fruit bowl and swung his arm in a circle toward Calvin.

"Bye, ladies," Calvin said quickly as he followed behind Nick.

"Wait, Nick—Wilson isn't going with me tonight so I need a ride." She spun to catch his arm.

"Cindy, you can drive. If not, call the service. They'll bring a car for you."

"Nick, come on," she pouted.

"Calvin has the Z4, it only has two seats," he argued.

"Why don't you leave the Z4 here, take the Sequoia, and drop me off at Jillian's?"

"I don't know about that. Max might kick my ass if I don't bring his car back," Calvin volunteered.

"Come on, you can pick it up tonight when you bring Nick back," Cindy tried to convince Calvin. "What's your brother's number? I'll talk to him. I know how to handle him." She grabbed her phone out of her purse.

"Calvin, I don't think that's a good idea. Cindy, he's your teacher after all," I piped up. I could feel the pressure building in my chest and across my shoulders.

"Yours too, Wilson, big deal; it's not like I'm trying to date him or anything, I just want to tell him about his car," Cindy snapped.

Calvin's eyes grew large and his mouth hung open. He must not have known the minor detail that his brother, Max—Mr. Goldstein—was, in fact, my teacher.

"You know what? I'll text him on the way. He'll understand. Nick let's just take the SUV." Calvin grabbed Cindy's arm and slid his hand down around her waist.

"Thanks, Calvin." She looked at Nick.

"Fine, but you're driving." Nick tossed him the keys and they all walked out the door.

My heart was on the floor, and my stomach teetered on the thin line between knotting in anxiety and twirling in excitement. I wanted to get cleaned up before Max showed. I ran upstairs, pulled off my clothes, and searched through my duffel bag for my comfortably tight Anne Klein jeans and my cute, off-the-shoulder, button-up cashmere sweater I'd gotten on sale at Nordstrom's. I'd just pulled my jeans over my hips when I heard the front door open.

"Max? I'll be right down," I yelled from my room. I didn't hear him say anything back.

"Wilson?" It wasn't Max's voice. My heart jumped into my throat. "I wanted to leave these with you." Calvin came up the stairs, dangling the Z4 keys in front of him.

I wrapped my sweater around my chest. *Oh my God, how embarrassing.*

"Oh. Thanks, Calvin. I'll make sure Max gets them." I shuddered a little as I reached for them.

"Should I tell my family you guys won't be making it to dinner tonight?" Calvin was staying very cool. His eyes locked on mine, not making an attempt to look below my chin. I didn't say anything. He nodded and turned to leave.

"Calvin?" He waited. "Thanks," I whispered. He didn't have to support what his brother and I were doing. He could've easily told Cindy everything he knew; instead, he didn't.

"Wilson, don't worry about it. No problem. Just have Max text me if he takes the car home." He turned and I watched him shuffle down the stairs and out the front door.

I stretched my sweater over my head and pulled it down. I stood there for a moment before I went into my bedroom and shut the door. With no idea how far away Max was or how much longer it was going to take him to get to me, I grabbed my phone off the bed and called Joanie. The last time we talked I had to cut her off because Max came over.

The phone rang several times before going straight into her voicemail. Surprising, considering from the last time I talked to her she had left me a gazillion voicemails and text messages. I threw myself onto the bed and left her a vague message only she would understand. I stretched my arms out to my sides and felt the muscles in my back pull and relax. I pushed my chin to the ceiling and closed my eyes. I didn't realize how sore I was until I stopped to lay down.

Have you ever fallen asleep only to be startled awake by someone standing over you? It's like you can feel their presence there before you wake up. They didn't touch you or say anything; all they did was look at you.

I opened my eyes to Max's face, staring at me. My heart curled up into my throat. He pushed his knee into the bed, next to my waist. My butterflies swarmed. His smell anchored low in my body. When he leaned over me, his hair angled forward across his forehead and his eyes soaked me in his presence.

"Hi, Wilson," he whispered, wetting his lips with the taste of mine.

He pulled up slightly from our kiss. My arms still stretched out by my sides.

"How long have you been here?" My words tickled his mouth. He pulled further away.

"Just long enough to hear you talk in your sleep." He smiled and his eyes followed suit.

"What did I say?"

I curled my arms around his neck and tangled my hands into the back of his shiny black hair.

"Something about a guy you're supposed to meet tonight," he teased.

"Did I mention his name?"

His hands slid under my shoulders and pulled me to his chest. The sounds of our desires rose from deep in our bodies. We could have picked up from where he left it on the phone earlier and I would have been perfectly fine. He opened his mouth and gently caught my lip between his teeth. I really liked when he did that.

He left me wanting more, dragging his mouth across to my cheek. He pressed his lips to my ear and tangled his words in my hair.

"Max. You said the name Max."

"Sounds right." I shivered as his smoldering breath occupied my neck.

He drew his hands up around my face, tracing my arms as he pulled me off the bed.

"What did I miss? Clothes on?" he groaned with his eyebrows raised and his head bent to the side as his eyes captured my entire body.

"This is what happens when you hang up." I teased him.

"Well, next time I'll remember to stay on the line." He slid his hands to my waist. My breath lingered shallowly as he pulled me in and kissed me. Finally tasting him, I was glad he hung up.

"How did you get out of going with Cindy?" he asked, sliding his hands along my back.

"I told her my head hurt and that I didn't feel up to it. Calvin helped by taking her in the SUV. Your brother left your car here and gave me the keys." I pulled them out from my front pocket and held them in the air. He glanced at them, shook his head, and lured his eyes right back to me.

"Gave *you* the keys, huh? You must've really charmed him." He bent to fit the curve of my body kissing down around my collar, as his hand browsed down my arm and collected the keys to his car.

"Or shocked him," the words soared out of my mouth. I was hoping he didn't catch the unscripted thought that had plummeted from my mind. Of course that was like wishing my parents were coming for me. It just wasn't going to happen.

"Shocked? What happened?" He leaned back to see my expression.

"He didn't know about us?"

"Yeah, he knew about you." His hands pushed my hair back from my face.

"He didn't know I was one of your students." Silence filled the room.

"No, I didn't tell him...you were my student." His skin dropped white, his eyes withdrew, and he shifted away from me.

A wedge was driven between us. Not about the feelings he had for me or I had for him, but the judgment he embodied with the choices he had made. The struggle he had with me being who I was. I understood it, and as much as I hated it, it was a reality we had to face.

I pushed my body against his center and wrapped my arms around him, feeling his heart pound hard and fast against my body. It was our last night together and I wasn't giving up now.

"Max, don't worry. Nobody knows. Calvin isn't going to say anything to anyone." I forced my hands around his face, making him look me in the eyes.

"It's not other people I worry about." He drank from my words and spat them back. His palms hot on my face, he stroked his thumbs across my cheeks.

"Don't worry about me. I'm fine. You need to know that, Max. Please," I choked as I grabbed his hands, holding them to my face. I wasn't about to let him go. Not now, not ever.

"Wilson, even a year from now—," he started to say something; I pushed my lips to his to stop him from telling me he was wrong. He wasn't.

I wouldn't let him pull away. The more he pushed his hands to release me, the harder I kissed him. I had to break him. Make him see we were worth fighting for. Dread dripped heavily from my heart, feeding the lost butterflies trying to decipher my emotions.

Then his body shifted and I knew the fight was over. I felt the rush of his desire flood over me. A switch had been clicked, and he was unstoppable. His hands found their way to the back of my thigh. He locked strongly around my legs, flung me on the bed, and stood staring at me. I didn't give him a chance to change his mind. I clutched his T-shirt across his chest and pulled him down on top of me. This was the one time I wasn't going to give in.

Words were all worn out. Nothing he was going to say could change what I wanted. His hand pressed down on my shoulder, pinning me onto the bed, his legs bestridden mine. His eyes tracked my body to my sight, while his other hand held me perfectly enough to feel his desire. He kissed my exposed shoulder. Lust rushed my skin as he tasted across my collarbone and up to my ear. My breath quickened; I wanted to feel his skin against mine. I pushed my hands down to his waist and yanked his T-shirt from his pants. He sat up, forced his hands to the back of his shirt, and pulled it off his body. I pressed my hands to his chest, feeling my way around his tight skin as he pressed his fingers to the buttons of my sweater. My heart thumped in the back of my throat. All I could think about was his lips kissing my body. He worked his way to the last button down by my waist, and then slid the sweater open. As I felt his mouth press against my stomach, sparks ignited low in my groin. His hands pressed lightly up my sides to my shoulders. He navigated my skin. His fingers clung to the straps of my bra, pulling them vacant my shoulders. His hands wrapped behind me and unsnapped the clasp. I was exposed. Cool air rushed across my chest. I closed my eyes and let him explore the topography of my body. Tasting the contours of my chest, he made feelings rage deep in my body.

My hands, owner of their own actions, pushed down below his navel to the first button of his Levi's. His arms anchored his body above mine, his muscles flexing; I pulled apart the waist of his jeans. Like dominoes, the other buttons followed. Calvin Klein was the only thing separating him from me. I slipped my hands between his jeans and Calvins, using my wrists to pull his Levi's off his backside. He was down to his boxers when he lowered his body and brought his hands to my jeans. His fingers warm against my abdomen, he hovered before unbuttoning my pants.

His intentions drifted from my waist, across my chest, and up to my expression. His eyes smoldered, waiting for me to tell him it was okay. I moaned his name soft through my lips. I took hold of the band on my jeans, lifted my hips off the bed, and pushed. He seized my hands—I thought he was going to stop me. Instead, he pulled down, all the way off my body; goosebumps raced across my skin. He skimmed his body gently against mine, up to my wanting lips. Our bodies fought hard to wait, seeing where our ambition was taking us. My hands caressed across his back, and he worked to learn my bumps and curves. His lips lingered long on mine, his sweet taste filled me. My butterflies stormed strongly through my body. His lips pressed delicately against my collarbone, sending signals through my arms to push him down my body. His warm mouth tickled me delicately. Pleasing moans grew loud from my throat. He pulled away, the cold air swirled where his mouth left, causing me to lose my breath. He noticed.

"Are you okay with this?" he spoke, almost apologizing. His hair hung long enough to tangle in his eyelashes.

"Max, I've never been more okay with *anything* in my life as I am with you right now." My body surged with waves of adrenaline in places I'd never felt before.

He pressed his mouth above my navel. I felt his knowledge and experience consume me. He knew how to dangle me over the edge without letting go. His hands tracked along my sides down to my thighs. He pressed enough to slip his fingers under the waistband of my panties. I felt my body quake deep. My arms clung to my sides; I didn't know where to put my hands. He plucked his mouth from my skin as his eyes drank up my body and he caressed his fingers along my hips. Shivers owned my legs. His lips followed, pressing enough to bring me to the edge of delirium.

"This is where we left off," he breathed as he slid off the bed. I looked at him; his Calvin Klein's worked hard to keep him covered. He let out a low, earthy growl as he clasped his hands around my ankles and pulled me closer to the edge of the bed. My hands trailed above my head. I left them there, frozen by him. His knees pressed in between mine while his lips explored my skin. His hands read my body before sliding down past my navel and behind the front silky panel of my panties. A craving flooded my body and my butterflies busted free. He looked at me, it was all unknown. I loved how thoughtful he was of my first experience. He watched my face as he brushed his fingers across the apex of my legs. I moaned a high pitched sound that must have given him the okay to continue—a language I was learning. He was brilliant with his hands. I pushed my head back into the bed and closed my eyes. I couldn't breathe. I didn't know what happened—scared or not, needy or independent—I grabbed his head, knotted my hands in his hair and pulled him to kiss me. He growled a deep, guttural moan before I shattered completely.

He smoldered with a confidence that hypnotized me into a comfort with him. I was changed forever. No more need to feel a sense of not belonging or weakness because of my age. I knew what he did was for me, and that was all I needed. He wanted me, and I was content in that. I could wait a month.

CHAPTER EIGHTEEN:

I loved how he held me. His hands refreshed my feelings and his body protected me from any guilt I had for having them. He smiled as I shivered.

"Are you cold?" he asked as he pulled me closer to him.

"No, I'm not cold, I just can't stop shivering." My body kept reliving the moment of pure ecstasy with him.

I don't know what he did to me, and quite frankly, I didn't care. He knew how to work the equipment and I was totally fine with his skills. As a matter of fact, it was my skills, or lack of them, that caused me to start feeling self-conscious. Inexperienced or not, it was my turn to learn what made him tick.

I stretched up to kiss him, my hands caught in his hair and I pushed him back. His hand wrapped around my body, pulling me on top of him. Our bodies molded together, I felt the cool fabric of his boxers against my skin. His fiery hands lingered on my lower back before they slid down further. I wanted to give him what he'd given me, but didn't know how. I left his lips, traced his chin, and kissed along his chest. My tongue left a cool, wet line down to his navel. His stomach flexed. I must have tickled him. I ran my hands down his sides and across to his waistband. I didn't look at him, I didn't want to know if he wanted it or not. I fit my hands in between his glistening skin and silky boxers. As I pulled them slowly away from his waist his hands caught me.

"Wilson, I'm okay. You don't have to do this." His hand pushed at my chin so I could see him speak.

"I want to," I told him.

I pulled his Calvin's a little lower to see the foundation of his happy trail. My hands shuffled around his boxers.

"What's wrong," he asked, breathy.

"Nothing," I huffed.

"Really I'm serious, you don't have to do this," he said low.

"I want to, Max; it's just…I've never…I don't want to hurt you." I pulled my hands away.

He tugged his boxers down and there he was. I leaned on my elbow and soaked in his entire body. He was so beautiful. Even the parts I'd never seen before were amazing. I didn't know where to start, so I did what I thought he would like. I carefully moved my hands to his stomach, awkwardly, to where they should go; he helped me overcome my inexperience.

He guided my hand to his body—he was so warm, and his skin was so soft. I slowly manipulated my way down to make him lose his breath. His hands pressed against my bare skin, he moaned deep, strong, short breaths. I tingled low and deep; he was making me excited again. I think I understood where he was and I wanted him to reach for the same place he'd taken me earlier.

He released a deep, beastly groan and I felt every muscle in his body tighten and release. He found my lips and kissed me hard. I forced my arms up around his neck. His hands pressed and rubbed over my entire body as he pulled me tight against him.

When he finally stopped moving and we lay in each other's arms, he giggled.

"What's so funny?" I asked him.

He pulled his boxers up and leaned back, looking down at our bodies. "Looks like we're gonna need a shower."

"Yeah, what's up with that?" I teased, "Because when I fantasized about it, nowhere did *that* happen." He lifted his chest into the air so our eyes met.

"Well, it's your fault. If you weren't so incredibly tempting, we wouldn't be in this predicament." He brushed his lips softly against mine.

He stopped moving. "You fantasized about this?" His eyes narrowed and his expression pulled at my heart.

"Yeah, and we took a shower too." I stretched up and kissed him.

"Really?" He slid down off me and stood, waiting for me to respond.

"Really. And if I'm going to meet your parents we'd better get a move on."

He grabbed my hands, hoisting me up from the bed. His arms wrapped around me and chills shot down my spine.

"It'll be a quick shower; I bet you won't even miss me. We're still going to try and make it to dinner, right?" I asked against his skin.

"If you want to," he answered. "Maybe we'll get there for dessert." He ran his fingers down the inside of my arm and snatched my hand. He pushed me toward the door.

"Let me get the clothes I want to wear tonight." I went back to my duffel bag. He pushed his hand into my folded clothes and noticed the cute slinky top I'd brought just in case I was going to see him. He pulled it up, hooking it on his finger.

"Wow, Wilson, what I wouldn't give to see you in this," he purred. I snatched it from his finger, his hands wrapped around my waist. I liked how comfortable I felt with him.

"I know something you won't give." I slid my hand down his stomach, stopping just above his waist.

"Hey, careful there, I don't think you want to start something you're not ready to finish." He pulled my hand up to his chest.

After what I just experienced, I'm totally sure I would have no problem with going all the way with him.

"We'll see in a month." I flicked him in the chest and walked toward the door.

"Ouch, thirty days." He rubbed his fingertips on the spot where I'd flicked him.

"Seven hundred twenty hours." I grabbed a towel from the closet and tiptoed through the hall and down to our special bathroom.

I swung the door open and I was back in the familiar area where we'd had our first kiss. The couch I cried into, the mirror I looked at him through, and the counter I leaned against when he kissed me. I walked past them like friends I'd outgrown. I appreciated each for where they'd brought me.

The shower looked incredible. I didn't have any curtain to pull or glass to close me in. Surrounded by shower heads protruding around me, they were pointed to every part of my body. Earthy tones of brown and tan braided through the stone on the walls. A perfectly sized rock bench sat precisely below the showerheads, finding the one spot the water missed.

My body craved a nice hot shower. I pulled off my panties and dropped my towel onto the oversized, velvety taupe antique chair. I twisted the knob to hot and the shower steamed as water flooded the space. I stepped into the stream and felt the water drench my hair; it was like someone took a pitcher and poured it over my head. The lower heads pulsated like hands caressing my entire body. I tilted my head back and closed my eyes, letting the water swallow me. I was reaching for the shampoo when a slight knock at the door pulled me away.

"Do you mind if I come in?" Max whispered against the door.

My throat went dry as I answered him, "No, come in."

He pushed the door open, slowly. His eyes focused on the slate floor. I stood there, waiting to see what his intentions were. His sharp black hair dangled across his face. There wasn't a curtain or towel to wrap around my body. I was exposed and all he had to do was look up, instead he waited for permission.

"Do you like your showers hot? Because I like my showers hot," I told him. He swallowed hard.

"Me too, really hot," he answered as his eyes took in my body bit by bit. He sauntered to the edge of the shower, mesmerized by the sights and sounds of the water as it splashed down my skin. I grabbed his hand and pulled him in, Calvin Klein's and all.

His body became wet and steaming; his boxers, translucent. Without words, he brought his lips to mine. The water traced down our faces and invaded our kiss.

I turned away, filled my hand with shampoo, then reached up and tangled my fingers in his hair. He caught my hands, collecting the excess shampoo and shared his lather with me, pressing his foam-filled hands into my hair. His strong fingers massaged my scalp with delicate intentions. I leaned back, closed my eyes and let the water flood me. His hands were careful not to pull my hair or brush my temple, and his lips were a pleasant surprise against my mouth.

He slowly pulled away and asked against my ear, "Do you want me to wash your back?"

I grabbed the soap and started lathering across my body. He shifted my hair away from my neck and started tasting below my ear. His hands ran up my stomach and across my breasts; I turned and kissed him. His body warmed me. We fit perfectly together. The water filled the gaps between our skins and I couldn't tell where he began and I ended.

"Um-hum, please," I moaned as his hands slid down to my waist; they were so warm.

"You're so soft," he said against my skin. He turned me to the wall, I felt his hands push and drag heavy across my back. I couldn't see what he was doing, but when I felt his mouth against my shoulder blade I knew where he was. His hands slid up under my arms and his body pressed against my back—his entire body. My head tilted back as his hands encased my stomach and worked their way down my inner thighs. A moment of desperation flooded my body. He was teasing me, and it was salacious.

His hands traveled low. His mouth close to my ear, I could hear his visceral breaths. It drove me wild; my hips pressed back against his exposed desire. I wanted him so bad. But even in the heat of the moment, somewhere deep in my soul I found a thread of responsibility and pulled away from him.

He snatched me back. The water created a cocoon around our bodies, bursting open the wings of my butterflies, and they were free to fly. He was perfect to me, and to him I was flawless.

He reached across, still tangled in my body, and turned the water off. His hands unwilling to leave my skin, I turned to face him. His hands wrapped tightly around my body. My face rested perfectly against his chest.

"I could stay like this forever." I tightened my arms around him.

"Me too," he whispered. "But then we'd miss dessert and my mom makes the best berry cobbler." He licked his lips in a boyish manner.

I noticed when he talked about his mom he had an inspiring innocence about him. *Oh, what she must be like, to still hold such a deep part of his heart.* Something I could only envy or dream of. My experience with having a mother—or the lack of one—was the day she dropped me off at my grandparents' house, kissed me on my forehead, got back into the car, and drove away. My whole life I'd blamed myself for making her leave. Maybe if I was less hyperactive, or if I liked her boyfriends, she would have stayed for me. Maybe if I was a better daughter then she would've come back for me. All the while, I never knew my grandparents had obtained a restraining order against her and that she was never coming home to me. Not then, not now. They died never forgiving their own flesh and blood.

I pulled away from him, grabbed the towel I'd thrown on the designer chair, and draped it around my core. I was cold.

"Let's go to your place. I really want to meet your mom," I choked on the words.

He stepped out, wrapped the towel around his waist, and shook his head, causing his hair to fluff and lie perfectly. He pulled me into his chest.

"Are you sure? We could stay here if you want to." He tried to understand.

"I'm sure. I want to go." I pulled away from and snatched up my clothes. "I'll be right back."

I opened a door that led to the toilet—not my favorite part of bathrooms, but at least in there I could hide the pain that I hated to own in my soul. I'd been so good at disowning it for so long, I thought I was immune to the jealousy that reared in my body, especially with him. I wasn't going to let the experiences of my F'ed up mother ruin what new memories I had created with Max. I wanted to see a family like his—where the choices of a mother spurred success in her son's life and she was there for him, really there. It was that reality I wanted to inhabit.

I got dressed and pushed the backs of my hands to my eyes, drying the useless tears from my cheeks, and worked at filling my mind with thoughts of what we'd just had together. *I'll be damned if I was going to let* her *win.*

Max knocked on the door.

"Wilson? You okay?" his voice was soft. I could hear that he was concerned. I guess I would be, too. He had totally made me unbelievably happy and I go pull the basket-case freak-out and run away to a toilet to change my clothes. At least it was spotlessly clean.

"Yeah, I'm fine." I opened the door. "Sorry about the disappearing thing." He slipped his hands around me and clutched me to his body.

He didn't say a word. He just held me until I was comfortable enough to pull away. It wasn't about sex or guilt. It was his understanding of how to treat a woman, when she just needed to be held. It was him being sensitive and concerned about me.

"Wilson, I think we should change your bandage." He pressed his fingers to the edges of the tape. "It's soaked."

"Okay, thank you." As he pulled the bandage from my temple, his eyes reflected less concern.

"How bad is it?" I asked, pushing my hand to the edge of my eyebrow.

"It's not bad at all. Smaller than I thought it was going to be. I don't even think you're gonna need a Band-Aid."

"Oh good," I said, relieved. The last thing I wanted to do was go meet his parents with a ghastly bandage taped across my head.

"You ready to go?" he asked low.

"Yeah, I am." I walked to the sink and washed my hands.

"Oh, I almost forgot," he said as his hand reached into his pocket.

"What?"

"This—I found it on your dresser, thought you'd want to wear it tonight," he answered as he held the key and heart necklace up in the air. He pulled it across my neck and fastened it. He pressed his hands down across my shoulders onto my forearms.

"It's beautiful, Max. Thank you," I whispered.

"You're welcome." He kissed the top of my head. "Something to keep me close to your heart."

It'll be the perfect symbol of him when we get back to Wesley. Even though, I didn't need a necklace to remind me to whom my heart belonged.

He held out his elbow and I wove my arm through his. He walked me through the hall, down the steps, and out to his car. My other hand pressed my new necklace against my chest.

Yeah, it was something that definitely kept him close to my heart.

CHAPTER NINETEEN:

I loved that he held the car door open for me and made sure my seatbelt was on before he shut me in. The drive to his cabin was comforting. He reached over to me and held my hand. His fingers were warm against mine.

"You should know something about me," he said after a moment. My heart dropped into my stomach. I knew this was going to be too good to be true.

"Yeah, what's that?" The words clung to my throat. *God please don't let him tell me something that would break my heart.*

"Well it's not really something about me; it's more about my family." He glanced over. My heart started to rise back to where it belonged.

"Okay—," I sang to him. I don't know why he took so long to tell me. Maybe it was something he was embarrassed about.

"I've never taken anyone to my family's cabin before—to meet my parents." He looked forward as he turned. The muscles in his neck bounced as he swallowed hard.

"Nobody?" I asked. I felt my lips pull into a slight smile.

"No, not a woman." He looked at me, his face tensed. "You're the first." He looked so vulnerable. *Reality check, he called me a woman.* It clicked for me, and I understood instantly: I wasn't a girl anymore.

"You, Max Goldstein? Not one girl?" I wrapped my hand over his and pulled it to my face.

"No, not one. No one was ever worth it before," he said looking straight ahead.

Did he even know what he was saying to me? If I could press heavy against and melt into him I would do it. Did he know that he made the butterflies and tingling parts of my body completely dedicated to him? Invade me with words, I'm here.

"Well, I'm honored. Thank you, Max. That means so much to me." I leaned over and kissed his cheek. He peeked at me. The muscles in his jawline flexed.

I could tell he was entering an uncharted area of his life. As handsome and worldly as he was, it was hard to believe he'd never brought a girl home to his parents before. Was he that private? What did that mean about me? I felt a bubble of spastic energy spin up into my throat. *I'm the 'one' he brings home to mom.*

"What if she doesn't like me?" I mumbled as my eyes focused on the glove box handle in front of me. I didn't want to look at him.

The car swayed to the right and rolled to a stop. He cleared his throat. I felt his eyes burn into my skin. He tickled the side of my face with his fingers as he pulled my hair away.

"How could she not? Wilson, she'll love you. She'll see exactly why I wanted to bring you home with me." He leaned over and kissed me softly.

"Yeah, but what if Calvin said something about us to her?"

He took a deep breath. "He would never do that to me. He's known about you for some time; I'm sure we'll talk later."

"What do you mean 'some time?'

"Well, he knew I was interested in someone at Wesley; but he didn't know the exact details."

"Oh." *Wait, he's been interested long enough to talk to his brother about me?*

"Okay, so are you ready?"

This was it. My heart throbbed fast in my chest. I was going to meet his parents.

He pulled my door open and helped me out. His arm circled around my waist where his hand had now memorized the space on my hip. He pressed his lips to my temple as he shut the door.

"You're so tense. Relax, there's nothing to worry about." He laughed against my hair. "Their bark is worse than their bite."

Simple for him to say, he wasn't the one in the hot seat. With me, he was getting off easy. The only family he had to face was my best friend, Joanie. And I do have to admit, she was very protective of me and could be a real pistol. She was also the only family I had.

I noticed a couple of cars parked in the driveway and none of them were the black Toyota Sequoia Nick had driven. Max directed me up the steps of the porch. He pulled open the front door and pressed against me to enter. I stopped breathing. When I was here earlier, we'd come through the garage; I never saw the entry—it was amazing.

The stone that greeted us on the porch continued past the door. Splashes of warm sunflower yellow wrapped the walls. A heavy but intricately delicate black iron chandelier hung centered from the ceiling. Its cascading arms held antique white candles and created shadows on the walls that flickered and danced. They looked so real. Rustic wooden loveseats stressed with stories to tell hugged a colossal armoire that matched.

Max pulled my jacket off and hung it in the closet behind the front door. I took off my boots and handed them to him. He just smiled as he pulled off his boots, too.

He shut the closet and, dragging his hand down my arm, he grabbed my damp hand. His eyebrows tightened around his eyes.

"Don't be scared. It's okay, they'll love you." He pulled me to his body, wrapped his arms around me and kissed me, determined to change my mood. It worked.

Voices filled the house as Max pulled me to the great room. His stride was fast; I slowed my pace pulling back on him. He stopped and turned to me, locking his eyes on mine. Without words, he reassured me. We turned the corner to the dining room and my heart leaped into my throat. His mom saw us and stood up.

"Oh Maxi, you made it." She came over to him and kissed his cheek. The room went silent as she stepped back to see me. Her eyes revealed her warmth. Her velvety brown hair wrapped picture perfect around her face. Max had her smile.

"Mom, this is Wilson. Wilson this is my mom, Nancy." He stepped behind me, keeping his hands secure around my waist and his chest against my back.

"Wilson, welcome to our home, it's my pleasure." She grasped my upper arms and pulled me to hug her. Instinctively, I wrapped my arms around her; she was so soft and smelled like a bouquet of spring flowers. All the fear I had was washed away in her embrace. She was genuine, and I craved that.

"Mom," Max mumbled. She let go of me first but kept her hand around my back.

"Wilson, this is my dad, Frank," Max continued. I waved to him.

"Nice to meet you, Wilson." He stood up, came over, and took my hand.

"Thank you for having me," I was barely able to speak. I was overwhelmed with their warmth. I felt Max tighten around my waist.

"My sister, Camille." He held his hand out to her.

"Nice to meet you, Wilson. This is my husband, Dan." She pushed the back of her hand to the chest of the man next to her.

"Hi," I said as I looked at them and gave a slight wave.

"Mr. and Mrs. Vaughn," Max introduced me to the other dinner guests. Mr. Vaughn stood up and nodded, his wife only smiled.

"This is our daughter, Emily." Mrs. Vaughn pointed across the table. My eyes caught her and I lost my breath. It was the same girl who'd been with Max today at the ski resort. She was even more striking than before. Her crystal blue eyes danced, her perfectly smooth complexion radiated, and she oozed a self-confidence she had to have been born with.

"Nice to meet you." Her eyes met mine for a moment and then looked right through me to Max. She smiled.

"Hi Max." Her head tilted and a sparkle appeared in her eyes.

"Hey, Em," he said to her. A familiar comfort bounced between them, something I wasn't prepared for. He slid his hands from my waist up to my shoulders.

"Oh, I wish you had gotten here just a bit earlier. You could have met Calvin." Nancy broke the triangle between us.

"Mom, she already knows Calvin. They met yesterday," Max told her.

"Oh, good. Well, come and sit, join us, we are just about to have dessert. Did you eat already?" She stood behind her chair holding the back.

"We had a small taste of something." He told her, pulling out my chair. "Wilson might be hungry still." He smiled at me.

"No, thank you. I'm fine, really." He sat next to me and grabbed my hand under the table.

"Well then, berry cobbler it is." She left to the kitchen.

Mr. Vaughn and Frank continued their conversation, inviting Max to join them.

My eyes traced back to Emily, who sat across from me.

"Wilson. That's an interesting name. Is it a family name?" I heard Mrs. Vaughn ask. My attention switched to her.

"No, it's not," I answered shortly.

Do you know how many people ask me that when they meet me? I used to get really mad and come up with elaborate stories about how I was named. Now I just tell them no and it tends to end the conversation.

"Have you ever thought about legally changing it?" she asked me with all seriousness.

Are you frickin' kidding me? The audacity of this woman to ask me something so ridiculous. Cindy was right about these Vaughns—they are so last season.

"No, never."

"Oh, I hope I didn't offend you," Mrs. Vaughn apologized. I felt Max grab my leg under the table and comfort me.

"Mom!" Emily looked horrified.

"I'm not saying I don't like it," Mrs. Vaughn piped in.

"Mom, I think Nancy needs your help in the kitchen," Emily told her, gritting her teeth.

"Fine." She stood up from the table and huffed off to the kitchen.

"I'm sorry about her. She tends to talk before she thinks. She drinks a couple glasses of wine and loses her manners. Right, Max?" She tapped his arm.

"Ah, yeah, I guess so," he answered.

"Oh, come on, remember last year when we were having the big dinner down at our place and she asked my brother's friend if he was gay? You have to remember that." She smiled trying to get him to remember. She grabbed his arm and pushed at him. "Come on, he threw a huge fit and ran out. Jeff chased after him. Remember?" She pushed him again.

"That's right, at the annual Gold-Vaughn family dinner. That was awkward." He pulled at my hand under the table.

"That was the moment we found out *Jeff* was G-A-Y." She spelled out the word. "My parents still can't talk about it," she whispered across the table, forcing a smile.

"Wow, a year later?" I asked.

"Yeah, and they still get all choked up about it," she said.

"That's right, I missed that one last year," Camille interjected.

Nancy came out holding her berry cobbler pie, meticulously cut into perfect pieces, with Mrs. Vaughn following behind her holding plates.

"Okay everyone, ta-da! Who's having a piece?" Everyone around the table raised their hands.

Max pushed his mouth to my ear. "Do you want to share a piece?" I shook my head yes.

"Mom, let me help with that." Max pushed his chair out.

"No Maxi, sit. Karen and I can do this." She placed a piece of pie on a plate and Mrs. Vaughn brought it over to Camille's husband Dan.

"Wilson and I are going to share a piece," Max told his mom.

"Okay, honey." She delicately put a piece on the plate and slid it over in front of me. Within minutes they had everyone served.

"Oh, I think the coffee is done by now." She got up to get it.

"Honey, sit down, visit; Max and I can bring it out." Frank looked at Max and shifted his eyes. "It will give us a chance to check the football scores. The Broncos were up by seven the last time I checked. Who wants coffee?" He counted everyone who raised their hands, including me, before he and Max disappeared into the kitchen.

"This is Maxi's favorite pie. He and Camille would fight over the last piece. You must be pretty special if he's willing to share it with you." His mom took a bite and looked up at me. My heart warmed, deeply.

"He's a great guy," I answered her compliment. I broke off a small piece and tasted it. It was phenomenal. Chunks of berries burst in my mouth, sweet with a small twist of tart.

"So how did you meet my brother?" Camille took another bite and waited.

The second bite almost didn't make it down my throat. Acid would have gone down easier. *Max and I talked about this, what was the plan?* My mind went blank and I shuddered all the way down to my toes. I didn't want to screw this up. Was it coffee or a party? I lifted my eyes from my plate and found everyone staring at me. A pin could have dropped and everyone would've covered their ears.

"Um, well. We took a class together." As the words left my lips I remembered we agreed to say a coffee shop. *We met over at a coffee shop, oh shit, what did I just do?* I'd better backpedal or start working this out to be truthful enough to twist it into what we wanted them to see.

"It was a government focus group." I tried to come as close to the truth as possible. I really liked Nancy and I wanted to be honest with her.

"So you're a teacher like Max?" she asked.

"You look way too young to be a teacher," Karen Vaughn interrupted.

"They have accelerated programs now. I remember seeing it on TV," Camille told us.

"No, I'm not a teacher," I answered.

Max came out then, holding a couple of coffee mugs in his hands. His face went a little white as he picked up where I left off, filling in the gaping holes in my lie and making it real to them.

"Wilson's a student. She doesn't have time to work. She's carrying some pretty heavy units this semester." He pushed the mugs to Emily and Camille.

"Oh, wow, what school?" Camille asked. She grabbed the cream and poured it into her coffee.

That's it, we're caught. Might as well just wrap it up and tell them the truth. I opened my mouth to come up with some random excuse for what we were doing.

"She's attending a small school in the East Bay," he rattled it off so fast it took me a moment to recognize what he'd said.

"What's your major?" Emily asked. I looked at Max and back at her.

"I'm undecided, but maybe sociology or childhood development," I said as Max's dad set a cup of coffee in front of me. Thank God it gave me something to focus on while they intently listened to what I said.

"So you want to work with kids?" Camille asked.

"Something along those lines," I said. Max didn't go back to help his dad bring in more coffee. In fact, he sat next to me, keeping his hand occupied with mine.

"Do you live on campus or with your parents?" Emily asked as she sipped her coffee.

"On campus." Drips of perspiration rolled down the back of my neck. This was way too hard to keep up.

"So are your folks nearby?" Frank asked keeping the conversation about me. A bubble large and rough stuck in the back of my throat. I looked at Max hoping he would help me; I didn't want to go there with all these people in the room. But what choice did I have? It was going to come up sooner or later. Might as well get through this fast—go ahead and rip the Band-Aid off.

"I don't have a relationship with my mother or father. My grandparents raised me." I felt the wounds in my heart tear open and a burning sting over come my body. I didn't want to say this in front of Max's mom. I didn't want her to know I came from a broken-down, shattered family, which was splintered even more by living away at a boarding school.

"So your grandparents live in California?" Frank asked. He was determined to find out if I had family or not. It felt kind of strange to have to answer his questions with words that didn't comfort his ideals about my heritage. Max kissed my temple and answered his dad's questions.

"Wilson lost her grandparents recently." He tensed his face, his eyes narrowed and the corners of his lips pulled down.

Out of the corner of my eye I saw Nancy stand up and walk over to me. She grabbed my hands and lifted them in the air so my body would answer by standing. She pushed her arms around my neck and hugged me with so much love I couldn't help but lock my arms around her.

CHAPTER TWENTY:

I know it was probably hard for most people to relate to the screwed-up type of emotional disconnect I had when it came to my parents. It was just easier to pretend they didn't exist instead of always trying to justify why they didn't want me. I was used to calling a spade a spade. I had no problem with that. My mother wanted to do drugs and drink firewater more than she wanted to raise me. She plopped me at my grandparents' house and that was all she wrote. Well, actually, she did write me one letter. Told me that someday she hoped I'd forgive her for leaving me. I never wrote back.

"Wilson, I'm so sorry," Nancy whispered in my ear as she let go. Her words filled the empty holes throughout my heart. She pulled my hair back from my face, holding it in a loose ponytail—something a mother might do when comforting her daughter. My hands ached to stay touching her, making her real in my existence.

"Thank you. I'm really glad I had a chance to meet you. I see where Max gets his compassion," I whispered, then smiled.

She let go of my hair and captured my shoulders.

"You are very sweet. Now, I think we've taken you away from Maxi long enough." Her hands floated off my shoulders and I went cold. Thankfully, Max replaced her warmth by protecting me in his arms. She passed him, tousling his hair. "Get your hair cut," she teased. His smile reached his eyes.

"I wanted to give you a tour of the cabin, if you don't mind me taking you from my family." He pulled me from my space and wrapped his arms around my back.

"I would like that." I turned and gave a slight wave to the panel of questioners and left the dining room. He held my hand as he led me to the great room. I looked around as he pulled me close.

"This is the great room. Over there is where you made me lose focus but I still beat you at pool." He bent close to me and pointed to the pool table

"Oh, wait—we never finished that game." I pushed his head off my shoulder. "Besides, I could have won if you weren't so focused on scoring," I said.

He shrugged and pressed his hands to his chest.

"Personally, I was very happy with the results of that game." He took my hand and pulled me through to the living room toward the stairs. "I want to show you something."

I happened to look at the opposite wall and noticed a clock: it was nine forty-five. A wave of disappointment crashed heavily across my chest. In a little over twelve hours we would have to separate and go our own ways.

He will go back to his classroom and me, my dorm. What if he didn't feel the same way once we were back at Wesley? I shivered deep in my body. I didn't want to think about that. *Live in the moment, Wilson.* I had to convince myself that everything was going to be perfect tonight. And whatever may happen later, I'd have to deal with it then.

He led me to his room.

"I've been here before. You don't have to fake it. Nobody can hear you," I whispered to him.

"I know that, but I didn't get to show you *this* the last time you were here." He pulled me through his room, grabbed a huge fluffy jacket, and wrapped it around me. "You're gonna need this." He pulled open his sliding glass door.

The freezing air fought its way into the room. It leapt and swirled around my head, trying to find a way down to my protected skin.

"Max, it's freezing out there." A chill spread throughout my body.

"I know, but it's worth it. Trust me." He went out onto the side balcony and held out his hands.

My teeth chattered, causing my jaw to tense. I reached for him and allowed the chills to take over my existence on the little deck off the side of his room.

"I hope so, because I can't feel my nose." He wasn't wearing a jacket. As a matter of fact, he was only wearing a hoodie that he'd pulled over his head after he stepped out into the cold. He reached up to light a tall standing heater, then turned to show me what he'd brought me out there to see.

"It's one of my secret passions." He went to the telescope he had pointing out into the clear night sky. His boyish eyes rounded, his hair tucked tight under his hood, and his lips stretched across his little smile.

I would look at pictures of black and white shapes if it meant I got to be close to him. I watched him aim and focus the scope to perfection. I wasn't cold anymore. He spun his hands in a circle trying to persuade me to come closer. His voice mixed with the cold, creating clouds of words that lingered and drew me in.

"Come here, look at this," he told me as I slid between him and the telescope. His hand wrapped around me, trailing across my back as I lowered myself to the scope.

"That's Jupiter. It's the brightest object in the Taurus constellation." He took a deep, thoughtful breath. "The Greeks believed that Jupiter fell in love with Europa, daughter of King Agenor. When she wouldn't have anything to do with him, he disguised himself as a white bull and sauntered up to her as she picked flowers. He impressed her so much with his gentle manner, he was able to lay down in front of her, and she climbed up onto his back." His breath caressed and wrapped hot around my neck. *The fact that I saw a bright, fuzzy circle in the telescope was interesting, but it's the idea that he knew the mythology regarding Jupiter, quite frankly, that turned me on.*

"What happened to her?" I stood up from the scope. His eyes lowered from the heavens to me.

"He charged straight to Crete with her on his back, then confessed who he really was and how much he loved her. She stayed and married him." His arms pushed into my jacket, his hands froze through my shirt. I lost my breath and jumped.

"Oh I'm sorry, you just looked so warm." He tried to pull his hands out; I held him right where he was.

"I didn't expect them to be like icebergs," I whispered. His eyes traced down to my neck.

"They aren't now," he answered. The tip of his tongue tasted the edge of my lips before he kissed me. He pulled away, teasing me just enough to make me talk.

"You taste so good," I mumbled across his lips. I felt him smile.

My stomach betrayed me and started to rumble.

"You're hungry. Let me get you something to eat." He leaned back, trying to read my expression.

"I'm fine," I tried to convince him. Although it wasn't like I was one of those girls who won't eat in front of a guy.

He grabbed my hand and pulled me into his room, heading to the little fridge next to his desk.

"Wow, how convenient is that?" I said as I sat on his bed and took off the gigantic jacket he'd wrapped me in earlier. He danced around a bit before naming off the limited items he had available.

"I have a half a jar of maraschino cherries…a half of a sandwich from yesterday…" he held it in the air toward me. I shook my head no. "Oh wait, I have sliced pepper jack cheese? Some apples? Oh, here we go, how about some whipped cream?" He shook the can and tilted it to his mouth. *Oh, Jesus, if he knew how badly I wanted to be that whipped cream.* He shifted his eyes toward me, reading my thoughts. He brought the can to me on the bed, straddling his legs between mine.

"Open," he said, holding the can above me. As I reached for it, he pulled it away.

"Don't you trust me? I won't give you too much."

He held the can above me again. I swallowed, parted my lips, and opened my mouth. He focused on my face; his eyes hypnotized me, and mine shut. I heard the can spray and felt the airy cream fill my mouth to overflowing. He tossed the can on the bed and brought his mouth to mine, making sure it didn't overflow down my chin. His tongue tasting around me, I swallowed the sweet cream. He pushed me down onto the bed. I felt his knee press up between my legs, his hand reaching for the can while he put his mouth to mine. I pulled the hood off his head and knotted my hands in his hair. He pulled back from me. My body ran cold.

"I'll be right back," he groaned as he jumped off me. I could hardly breathe. He didn't give me a chance to ask where he was going before he was gone.

Great. Exactly what I didn't want to be: left alone in his house. I didn't want the awkward gap of time and space that I had nothing in common with. I wanted to be with him as much as possible. By myself, in his room, my thoughts played tricks on my psyche. *Where did he go? Why didn't he tell me? What if his mom comes in here and I am spread out, lying on his bed? Clothed or not, that would leave a bad impression with her. I didn't want to mess this up. I really liked her.* I sat up and looked around the room. I caught my reflection in a mirror on the bathroom door. My hair was completely jacked. I stood in front of the mirror trying to flatten the frizzy mess. I pulled it back, twisted it into a small tight roll, and stuck a pencil from his desk in my hair.

When the bedroom door swung open, he had a plate of food in his hand and two frosty glasses stacked together. He froze looking at me standing there; he licked his lips and his throat bounced as he swallowed. He slid the plate onto his desk and set the glasses next to it. He sped to me, pressing his lips to the back of my exposed neck. His hand wrapped tight across my stomach.

"Mmmm, I've never seen your hair up like that before," he breathed warm against my skin below my ear. His hand, cold from the frosty glasses, slid up across the back of my neck. Chills owned my skin.

"Really? That's all it takes to bring you back to me?" I watched him in the mirror before I spun to face him. "I think I'll wear my hair up around you more often. How about Monday, 12:45?" I asked low. He froze against my neck.

He pulled away from me, looking me straight in the eyes. His jaw tightened and his lips pressed hard.

"That's not fair. I'll have no control. I keep trying to figure out how I'm going to make it through Monday. I already know that I'm gonna have a hard time keeping my hands off of you—to be honest, I'm beginning to worry about returning to Wesley." He grabbed my wrists and space opened between us.

"Me, too. What are we going to do? It's not like I can drop out of your class." My stomach ached when I said it. Because I couldn't guarantee I'd be able to control myself either.

"I wouldn't let you drop out, that's not a solution. Besides, I need to see you." He tugged at my chin, bringing my face up to his.

"We'll cross that bridge when we come to it, right?" I told him, pulling him to his desk. I didn't want to focus on a day that was already too close to changing everything about our weekend. "What did you bring to eat?" I asked.

"Food," he teased. He picked up the plate held it high in the air so I couldn't see it, twisting his body away from me.

I pressed my hands slowly up his sides, tickling him as he tried to keep me from seeing. He was ticklish. He let one hand go of the plate and wrapped it around me. Pushing me, the back of my legs found the bed; our bodies tilted. He landed perfectly on top of me—not too heavy, but just heavy enough for me to feel his want. He'd saved the plate from falling, he was so good. He looked deep into my eyes. Then, blinking slowly, he looked away to the plate.

He pulled a low, smooth breath in, "Close your eyes." I did.

I opened my mouth slightly, pushing the tip of my tongue against my bottom teeth.

"No peeking. Here, taste this. Don't bite me." He pressed his finger into my mouth; I closed my lips and sucked. Milk chocolate melted on my taste buds.

"Mmmm," I moaned from the back of my throat. I opened my eyes, he was watching me. He pulled his finger out of my mouth and tapped the tip of my nose.

"No peeking." I closed my eyes and opened again. Cold air rushed my mouth. He pushed something cool and wet against my lips, dragging it across to my bottom lip before resting it on my tongue. I closed my lips around it and pressed it against the roof of my mouth. Strawberry's sweet nectar flooded my throat. He kissed me, making my lips warm again. He tasted like milk chocolate. His hands pressed into the bed, pushing his body up to hover above my chest. I grabbed locks of his hair, trying to force him back down to me but he resisted. He bent to lie on his side next to me. His long fingers caught my hair and pushed it off my face. He brought his hands to the collar of my shirt and slipped his fingers down under the front. My breathing quickened as tingles raced down my body, low. His eyes didn't drop from mine. His fingers pressed the charm against my skin before he picked it up.

"You know, when we get back to Wesley things will have to be different." His eyes dropped to the pendant.

Why did he go there? It was our last night together, I didn't want to worry about Monday or even the rest of my life. I just wanted to live right now.

"I know. But we aren't there right now." I turned toward him.

"I want to make sure we're on the same page. This is the only time we're going to be able to talk about it before we get back." He broke his gaze from my pendant and examined me, his eyes capturing my expression.

"Yeah, I know." I rolled onto my back. My necklace fell against my skin and slid behind my hair. I closed my eyes, stopping the rush of heartbreak that tried to take over.

"Wilson, I wish we didn't have to think about it," he whispered, the tips of his fingers brushed around the side of my face.

"Me, too." I opened my eyes.

"We are going to have to really watch our actions around each other. No touching." His eyes tightened as he swayed onto his back.

I wasn't going to let this mess up my last night with him. I rolled up, pushed my chest against his and wrapped my arm around to the other side of his head, twisting my fingers into his hair.

"I can't touch you like this?" I asked low.

"No," he let out a breathy sigh.

"How about this?" I unzipped his sweatshirt and slipped my hands up under his T-shirt.

"Definitely not." His hands tucked around me. His stomach tightened.

"What if I did this?" I stretched up and kissed him. This time, I pushed my desires on him.

His arms tightened and pulled me closer to him. I felt his body give up and surrender to my way of explaining. We both had a grasp on how we were going to act back at school—I think.

CHAPTER TWENTY-ONE:

Sometimes I think honor should be compromised. I *know—hard to see where that is logical. But in certain circumstances honor just gets in the way. Tonight it was so in my way and I couldn't seem to find a way around it. Maybe, if I was one of those paratroopers, I could scale it with my bare hands and discover what's on the other side. But I am not a paratrooper. I'm a seventeen-year-old girl with a twenty-two-year-old boyfriend who wants to wait until I'm eighteen to go "all the way" with me.*

I understand why, I'm not stupid. His career, my education, his freedom, my innocence…all tied together in a nice little package of morality.

"What are you thinking about?" Max whispered across my neck.

"My eighteenth birthday," I answered. He stopped kissing my neck, the tip of his nose pressed firmly against the edge of my ear.

"Really, what did you want to do?" he laughed just enough as he asked.

"Celebrate Christmas," I said.

"Okay, what else do you want to do?" He pressed his lips up behind my ear. I was going wild. He knew what else I wanted.

"Open my present from you," I breathed. He growled hot against my skin. My butterflies twirled. It was exactly what he wanted, too.

"I want to give you your present so bad." His face tensed as he pressed his fingers light on my neck. "Twenty-nine days from now."

"How about a sneak peek? Just a little something." I was done waiting. I just wanted him entirely.

"This whole weekend you've been sneak-peeking." He adjusted his body on top of mine and I could tell he was aroused.

"I like sneak peeks." I slid my hands into the back of his Levi's and felt his muscles tighten.

"Me, too." He navigated his lips down the front of my neck toward my chest.

"Whoa, you're vibrating." The phone in his pocket rang. He didn't stop kissing me as he reached between our bodies to pull out his phone.

"Sorry," he spoke against my skin as he set it next to me on the bed. He didn't check it. He slid his hands down to my waist and pulled at my shirt instead.

"Max? Don't you need to answer that?" I asked as he ran his hand up my side and over across my stomach.

"No. Whoever it is can leave a message." He pulled my shirt up to expose my chest. He ran his hands across my bra, his lips kissing the exposed edges. Nothing better than a man who knows how to change the subject; however, there was something desperate in the ring of his phone.

"Don't you think you should find out who called? What if it's important?"

He pressed his ear to my chest, listening to my heart pound. My hands, comfortably tangled in his hair, held him against me.

"Well, your heart is telling me you'd rather have me continue what I was doing." He turned his head to look up at me. His hair ticked across my skin.

His phone chimed with a text message.

"There you go, now that's a sign you need to find out who's calling you." I grabbed it and put it in front of his face.

He snatched it. I watched his eyes shrink. His hands worked hard to answer whoever contacted him.

"Send. Okay—happy, right?" He held his phone up in the air then set it down on his night stand. I heard it shut off.

"Yeah, so it wasn't an emergency?" I sat up.

"No. Now, where were we?" He leaned me back, adjusting his body to press where it was before he'd gotten up. "About here?" He brought his lips to my neck.

"Yeah, about there." I slid my hands back in between his underwear and his muscled backside.

"Because you looked pretty intense when you texted back," I continued.

"Wilson, the only person I would want to talk to is here with me." He stopped kissing me and looked into my eyes. "Besides, it was only Calvin telling me he's at Nick's and he needs me to pick him up." He pressed back against my neck.

"Oh shit, are you kidding me? Oh my God! We've gotta go. I told Cindy I had a headache." I pushed him up and slid off the bed. My head was swimming. Exactly what I didn't want— Cindy to come home and find I wasn't there. Max stood, watching me bounce around his room talking to myself. "What am I going to tell her? What excuse will she believe? What the hell? I'm so stupid." My arms tingled hot, and I wanted to throw up.

"Why are you freaking out? There's nothing she'll do. She's too chicken-shit." He stopped me, holding me by my shoulders. He took a deep breath, lifting his head, telling me to take one too. I did.

"You underestimate her. If she's pissed enough, she'll attack. And *leaving* after I told her I was staying home just might be the thing that pops her bubble." I pulled him toward the bedroom door. We had to get back.

"Well, it's about time her bubble was burst. I don't like how she treats you. You deserve so much better." He grabbed me and his eyes captured mine. "Slow down. Don't worry, I'll take care of it." His arms wrapped tightly around my body and his lips pressed firmly onto the top of my head. I melted into his embrace. I believed him.

"Grab that jacket. It's cold and I don't want you to catch a chill." I snatched the puffy jacket I'd worn earlier and hung it over my shoulders. It smelled so good, just like him. I'd have no problem keeping warm in his jacket. He pushed my arms through the sleeves and zipped it up to my neck. He grabbed my hand and pulled me downstairs to the great room.

His whole family was there, except for Calvin. Max swung his hand in the air and gave a firm wave.

"Well, I have to take Wilson home. I'll be back late." His mom scurried over to us and held out her arms. I let go of Max and hugged her.

"Oh Wilson, it was such a delight meeting you. Come back tomorrow, you and Maxi. We'll have a nice brunch." She let go of me, I wasn't ready. I held her tight against me a moment longer. Her embrace was something I've longed for my entire life. I felt her arms wrap back around me. Finally I got to feel what a mother's embrace could be like. The smell of sweet peas and the weight of a sun-soaked hot day saturated my body.

"Okay, I would love that. And thank you for opening your home to me," I answered back instantly.

"Mom, we're leaving tomorrow," Max told her.

As I let go of her, a flood of vacancy washed across my soul. I didn't want to forget how she felt.

"Well, you'll just have to find time to come back." She looked at Max and pulled at the back of my hair, lifting it off my neck. "You have the prettiest hair." She focused back to me.

I wanted to pack her in my suitcase. I'd found what had been missing my whole life.

"Thanks," I whispered to her.

"Frank, Camille. Max and Wilson are leaving, come say goodbye." She swung her hand in a 'come here' motion.

"Don't worry. It's okay; they're deep in their game." I waved at them. They were playing pool and I didn't want to pull them away from it. Frank and Dan waved and said something I couldn't hear. Camille came over and gave me a light hug.

"I don't know where Max has been hiding you, but it was nice he brought you here."

"Nice to meet you," I exhaled. She winked at Max and popped him in the chest with her fist before she went back to the pool table.

"Okay honey, drive safe, it's dark and icy out there. I'm not going to wait up. I'm pretty tuckered out." Nancy gave Max a kiss on the cheek and pulled at the collar of his hoodie.

"That's fine, mom. Thanks." He kissed her back.

I loved him. I really wanted what they had. The way she fussed over him and he let her.

He pushed his arm around me and led me to the entry where we'd left our boots. I held him and slipped my feet into my fake UGGS. Not too bad, only lost my balance once.

"We'd better hustle," he whispered in my ear. He opened the front door and the stinging-cold air rushed against my face and hands. I really was leaving and I truly didn't know if I was going to make it back tomorrow. He grabbed my hand and pulled me to the car.

He drove fast through the cold, dark, icy roads. It was a good thing all I could focus on was him. He stole glances on the straightaways.

"So I've been thinking about how you can explain to Cindy why you weren't there." Max turned down the radio, which was playing some bass-heavy song about love and drugs.

"Good, because she's probably really pissed off right now. I'm surprised she hasn't called me yet." I pulled my phone from my pocket and checked.

Cindy wasn't one to text or call me a lot. She was usually busy with other people. Which—don't get me wrong—I didn't mind. I wasn't one who liked to talk on the phone much. I'd rather talk to people face to face anyway.

"I think we should tell her the truth," he said. I felt my gut tie in knots.

"You're joking, right? Or you've lost your mind. We can't tell her." I pushed my hands through my hair and rubbed my eyes. Something I do when people come up with totally insane ideas.

"Wait, now hear me out. What if…by telling her about us, we are giving her the power to prove herself trustworthy. You know, kinda like creating responsibility and ownership to something she has access to. Does that make sense?" He pushed his hand in the air between us, glancing over when he could to field my reaction. I sat silent for a moment before I answered.

"I think if we did something like that, you would be in jail and I would be lying on a psychiatrist's chair explaining, in detail, what you did to me and why I let you."

I was as calm as I could be. The fierce fire storm raged hard and chaotically in my body. *There was not an ice cube's chance in hell she could keep us quiet. She is all about personal and private PR. I remember the time our friend Tracy told her about kissing some random guy behind the bleachers at a football game and, by half-time, everyone knew about it. She is the last person you would want to tell anything to.*

His jaw tightened and I waited for him to argue his point. But instead he exhaled slowly, tilting his head to the side.

"I wish we could be open with her, I really do. But I think—no, I know—she would warp it into something bad or wrong and use it to her own twisted advantage. And to be honest, I don't think I could handle that." I was glad I told him my feelings about Cindy. Hopefully he'll see my logic. If not, God help us.

"It doesn't feel wrong to me. *You* aren't wrong for me. What is a month from now? You and I will still be the same people. But it's all about the numbers and that's what matters to the law. You're right, we can't tell her." He slid his hand across my thigh after he shifted. "I don't know what I was thinking." He twisted an awkward smile.

"How nice it would be to *not* have to hide. If it was a normal situation, we could go anywhere and do anything without a second thought. But it's not that way. So right now, we have to take what we can get and protect what we have." I stared at his profile. His eyebrows lowered and his jaw clenched.

"So what are you going to tell her? About not being there when she came home, and the fact that you are here, with me, in my car." He stopped driving. I turned away and looked out the window. We were at the gate to Cindy's cabin.

"I don't know." Knots of dread tangled around my confidence.

Max pulled out his phone and texted Calvin. His thumbs bounced and clicked the keys quickly.

"I told Calvin we were here." He laid his phone on his thigh. I watched, waiting for it to chime and vibrate. It was forever before it responded. He grabbed it and read it to me.

"Come down. Nick pressing button. Cindy not here yet," his voice lightened.

"Oh, thank God; Cindy must have hooked up with someone from the club," I breathed. The huge block of stress that weighed heavy on my shoulders dissolved to nothing. The gate swung open and Max drove the car through. We were so lucky Cindy wasn't there yet. We dodged another bullet. He drove through the pitch black night down the long driveway to the Browler's mansion. The beams of our headlights bounced and danced off the snow around us as we turned and twisted through the acres and acres of front yard. I was able to breathe deeply and the muscles in my neck released a wave of pressure across my back.

We could actually walk up to the front door together, hand in hand, to say goodnight. Not that I wanted to do that, but it was reassuring that it was a possibility.

He came around to my door and opened it. I grabbed his hand and slid out of his car. He, like every time before, wrapped his arm around my waist and pulled me against his hip—a comfort I was getting used to, something I was going to miss back at school. He pulled me up the steps to the front door of Casa de Browler and stopped me from going in.

"I want to kiss you good night." He pulled me close. My heart fell to my feet.

"No, I don't want you to go," I mumbled. I balled my fists and tapped them against his chest as he held me. When I stared into his eyes, they danced for me. He had a twinkle that told me he was teasing and a smile that roped me in.

"I want to know what it feels like to kiss you goodnight on the front porch," he said as he leaned into me and pressed gently against my lips. It was as good as I could have imagined it. I twisted my fingers around the hair on the back of his neck and pushed up onto my tiptoes. He slid his hands up, pressing them below my ears and cradling my face. He tilted his head to one side and opened his mouth.

"Mmmm, feels good," I breathed. My entire body was smiling. I tasted the excitement of our first porch kiss and the disappointment of it being our last.

There is no porch at the dorms and, when I graduate, who knows where I'll be for college. But I could almost bet that not one of the colleges would have a huge, beautiful porch like the Browlers'. My heart pushed for him, but at the same time, was broken by the thoughts of our Monday morning existence together at Wesley. I tried my best not to think about it. I pushed myself against his chest and wedged my head under his chin. His arms pressed heavily across my back. I felt the muscles in his body tighten around me. I never wanted to let go.

He loosened his arms from around me. Suddenly, his head snapped up and he reached for the door. Instantly he had me through the entry and was pulling me toward the stairs.

"What are you doing?" I stumbled over my boots. Max tossed Calvin the keys to the car.

"I'm not here," Max told him.

"Okay, bro," Calvin played cool.

"There's a car coming down the drive. Might be Cindy," Max told me as he pulled me upstairs.

My heart leapt high into my chest. Selfishly, part of me wanted it to be her; that way Max would have to lock himself in my room and wouldn't be able to leave until she was asleep. Or better yet, he'd have to stay all night. At the very least, I would be guaranteed one last night alone with him. We hurried into my bedroom and pushed the door shut, pressing the lock. I grabbed the chair from the desk and propped it tightly under the knob. I'll admit, it might have been a little overkill, but there was no way I was going to let anyone interrupt my last night alone with Max, especially Cindy.

CHAPTER TWENTY-TWO:

"Wow, you're serious," he said after I double-checked the force pressuring the chair against the door. His fingers ran across the top of the chair and down the spiral dowel, finally reaching my hand. "Do you really think Cindy's gonna bust in here?"

"I'm not taking any chances. Tomorrow we fly back to California, and that's a reality I'm not ready to deal with," I said. He pulled my hand and pressed it against his chest.

"Wilson, you'll be fine. We will do what we have to until we don't have to anymore." His heart pounded an excited rhythm against my skin. My feet shuffled forward to him as he led me gently to the middle of the room.

"I don't know Max, I can't stop thinking about tomorrow. I don't want to go back right now. I'm not ready to let *this* go." I pushed my hand between us. I felt my eyes well up with anticipated disappointment. My tears tasted desperate.

I visualized us in his classroom. He totally ignored me, wouldn't even look my way. He helped Bonnie Wente with her questions and his hand pressed against her back. His smile warmed his eyes as he spoke to her. Painful thoughts tarnished my visions of him touching her. Irrational thoughts, desperate wishes, and heartbreaking nightmares took over any normalcy I had. The door wedged closed with the chair was the only thing I thought could keep him here with me, away from tomorrow.

"Wilson, please don't cry. I'll keep tomorrow away as long as I can. I promise." He cradled my head in his hands and pressed his lips to taste my tears. His fingers pressed solidly against the back of my neck as his thumbs cleared what his kisses had missed.

"I'm sorry. Stupid isn't it? Crying for something I haven't even lost." I grabbed the waist of his sweatshirt, clinging to any hope that he would agree to stay forever with me in Aspen. *Was it crazy? Yes, but it's the only thing I could rationalize in the moment of pure lunacy.*

"Not stupid, I wouldn't call it that—meaningful, significant, even emotional—but not stupid. Far from that." His eyes studied the expression from my lips to my eyes as he spoke. He pulled me close, his lips warmed my forehead. His sweet aroma flooded my body, finding its way to my heart. He held me standing in the middle of the room.

"I swear, throughout my entire life, I've never cried as much as I have this weekend." I looked up at him, my head still weighed against his chest.

"Is that a bad thing?" He smiled down at me. His hand stroked my hair away from my eyes.

"No. It's a safe thing, a trust thing." I rose to touch his lips to mine; they tasted as sweet as they smelled.

"Wilson, I won't hurt you," he whispered across my lips.

"I know," I answered. His arms tightened across my back. His words were my aphrodisiac, carrying endorphins throughout every part of my body.

I trusted him. It was strange to have such an unfamiliar feeling. I've never trusted *anyone* like this. With him it was instantaneous. I don't think I could have experienced him the way I did this weekend if I didn't trust him. Completely unprotected, open, and raw; it was sometimes painful to face, but he made it okay to own who I was and where I came from.

I elevated my hands up around his neck and kissed him, allowing him to taste my desire for him to take me. He pulled his mouth from mine. Cool, empty air blended with my skin as he took off his shirt, then mine. We both hurried to unbutton each other's pants. I knew what he looked like in tight boxers and welcomed that view again. We shuffled and kicked to be free of the tangled pants at our feet. I felt his weight press me toward the bed as the back of my legs hit the edge, and my body tilted to fall. He crawled up slowly and deliberately, heavy against my body. I felt his desire through his Calvin Klein's. His body swayed as his mouth climbed to breathe in my ear.

"Wilson," he inhaled. "It's a good thing I'm not seventeen." He pushed his hands heavily into the bed above my shoulders, raising his chest off mine. Pressure filled the low space between our bodies. "Because I don't think I could wait to be with you if I was." He pressed his hips against me again.

I lost my breath. I felt the same way. I thought about being alone with him like this. Nobody would know. I could be with him and share that part of me that ached to have him take me, *completely*. I dug my fingertips into his lower back; he bit his bottom lip and studied my expression. His lust-filled eyes danced purposefully and slowly before he dropped his head. His hair fell toward me. His breath paced fast as he moaned. His motion snared my butterflies in his net. He owned them and they were ready to go, willingly.

I let out a deep, instinctual growl as the space between our bodies vanished in rhythm. My mind swimming in his pool of confidence, I was his entirely. He brought me to teeter on a razor-thin edge of anticipation and ecstasy. The only thing separating us was the thin, snug fabric of his Calvin Klein's and my panties. My mind raced with the thoughts of his weight heavy against my body on my eighteenth birthday with nothing between us but my own inhibitions about my virginity.

My soul found its mate, causing us both to shudder and twitch in pleasure. He pushed his mouth hard against mine. His arms circled my shoulders as his muscles tightened around my body; he laughed as I raked my hands down his back. Ticklish, he adjusted to lie next to me. My body rippled with chills as the cool air danced on my uncovered skin. Max noticed and pulled a blanket over us from the foot of the bed.

"Thanks," I breathed.

"You're welcome," he answered as he pressed his forehead to my cheek, his nose dragging across before his lips tasted my face.

A wave of fatigue splashed fast through my body and my eyelids became victims of the weight. His face pushed against the side of my head, his breathing slowed and became deep.

"Max? Are you sleeping?" I asked, fighting to stay awake. His arm had become heavy across my waist.

"Hmm? No," he mumbled as his breath quivered into a yawn.

"You have a nice family," I mentioned to him.

"Mm, hum," he breathed. He tightened the space between us and pulled his arm across my stomach.

"I'm serious. You don't know how lucky you are to have such a nice family." I pushed against him.

"Wilson, what you saw was what they wanted you to see." He rolled over onto his back. The soft sheets tugged at my side. He tucked his hands behind his head and stared up at the ceiling.

"Well, Max, I think your mother is amazing and I loved her." I rolled over. My arms draped his chest and my hands held my chin firmly as I looked at him. "And your sister was sweet."

"Don't think that my family hasn't had its own sets of problems. I had a lot of pressure from my father to follow him into the family business. When he found out I had different ideas for my life, watch out." He glanced at me before looking back up at the ceiling. The muscles in his jaw flexed.

I'd hit a nerve. *What was it with me and putting my foot in it? Great, I was so wrapped up in my own pathetic life story I didn't give him a chance to tell me his. How frickin' selfish. This whole weekend it never crossed my mind that, even with two parents, his relationship with them might not be perfect.* He sat up and leaned against the head board. His chest rose with each deep breath.

"I'm sorry, Max. I just assumed—that wasn't fair of me." I sat up next to him and pushed my fingers through his hair, wedging his thick black locks behind his ear.

"You didn't know. My dad always thought I was the golden boy. See, I was the one that was supposed to work my way up through his company then eventually take over for him when he retired. And, of course, I didn't do it." His shoulders rounded.

"You became a teacher instead," I whispered.

"Yep, I saw what the oil industry had done to my dad. It ate him up fast and consumed every part of his life. It wasn't what I wanted." He shook his head back and forth.

"I'm certainly glad you became a teacher." It was awkward to say, considering my relationship with him outside of Wesley. I rubbed at my ear and scratched the back of my head. A lump sat perched in the back of my throat.

"Me, too. I'm sorry if I sound selfish. I don't mean to, I just want you to know my family isn't as perfect as it appears to be." He grabbed my hand and spread my fingers with his as he held them tight.

"I know, *that* Calvin. He's a piece of work!" I leaned against him and smiled wide, attempting to lighten the mood.

"Well, he's his own worst enemy when it comes to people skills." He cleared his throat and ran his hands through his hair. "The fact that our father asked Camille's husband, Dan, to help run the company and didn't offer it to Calvin made their relationship a lot worse. He's pretty bent about that." He looked at me; his eyes constricted and filled with pain for his brother.

"That must've devastated him." The lump I'd cleared seconds ago clogged the back of my throat again.

"Yeah, and Cal is the type who acts like it doesn't bug him. But I know it's eating him alive. I do as much as I can to keep him involved with the family. One day he's just going to leave and not come back, and that's gonna crush my mom."

"As sad as it sounds, I know how that feels." I pulled the comforter up and tucked it under my arms to cover my chest.

He stroked down the inside of my arm with his fingers, tangling them around my hand as he lifted my wrist to the tip of his nose. He inhaled and pressed his lips to the delicate part of my wrist. The temperate air breezed cold across my skin as he pulled away. He looked into my eyes and I knew—if he could—he would heal me.

CHAPTER TWENTY-THREE:

We lay tangled together watching the bottomless orange sun rise up over the snow-covered, rolling hills glimmering outside my window. My voice was hoarse and my throat was dry from talking with him all night. The edges of my eyelids stung from the thin, crisp morning air and lack of rest. Unfortunately, we couldn't keep the morning from coming.

"What time is your flight today?" Max leaned over me.

"I don't know. I'll grab my ticket." I pressed my hand over my mouth as I answered. I didn't want to scare him off with my morning breath. I shifted my legs to the side of the bed and was just about to roll up when he held me down, pushed my hand away, and gave me a light kiss.

"Oh my God, Max, my breath is so bad." I grabbed his hoodie from the floor and slipped it on. He caught my waist and pulled me back to the bed.

"I don't care, you smell good to me." He kissed me, deep and slow. The self-conscious thoughts of my stenchy breath evaporated instantly. His hand pulled at the zipper of the hoodie I'd just put on. My hands curved around his ears, my fingertips curling into his messy black hair. The ticket could wait.

He slipped his hand past the open zipper on my hoodie; I lost my breath. He was ready for our last moment together before we had to return to the Bay Area. I pulled away from him—the perfect opportunity to tease him one last time. Standing on the bed by his feet, my hoodie fell open just enough to show the curves of my breasts.

"Okay, so what are you willing to do to get me to take this off?" I held the front collar of his hoodie in my fists.

"Hmm, how about kiss your feet?" He grabbed my ankle.

"I don't know, that doesn't seem like a fair trade, what else you willing to do?" I shifted my feet.

"This." He pulled my ankle and I went down screaming. As quickly as I fell, his hands slipped under the bottom of my hoodie. Navigating across my stomach, clutching at my waist, he slid me down to even out our bodies. My hair trailed behind me and my hoodie pulled up to expose my stomach.

"That's really unfair. I'm not as strong as you," I complained before he tasted my pouting lips. He was such a good kisser. Chills rippled through my body as he bit my lower lip, causing my mouth to open for him to explore.

"Sorry, you're a weakling. Survival of the fittest right?" he said, his lips slightly touching mine. I let out a low whimper.

The handle on the door shook and I heard Cindy's voice through the solid wood door.

"What the hell? What's she doing locking the door. It's not like she went out last night and brought some random guy home. Frickin' Wilson." Her hand banged heavy against the door.

We froze, staring at each other listening to what she was doing. Her voice trailed off as she moved down the hall and yelled for Nick. We broke the silence with laughter. It was the first time we weren't stressed out by her. I think the chair wedged under the door handle had something to do with it.

"Did she just curse me?" I turned to look at the door then back at him for his answer, trying not to smile.

"Yeah, I think she did. And she called me some random guy." He twisted his face to look pissed before he broke with the smile that always captured my heart.

"Well at least we're frickin' random." I went to grab my ticket. I guess it would be good to see what time we were going to leave today. "What time is it?" I pulled open the top drawer of the dresser and found my ticket. He grabbed his phone off the nightstand.

"It's a quarter to seven." He slid the phone open and checked his messages.

"My flight leaves at 3:15," I rambled to him.

"That doesn't leave much time. You're a little over four hours away from the airport." He flipped the covers off and collected his clothes off the ground.

"How much time do we have?" I laid the ticket on the dresser next to me. Reality hammered down solid against my expectations and I flushed with panic. I hadn't thought about the travel time and the extra two hours you have to allow for check-in.

"You need to leave by nine." He slipped his shirt over his head and reached for the Levi's he'd tossed on the bed.

His words burned harshly in my head. The regret scraped down my throat as I swallowed. Just throw me down on a sharp, prickly cactus—probably would have been less agonizing. I had less than two hours before I had to leave and, of that couple of hours, Cindy would monopolize ninety-five percent. All I'm left with is *right now* to create a memory that will sustain both of us until we can be together again.

It was the uncertainty of our future that kept me on edge. *How are we going to sneak time together? Can I hide my feelings for him while in his class? How will I react when other girls flirt with him? Seriously, less than thirty-six hours ago, I didn't even know if he would have recognized me outside of class. Now, in less than two days, we are full-on making out.*

"Wilson? Earth to Wilson." He slipped his hands around my waist, shifting me as he searched my eyes.

God, when he looks at me with his curious eyes, I shiver and melt. If he ran his fingers through his hair one more time, I swear I'd never leave this room.

"Wow, you were just completely somewhere else." He pressed his hands to the sides of my face. "Where did you go?" He pulled my attention to him and smiled.

"School on Monday." I bit my lip, trying to stop from showing him how stressed I was about leaving Aspen.

"Monday, huh? How do I bring you back to right now? I don't want to lose you to some experience we haven't even lived yet." His eyes danced around my expression, soaking up every uncertain thought that flowed across my lips.

"How are we going to be in class together without totally blowing it? I can't look at you without *everyone* in that room seeing how I feel." I lowered my head and dropped my eyes from his.

"We'll have to figure that out on Monday." He pulled up on my chin and kissed me. He lived in the *here and now* and knew how to bring me right back.

I ran my hands through his jet black hair and he dropped his hands around my waist, pulling me close. His aroma bathed my mind with want, and his taste pulled at my desires. It was his instinctive, masculine growls that hurled me over the edge. With all my strength, I pushed him to shuffle back and drop onto the bed. I wanted to make sure he left with one last piece of *our* Aspen that would keep him interested and wanting more. He flipped me onto my back, his lips tracing the outline of my chin up to my ear.

"You make it so hard to wait," he whispered.

"Twenty-eight days," I reminded him as I ran my hands up his back under his T-shirt.

"I'm counting the days," he answered.

I heard the lock on the door knob turn and twist. Cindy had gotten the frickin' key to unlock my room! My limbs ran cold and chills flooded my entire body. She pushed on the door but it didn't budge. The chair did exactly what it was supposed to do. Max was in the closet within seconds.

"Wilson. What the hell is going on? Did you block the door? Open this now!" She pounded on the door.

"I'm coming. You have to close the door first." I pushed against the door, looked back at the closet to make sure he was in it, and dragged the chair out from under the door knob. When I opened the door, Cindy pushed past me hoping to catch whoever she was sure I was hiding.

"What in the hell did you do? Why would you need to blockade yourself in this room? Where is he?" She looked out the window and pushed the curtains back looking for my 'mystery man.'

"I don't know what you're talking about, Cindy. I've been alone. I heard strange noises last night, I was the only one here, and I got freaked out." I followed her to the other side of the room.

"You wedged a frickin' chair against your door because you were freaked out? Why didn't you text me? I would've gotten Nick to check on you," she was serious.

How sad was our friendship? If that's what you would call our association. She'd send her brother to see if I was okay? God forbid she would leave a club—or drinks, or a guy—for me. I was her failed project and she was my ticket to Max. That was the extent of our parasitic relationship.

"I'm sorry, I should have called you." I tried to move her toward the door but she plopped on the bed. She wasn't going anywhere until she told me what she had to say.

"Oh, Wilson, there were so many hot guys last night. You could've had your pick and there still would have been leftovers for seconds." She smiled wide and bounced up and down on the bed.

"Sorry I missed it. My head feels better, though." I rubbed the gash up by my hairline. It hurt when I touched it. Visions of Max's family flashed in my head. They never said anything about it; I guess it really wasn't that bad.

"Where did you get that necklace? I've never seen you wear it before." She plucked the heart charm up from my skin and pushed her head close to my neck.

I swallowed and felt my blood speed through my veins. I pushed my hand to hers and took over holding it. I didn't want her to touch it and tarnish the feelings it held for me.

"This is the first time I've worn it. That's probably why you've never seen it before." I pulled the chain across my chin and pressed the charm to my lips. The tiny key dangling in the middle of the heart tickled at my lips as it moved.

"Was it your grandma's? Did your grandpa give it to you after she died?" She acted involved. The one time I hoped she would brush me off she became interested in my life.

"Something like that. Hey, what time do we need to get out of here?" I struggled to engage in a meaningless conversation with her. I went to the dresser and started pulling out my clothes.

"We should be on the road by nine, nine-thirty at the latest." She held up one of my shirts. "Wilson, I'm sorry I left last night. I probably should have stayed with you." She balled it up and tossed it back onto the bed. What a big step for her. She doesn't admit to very many wrong doings, especially this type.

"Don't worry about it. Not really worth thinking about. I survived. No permanent damage done, right?" I started folding my clothes. I didn't want to make it a big deal; I just wanted her to leave so Max could come out of the closet.

"You're so right. You handled it. Crazy to prop a chair under your door knob, but who am I to say?" She must have talked to her dad; for some reason, anytime she talks to him she adjusts back to the "bearable" Cindy.

"You talk to your dad this morning?" I pulled at the next drawer down.

"Yeah, he is coming into Denver around one o'clock. I told him we'd meet him and have lunch." She stood up, waiting for me to argue.

"Okay, sounds good." I snapped my jeans in front of my body and continued to fold them.

"Oh-kay—so you keep packing. I'll tell Nick to have the car ready by nine o'clock sharp." She held up my black lacy bra and spun it around her finger before dropping it back onto the bed. "Nice, Wilson."

My face burst red as the heat flushed to my cheeks. *Why does she do that to me?* I followed her and shut my door. I didn't wait to prop the chair under my door handle again.

"You can come out. She's gone," I whispered before I pulled the door open. His hair was tousled and messy with random pieces across his face. His smile—so wicked—rose to his eyes as they convinced me to join him in the huge, livable walk-in closet.

"She left, but I have a feeling it won't be for long," I told him as he wrapped his hands around me and spun me to the bench in the center of the closet.

"If I had known this room existed, mmmm, what fun we could have had." He sat me down on the bench and crouched down between my legs.

"Max? What are you doing?" I asked before he kissed me.

"Close your eyes," he told me, kissing my eyelids.

He left me sitting there. Cool air wrapped around me as he passed behind. Weight pressed against the crown of my head; a rush of air swooshed around my face as something tickled my neck.

"Open your eyes." I looked at him: he had taken off his shirt and was wearing a huge, black cowboy hat.

"Mmm, you make one hot cowboy." I grabbed at the waist of his jeans, pulling him closer to me. "It's *this* I worry about." I looked at the full-length mirror at the other end of the closet. I had on a pink cowboy hat with maroon-dyed feathers across the front. Tiny clear and pink beads created a pattern of zigzags covering the lower part of the feathers. Around my neck was wrapped a deep blue feather boa. I raked my hands up and down across the space in front of my head and shoulders.

"Really? A pink cowboy hat—really?"

"It's that or the bright orange Caltrans beanie I found." He reached across me and snatched it up. The fact that he had it next to me means he'd actually considered putting that thing on my head.

236

"You made the right choice." I wrapped my arms over the hat and held it to my head.

He backed away and swung the beanie in circles on his finger, the muscles in his stomach flexing and relaxing under his perfect skin. I didn't even notice when he tossed the beanie across the closet. All I saw was his body move and I was hooked. I'd be his cowgirl, Caltrans worker, or whatever else he wanted me to be if he would just keep moving for me.

He tilted his hat and held his hand out to mine. "Ma'am, would you honor me with a dance?" He caught my hand and pulled me up from the bench.

"Why, I don't dance with cowboys." I told him in my best southern accent as I fluffed the end of the boa at him.

"Well, it's a good thing I'm not a cowboy." He pulled me against his bare chest and my hand pressed firmly there before I slipped it up behind his neck and tangled my fingers in the back of his hair. With his hand around my waist, his other covering mine against his chest, I felt his body sway and push against me. I swear I could hear music.

CHAPTER TWENTY-FOUR:

We danced to a whole song in my head. Our bodies, sexy and smooth, fit as one. His rhythm tamed me and his smell intoxicated my senses. The deep, rumbling breaths he took as we moved vibrated through my body, awakening a desire so profound; if he asked me to make love to him I would, without hesitation, take a chance and live with the consequences. Bring. It. On.

I felt his phone chime with a text.

"It's Cal. He's at the gate." He held me tight against his body. My arms tightened around him. I wasn't ready to let go.

"How are you going to escape?" The words hurt as their edges scraped at my throat.

"Nick gave Cal the code. I need you to keep Cindy busy while I leave." His breath chilled my ear. Why couldn't his words get tangled in my hair for awhile? Just long enough so I could feel his kiss once more before he left.

"I'm not ready for this. Don't leave," I whispered. His hands navigated up to my head as he pulled away, waiting for me to open my eyes. He stared at me, studying every bump and curve of my face.

"Wilson, trust me, I will not let *this* go." His eyes shifted back and forth, watching me, as he drew close for our last kiss.

I don't know if it was because of the anticipation of the weekend coming to an end or the pure want that fluxed through my body, but his touch was extra sweet. With just enough sour to make me ache.

I knew I would still see him every day, and that those *every days* would be different. It wasn't that. I didn't want us to change. I didn't want to watch all the Bonnies and Jackies gushing over him. I wanted them to know he was with me.

"Max, I want to trust you. I really do, but how can one weekend convince you to wait for me? What happens when you decide—I'm not worth it?" Insecurities tumbled from my mouth. His face drained white, his eyes narrowed, and the muscles in his neck flexed roughly as he swallowed what I'd said. I ran him over with a cement truck filled with every rock-hard moment of my life when I've felt like I wasn't worth it.

"It hasn't been just a weekend for me, Wilson. I've wanted you for so long. I fought off the thoughts every day, exhausting every option to keep you off my mind; I can't do it anymore. I want you right here." He pressed his fingers to his chest, "All the time."

His energy was genuine and intense. If he was lying, I would have known it.

"This has been the most amazing weekend of my entire life and I am right there with you." I pushed my hand against his heart. "I've been there all along." I kissed him, tasting the sincerity of our words.

Our hands explored each other's bodies. I reached down to unsnap his jeans. I wanted to feel him one last time before he left, but he caught my wrists.

"Wilson, I want to—so bad. But if we don't stop, you'll miss your flight." He pulled my hands up to his chest. Tears welled in my eyes. I wasn't supposed to cry; I thought I was over that. I was wrong. The salt-drenched tears trickled down my cheeks.

"I'm sorry," I told him. His eyes filled with disappointment as our weekend came to an end. His fingers wiped away my tears.

"I'll see you later." He kissed me. I closed my eyes and my lips grew cold.

He was gone.

I was alone in Aspen, standing in a huge walk-in closet. His words flooded my mind. *I need you to keep Cindy busy while I leave.* I hurried to the door and peeked into my room. The door was shut and the window was closed. I went searching for Cindy. It was my job to keep her from seeing Max, and I'll be damned if I was going to fail.

"There you are, Wilson. Are you packed?" Cindy grabbed my arm; I shuffled and tripped as she pulled me back into my room.

"Whoa, I just have a little more to go." I told her. She went to close my door, peering around. Come to think of it, she was acting super weird. "What's up with you?" I didn't complain because at least she was being preoccupied.

"I don't want someone to find me." She stared into my eyes before she turned to the pile of wrinkled clothes on my bed. "He was a lot better looking last night," she whispered under her breath, but loud enough to hear.

"Who is this *someone* and how much did you drink last night?" I followed her.

"The *someone* is Alec, his last name is not important, and to answer your second question, way too much." She grabbed my duffel bag and started stuffing my clothes inside. "Why do I end up with the strays?" She focused on my bag. "It's not like I plan it; most of the time it just happens. We start dancing, I get excited, and boom, I end up sleeping with the guy." She looked at me, I just shrugged my shoulders.

"I need to be more selective like you." She balled up my favorite green shirt and shoved it into my bag. "I bet you can count on one hand how many guys you've been with." She looked up at me, waiting for me to answer.

I've never been one to kiss and tell. The only person who knew anything about my whole world was Joanie. Now, suddenly, Cindy wanted me to talk? The only problem was I couldn't even count on one hand because, technically, I was still a virgin.

"Yeah, one hand." I grabbed a pair of my jeans and rolled them up. Something, anything, to keep my hands busy and my mind clear to handle the next bullet she was going to fire at me.

"So do *I* know him?" She stopped twisting my clothes.

"Who?" I snatched another pair of pants, shaking them up in front of me before rolling them up.

"Wilson, come on. We're bonding here." She tossed my shirt down. "Okay, fine, my first was this guy, Robert. We met at summer camp my ninth-grade year. He was a camp counselor for the younger boy's group. He and I flirted all week, talked about stupid things. The last night, there was a dance. We snuck out to his car. Did you know Mini Coopers had back seats?"

Too much information! I didn't really want to know about Cindy's first time in the back of a Mini. As a matter of fact I wish she would leave so I could pack my on stuff and wallow in the self pity of my major loss. No such luck.

"No, never really paid much attention to whether a Mini had a backseat," I mumbled.

"Well, it wasn't the most comfortable way to—you know. Anyway, after that, I vowed to never date a guy with a Mini *anything* again." She laughed and held up her index finger and thumb apart about two inches. "So how 'bout you?" she pushed.

What was I going to say? I don't have a 'Mini' story or a one night stand I regret. I'm a virgin who's come so close that I feel like I should be an honorary member of the 'de-flowered' club. It wasn't like I didn't want to join. I just didn't have a valid membership for another twenty-eight days. Don't even think about driving until you're sixteen, can't vote until you're eighteen, and no drinking until twenty-one. Oh, and by the way, no sex with Max for another six hundred and seventy two hours. Problem was, other girls around me were joining that club long before I even considered it.

I cleared my throat to come up with some random excuse to change the subject when Nick pounded on my door.

"Wilson, we need to get a move on. It's after nine. Cindy in there with you?" His fingers tapped on the door so fast it was completely frickin' annoying. But I was grateful he distracted us from *that* conversation. Cindy pulled the door open a crack to see him.

"Is he gone?" she asked low.

"Who?" Nick's voice broke with a high pitch.

"He was here last night." She pulled the door open wide. Nick looked back at me. His eyes bounced between Cindy and me. He swallowed hard. His eyebrows curved down, his jaw tightened with worry lines faint on his forehead. I couldn't take the chance he would say the wrong thing.

"Alec. Right?" I said, looking at Cindy and shaking my head yes before I looked back at Nick, hoping he wouldn't say anything about Max being here. "The guy that came home with her last night," I continued to coach him.

"That guy? Yeah he left awhile ago. Where did you find him?" His eyes grew wide and he gave Cindy a cocky smile. He must have been used to her repeating the same pattern in Aspen. "Let me guess, the Polaris? The club where, if you are a *somebody,* you'd be there." He laughed.

"Very funny, Nick; keep laughing—jerk. At least I can bring someone home, unlike you." She wrenched her nose at him. "Wilson, you need to hurry up. We're going to be late. Nick, make yourself useful, grab my bags for me." She pushed past him.

"That's why I can't stand her. She is such a bitch." He sat on my bed next to my duffel bag.

"Well, she's leaving so you'll get a little break from her." I shoved the rest of my clothes into my bag and grabbed the miscellaneous things I had lying around. I really didn't feel like entertaining him while I finished packing. I just wanted to move on.

"I wanted to catch up with you before we get stuck in the car with Cindy for four-plus hours. Even though we just met, I feel a connection with you."

Oh, great, here we go. I like Nick as a friend, that's it. Why now? My whole life—nothing. Now that I really like a guy, suddenly all these others start to come out of nowhere. I have to break this to him easy.

"I feel like I need to look after you. I know, a little strange, but I was thinking this morning I should have found out if you were okay last night. And well, I didn't, so I'm sorry." He looked down at the floor. I was totally confused.

"Why are you sorry? I was fine last night. You're too sweet." I stood in front of him and ruffed up his hair. He caught me around my waist and lifted his body up against mine, his eyes smoldering. He pushed his hands against my face. Tangling his fingers into my hair, his lips pressed unyieldingly against mine. I pushed him away. *Oh God—what just happened? Not a good thing. Wrong message, total miscommunication here, we were on completely different pages. I didn't think of him that way.* I rubbed the back of my hand at my lips.

"I'm sorry, I couldn't help it." Nick took a step toward me. His eyes constricted, his face raced to a light shade of crimson.

"Nick, please don't go there with me," I whispered, stepping back holding my hand out for him to stop.

"I had to see if there was a chance you'd feel the same." He lowered his eyes to the floor before he sized up my body. "Wilson, tell me I don't have a chance, and I will leave you alone." His eyes met mine. It must have taken everything inside of him to do what he did.

"Nick, I really like you, as a friend. But there is no chance for you and me." I made sure to keep space between us. *Damn it, I didn't want this. I wanted to be his friend. Now everything was awkward and I had a four-hour drive with him.*

"So this thing with Calvin's brother is pretty serious?" He shifted his stance and brought his hands to his waist.

"Yeah, it is. But I would appreciate it if you wouldn't say anything to Cindy about it."

"Don't say anything to me about what?" Cindy piped up as she closed the door.

My heart dropped to my feet. Every ounce of blood that flowed through my body drained to my legs. Chills vibrated across my spine and down through my arms. I kept looking at Nick, waiting for him to pounce on the opportunity to expose everything he knew about Max and me to Cindy. Nick took a breath and started telling her what happened.

"I kissed Wilson." He stepped away from her. She turned really fast toward me. "She didn't kiss me back. I guess I'm not the one for her."

"Damn straight you're not. What the hell were you thinking? Stay away from my friends, Nick." Cindy's face burned dark red as she looked into my eyes. "Don't tell me, you're into *him*." She flung her thumb over her shoulder, pointing to Nick.

"No, we're just friends. Nothing happened between us." I felt relief spread throughout my entire body.

"Good. Because if you were, I'd have to really rethink our friendship. There's not one thing you could say that would make *that* okay." Cindy twisted her body to stand between us.

"Oh come on, Cindy, like you're this great catch. Give me a break. You can't even keep anyone long enough to learn their last name," Nick spewed as he headed for the bedroom door.

"Screw you, Nick," Cindy blurted out. Her body heaved and waned with such hatred, it made me glad I was an only child.

"No thanks, I don't screw skanks." He flipped her off and turned to me. "Sorry I can't drive you to Denver." He left.

I had to take a moment. Guilt started swelling from deep down, bulging and overflowing my conscience. This whole argument had started because of me. I've got to fix it. I can't have this on my head.

"Wait, Nick." I ran after him. He was already down the stairs and heading out the front door.

"No, Wilson, I'm not waiting. I'm done with waiting. All my life I've waited; not anymore. Go back to your friend." He turned and walked out the front door.

I stood unmoved and mortified. He'd saved me from the heat by throwing himself in the fire, and now there was nothing I could do to change it. I turned to go back upstairs to finish packing.

Cindy held her hands tight on her waist, "If he thinks he can talk to me that way and get away with it, he is so mistaken."

"I've got to finish packing. Give me a couple minutes." I passed her at the top of the stairs and closed the door to my room.

I just wanted to throw myself down and cry, but I only had a few more minutes before we had to be on the road. I figured I was the next in line to drive. I was already beat from staying up all night with Max, and now I was going to drive for four hours. Not my idea of a good start to the day. Especially when all I wanted to do was sit in the backseat, close my eyes, and relive my weekend with Max.

"Come on, Wilson, we've gotta go," Cindy whined as she banged on my door.

I grabbed my duffel bag—it was packed so crappily I could barely zip it closed.

"Okay, let's go," I told her, struggling and tripping as my duffel bag bounced off my leg. She rolled her suitcase down the stairs. *Bang, bang, bang.* I wished she would have just picked it up. Her demeanor was silent and cold. No doubt it was my punishment for Nick kissing me. She opened the front door and rolled down the stone steps. *Bang, bang, bang.* I wasn't paying attention to what she was doing so when she stopped, I ran into her.

"What is he doing in the car?" She pointed to the Sequoia. Nick was waiting in the driver's seat. "I am NOT getting in the car with *him.* You can drive us, Wilson." She didn't move.

"No, I can't drive. I'm exhausted and I don't know my way around. Come on, Cindy, give him a break." I walked past her and threw my bag in the back. Cindy followed.

"I'm only doing this because you rejected him." She tossed her suitcase into the back and got into the car. I opened my door and slipped in behind Nick. Not one word was muttered between any of us. He put the car in gear, Cindy plugged her ears with American Idol music from her iPhone, and I pulled the hood up on Max's sweatshirt. Wrapping my arms around myself, I closed my eyes. Four hours of silence. Wouldn't that be nice?

CHAPTER TWENTY-FIVE:

The sway of the car put me to sleep. The smell of Max on his sweatshirt as I held the sleeves to my nose took over my mind. I saw his eyes, filled with lust. We were at school in his class. Nobody was in the classroom with us; just him and me. He had on tight black jeans with a black T-shirt that showed every muscle. He was wearing the sweatshirt I had on and the hood was over his head. He was standing at the board, wiping them clean.

"Hey, that's my job," I told him, grabbing for the eraser. He held it in the air, too high for me to reach.

"Not anymore," he whispered into my ear and wrapped his hand around my waist.

"Hey, you're going to get us in trouble. Remember, no touching." I pushed him away just enough to tease him. I had on a very short, pleated black skirt with red stiletto heels and a real low cut, white V-neck top.

"No, I won't. Not anymore. I took care of it. Now we don't have to hide, ever again." He pulled me close and I breathed him in.

His lips found my exposed skin right above my heart. His hand slid softly up the back of my thigh under my skirt. It was such a turn-on to make out with him in his classroom. He pushed me against his desk. I pulled my hands from his hair and yanked at his jeans; he didn't stop me this time. He pulled my legs apart and lifted me onto his desk. My hands lost his buttons for a moment until he pushed his body between my knees. His lips pressed, kissing gently, against mine. I pushed at his jeans, sliding my left hand down in between his skin and boxers; it caught on the waist band. Pressure cut across one of my fingers. The more I tried to push my hand down into his pants the more my finger hurt. I pulled my hand from the back of his jeans. It was a huge diamond ring set in a white gold band half as thick as the space between my knuckles. My mouth dried, my heart galloped, and my eyes flooded.

"What's wrong, Mrs. Wilson Goldstein?" He smiled with his smoldering eyes, proud to be calling me the name I'd practiced for months.

My breath caught hard as I swallowed the images of what I hoped for someday. My eyes sprang open and I was in the backseat of the Sequoia. It took me a moment to realize Cindy was asleep with her ears plugged next to me and Nick was swerving, taking us off the road to a gas station.

My heart pumped blood so fast through my body, I swear I had none in my head when the car rolled to a stop. Light-headed, what had I just seen? I thrust my hands in front of my eyes and focused: nothing, no ring. A wave of fatigue flooded my body.

"I have to stop," Nick was short. I kept squeezing my eyes shut and reopening them. "Are you okay?" He stood between his door and the front seat, looking back at me. The freezing air replaced the warm as it swirled around us.

"Yeah, I guess. I think I should get something to drink." I still was in the dazed fog of a dream I wanted to remember.

"What do you want? I'll get it. I'd rather do it so we can get on the road faster," he came off bothered.

"A Coke. Thank you." He slammed the door, not asking Cindy if she wanted anything.

"Where are we? Why are we stopped?" Cindy woke up. She pulled her earphones from her head.

"I don't know. Nick needed to stop and get something to drink," I told her.

"What time is it?" She checked her iPphone. "Eleven fifty-five. I've been asleep over two hours?" She stretched her arms above her head.

Great, she is awake now and we still have another two plus hours to get to Denver. Find the happy place Max took you to and live there now, Wilson.

"Is Nick all wigged out? He can be such an ass." Cindy wrapped her earphones around the back of her neck.

"I don't know. I was asleep too." I pushed the sleeves of Max's sweatshirt up my forearms. I didn't want to be put between Cindy and Nick's dysfunctional relationship. My door swung open; startled, I just about jumped out of my skin.

"Here Wilson." He pushed a Coke at me. I thanked him and he slammed the door. He shuffled to the front driver's door slid in and didn't say another word.

I looked over at Cindy and mouthed. "I think he's still pissed."

"Whatever!" she said out loud.

I looked up into the rearview mirror to see his reaction. He glanced at me, leaned forward and turned the Green Day song up on the radio.

"*Do you know your enemy, your enemy*", repeated over and over. He definitely made sure Cindy heard the chorus of the song.

In minutes we were back on the road. I wish I had my iPod to help me escape the one-sided conversation Cindy insisted on having.

"Wilson, where did you get *that* sweatshirt? I've never seen you wear it before." She stared at me, almost like she waited for a lame excuse to cross my lips. "Don't tell me it's Nick's. I know for sure you didn't have it before you came to Aspen." She pushed her earphones into her ears, not waiting for my answer.

I didn't even bother speaking. I turned and looked out my window. The white frosted-whipped mountains speckled with sharp evergreen pines and earth brown jagged boulders made me think of my grandparents; I missed them. I rolled towards the door, wrapped my arm under my head and closed my eyes. I wanted to think about Max, instead I fell asleep.

"Wilson. Hey, wake up, we're here." I felt something tap my leg. I felt the muscles in my back pull up through my shoulders blades as I stretched.

Cindy grabbed her bag from the floor. I wanted to be motivated to get to my flight, but something inside me clicked into slow motion. I guess the fact that as soon as I left Colorado, the faster my weekend faded into a memory that I tucked into a corner of my mind. The flutter of the first butterflies Max freed in my body will become dull reminisces of empty cocoons and I wasn't really ready for that.

My phone vibrated with a message. My heart leapt into my throat. It had to be from *him*. It was about time! I pulled it from my pocket, my hands shook. Cindy had already closed the door and was pulling her suitcase from the back of the Sequoia. I unlocked the keys and waited to see what he texted me. A flood of disappointment reigned heavy across my body. It wasn't from Max, it was from Joanie.

WHEN R U BAK? CAN'T W8 2 HEAR ABOUT UR WKND W/MG! MISSED U.

Don't get me wrong, I was glad she was thinking of me and I was happy she texted me, but it wasn't Max.

MISSED U 2 @ AIRPRT NOW- FLT LEVS @ 3:15. C U ASAP. LOTS 2 TELL. I sent back. I went to the rear of the car where Cindy was still standing and grabbed my duffel bag. My phone chimed again.

I WANT JOO-C D-TALS-CANT LEV ANY OUT! K. Another message from Joanie.

K. GOTTA GO. LUV YA. W. I texted back.

"Who's that?" Cindy leaned over to read what I was texting. I pulled my phone against my chest. Cindy gave me the *after all that I've done for you* look. She was a master at the guilt trip.

"It's Joanie. Asking how our weekend was." I tried to fix the huff I created when I pulled the phone away from her sight. Cindy was manipulative to the core.

"Make sure you tell her I miss her and *next* time she should come with us," Cindy bubbled, snapping the handle up on her suitcase.

She was such a piece of work. First off, she never invited Joanie and besides, she would never let someone come that would take the attention away from her. Joanie and I are BFF's so our connection would just kill her. It's hard enough being her roommate. I faked a text back to Joanie.

"Okay, told her next time she's gotta come with us and we miss her." I shoved the phone in my pocket and anchored the duffel bag across my chest and up over my shoulder.

"You know where you're checking in, right? I've gotta go," Nick asked me, ignoring Cindy.

"Nick, don't do this to your sister, not before she leaves. Make up with her. Be the bigger person, for me?" I told him. He reached up and grabbed the back hatch, the muscles in his neck tightened.

"Sorry to let you down. But I'm done being the bigger person. I've done it my entire life and look where it's gotten me. I'm a chauffeur for my bitch half-sister and sadly enough, I didn't end up with the girl." He pulled the hatch closed and passed around me to the driver's side of the Sequoia. He might as well have punched me in the stomach. The blood pulsing through my body pooled low in my gut as I tried to catch my breath.

"Nick, I don't want to leave knowing you're upset. Couldn't we meet half way? Find someplace where we both feel comfortable with something more than strangers? Maybe even friends?" I pushed my hand out to him. I figured at least I could get a handshake from him. He looked over at Cindy who was already talking with the skycap about her ticket.

"Friends." He grabbed my hand and pulled me close, bent towards me and kissed my cheek. "I guess I have to be satisfied with what you're willing to give me. See you, friend."

"Thanks. See you." He hopped into the car and with that, I watched him drive away.

"Alright ladies, your flight will board from Concourse C, gate C41. It's the last terminal past the metal detectors. Gate C41 will be on the right side, closest to the middle of the airport. Thank you for choosing Southwest Airlines for your traveling needs." The Skycap smiled and handed back Cindy's ticket. He loaded her suitcase on the carpeted rollie cart.

"Thanks," I responded for the both of us.

Cindy stuffed her ticket into her backpack and entered the airport without acknowledging him. She only stopped her brisk walk to answer her phone.

"Hello? Hi dad, where are you?" She pushed her finger into her ear to hear him. She wrinkled her nose and scowled bending forward. I could tell it was going to be bad, another blow off situation. "That's fine. I understand. No our flight leaves after 3," she paused to listen. "Okay, well if you're stuck in Albuquerque, I understand. See you another time. Bye." She slipped her phone into her backpack.

"Your dad stuck in New Mexico?" I prepared myself for the blow up.

"Yeah. What's new? Bummer," she played it cool as we waited in line at the security gate.

"Sorry Cindy. I know how much you were looking forward to seeing him," I mumbled.

"You know what Wilson? I'm pretty used to being screwed by my family. So when you apologize, it's mainly to make *you* feel better. Words people use to fill an awkward moment, that's what an apology is." She pulled off her shoes and waited to be cleared as a threat to our country's air space. *What was I going to say to her response? She was kind of right. In that instance, I was a guest in her awkward situation.*

We made it unscathed through security and shuffled our way down to the very end of the airport to Concourse C. Winded, we found a couple of seats and waited to pre-board the plane with an hour to spare.

"You know, Nick can be such an ass. He really needs to grow up. What if my plane went down and I died?" She rummaged through her backpack.

"Cindy, can you not talk about planes going down, especially when I'm going to be on it." My heart pounded hard. She pulled out Chapstick and rubbed it across her lips.

"Oh come on Wilson, like *that's* going to happen." She tossed her lip balm into her backpack.

I was already a pretty inexperienced traveler, so my nerves were dragging about the whole process. A voice came across the speakers asking anyone who needed extra assistance to board first. Of course, Cindy tried to say she needed extra time. It didn't fly.

Eventually our numbers were called and we got on the plane. After adjusting our bags and spots, Cindy ended up on the aisle seat and I chose the window seat, which left an open one in the middle. I just hoped the flight wasn't sold out. We sat waiting for the plane to finish filling up. I watched as people of all kinds scurried down the aisle, looking around to find the open seats left. Lucky enough, no one was looking at the seat between us. Just as the trickle of people slowed I figured we were safe. The flight attendants were taking their places to tell us what to do if the plane went down, when one came and bent down to Cindy.

"We have one passenger that was bumped from an earlier flight and will need this seat. Sorry, ladies." She stood up and walked to the front of the plane and greeted him.

He was out of breath from running and unbelievably gorgeous. Butterflies woke and twisted in my stomach. He smiled at the attendant and ran his hand through his hair pushing it back out of his eyes as he sauntered down the aisle toward us. My heart stopped. How lucky was I? If I'd played the lottery, I would have won.

"Oh my God. Mr. Goldstein! First my house, then skiing, and now the flight home. Are you stalking us?" Cindy stood up and let him in.

"Hi Cindy; Wilson. Wow, what are the odds of sitting with you ladies?" He turned to each of us as he fastened his seatbelt.

He smelled really good as I tried to swallow. My heart had risen into my throat. I was so close to him, his elbow pressed lightly into the bend of my arm.

"So how was your weekend, Mr. Goldstein?" Cindy pressed his knee. My eyes burned holes into the back of her hand.

"Great. Yours?" He looked at Cindy almost totally ignoring me.

"Good. Other than Wilson wrecking her first time skiing." She leaned forward and looked at me.

"That's right, I was there. You okay?" Max turned to me. He gave me a slight grin, and narrowed his eyes pitching one of his brows.

"Yeah." I bit my lip to stop from smiling.

"Oh come on, you had a huge gash in your head, Wilson." Cindy interrupted.

"Really? Where?" He looked. I pointed to the side of my head as he tangled his fingers in my hair above my forehead. He was touching me. He let out a masculine sigh. My butterflies went spastic and crazy throughout my body. I wanted to kiss him.

"It wasn't that bad. I'm okay," I whispered as his fingers left my skin. The hair at the nape of my neck stood on end and goose bumps rose on my arms.

"You stayed home with a headache. I would say it was bad enough to flake on me." Cindy was still annoyed about that.

"Hopefully you weren't too bored staying back," he winked at me. My butterflies leapt high in my chest, climbing into my throat.

"What did she flake on? If you don't mind me asking." He looked at Cindy.

The plane started to move and the flight attendants started their spiel about how, if the plane goes down, we can use our seat cushions as floatation devices. The oxygen will fall from the ceiling, put yours on first then help the person next to you. Exits are on either side of the plane. We were exactly in between the front door and the back exit, down by the wing. Great, which exit's closer? I guess we'll go to the shorter line of people trying to escape.

"I went out to Polaris last night. I felt kinda bad she was all alone at the cabin, but it was my vacation too and I wanted to go out. Besides she told me to." She looked away from Max across the aisle at a little girl clutching to the arm rests. The plane stopped.

"Well it looks like you survived staying home from Polaris last night." He looked at me and squeezed at my knee. I felt the plane take off and my butterflies flew south.

CHAPTER TWENTY-SIX:

He had to know that when he touched me it caused a chemical reaction in my body and I couldn't stop myself from shivering, deep in my core. My butterflies were so controlled by him. If he asked them to fly into the flame of a candle, they would do it without hesitating.

"So what did you do last night, Mr. Goldstein?" Cindy grabbed her bag and started digging around, peeking up at him when she thought of it. I whipped my head toward him. My skin went cold and I felt a surge of adrenaline rush throughout my body.

"Well, um. My *girlfriend* and I hung out." He looked at me when he said the word that sent my head spinning.

Cindy stopped digging. "I didn't know you had a girlfriend. Does she live in Colorado?"

"No, she doesn't." He didn't offer any more explanation.

"Well, where does she live? How long have you been going out?" Cindy prodded at him as she pulled out her iPhone.

"Cindy! You can't ask him questions like that," I interrupted her as she stared at him.

"Why not? We aren't at school. He has partied with us, at least he can tell me about his girlfriend." She stared back over at him, waiting for him to answer. "Why didn't you bring her to my party?"

I watched Max shift his body to face her. He was actually going to engage with her about this. I hope he's ready to protect our secret. She was so manipulative she could get a Tibetan monk to talk.

"Max—Mr. Goldstein, you don't have to answer." I swallowed hard. I prayed she didn't catch that I slipped.

"Max? You called him Max. On a first name basis are we?" She glared at us.

"I told her to call me by my first name. It seemed crazy to have her call me Mr. Goldstein at your party that night." He looked at me then back over at Cindy. "She lives in California and I didn't bring her to your house because she was with a group of friends that night. And about that night, I wasn't there. Right?" He peered into Cindy's eyes, convincing her to believe his simple lie.

"Alright, if that's the case, do I get to call you Max, too?" She batted her eyelashes at him and wrapped her arm through his, resting her head on his shoulder.

What the hell was she doing? Touching him, flirting with him…he wasn't her type at all. He tells her about his girlfriend and she comes onto him? I cleared my throat, I was ready to pounce.

The seatbelt light chimed off and the captain came over the loud speaker, inaudibly, telling us all about our flight.

"Oh good, I'll be right back." Cindy stood up and left toward the back of the plane. The moment she was out of sight, Max pushed his face into my hair and inhaled. His hand slid up the other side of my face.

"I missed you. You smell so good," he whispered. I turned and he pressed his lips hard against mine. Our mouths opened and for a moment of time, he and I were the only ones that existed. He tasted extra sweet and more forbidden today. Our kiss was filled with sparks and explosions that still mapped through my body when he stopped and pulled back from me.

"You taste so good. I wasn't done," I told him against his moist lips. He gave me one last kiss. My cheek, fiery hot, was doused with an ice cold chill as he slipped his hand from my face.

"No, we aren't done. It's driving me wild to sit next to you. Not being able to touch you is torture." He leaned back in his chair. "I want to see you tonight, when we get back. Will you meet me?" His eyes blazed a sensuality that pulled my butterflies toward him. I looked back at the restrooms, Cindy wasn't out yet.

"Okay." I didn't mention to him I had a Romeo and Juliet essay due tomorrow for Mrs. Clouser's class. I'll just do what I can before we meet, then get up early to finish it. He probably would not have asked knowing I had weekend homework. "I'll text you when I'm settled." I added.

"You're so beautiful, Wilson. How did I get so lucky?" He ran his hand down my wrist, folded his fingers in between mine, and pulled my hand to his lips.

Out of the corner of my eye I saw the Pepto-Bismol pink shirt Cindy had on heading toward us. My heart thrust anxiety through my veins as I pulled my hand down from his. My body stiffened and I turned to look out the window. *Come on, Wilson, don't make it too obvious.*

"Okay I'm back. What'd you two talk about? Hey, Max, you never told us your girlfriend's name." She lowered herself into the seat and looked over at Max.

"We just talked about the huge government test he's giving tomorrow in class." I smiled; she laughed tightly.

"Wilson's kidding. No test tomorrow," he told her. "Cindy, please excuse me, I need to get out." She pushed herself out into the aisle. He stood up, leaning, and worked his way out. I took advantage and got up also. If nothing more than to stretch my legs; I walked down toward the restrooms, following Max.

"I had a great time this weekend," I told him as he stopped to wait for an open lavatory. He turned to face me, glancing back at Cindy he smiled and answered me.

"Me, too."

"I am really glad you took me to meet your family. I really liked them," I choked up slightly.

"They really liked you too. Which reminds me, my mom invited you to come out over winter break." He leaned back and forth as he shoved his hands down in his pockets.

"Do you want me to come, too?" I looked at the brown and blue diamond-patterned carpet.

"No, actually I don't. I said that to torture you, Wilson. Of course I do. But I have to tell you, my family doesn't celebrate Christmas, hence my last name." His eyes met mine before he dropped his glance. His hair shifted forward.

"Well that's great news for me, because then I won't have to compete to celebrate my birthday with Jesus. It will be a first!" I smiled at him. He looked up through his jet black hair. His eyes glowed with acceptance and his lips formed a slight smirk, sparking my sexual desire. *He can't do that when Cindy is so close. It would only lead to bad deeds.*

"So we can celebrate you and only you on December twenty-fifth." He grabbed my hand and pulled me a little closer. Good thing there was a partition wall between us and

Cindy. His eyes were fused to mine. He took a deep breath, his exhale constricted.

"We can celebrate the new freedom eighteen gives us." I glanced toward Cindy and didn't see her looking back. I leaned against him, sneaking a kiss before the lavatory door opened. He pulled away, captivated, before he went into the small room. I stood there, alone, waiting for the next one. I leaned against the wall, thinking about my eighteenth birthday in less than twenty-eight days. A door swung open, I grabbed it and went in.

What the hell was this? Okay so I've never used an airplane bathroom before; however, this was horrifying. Smaller than a closet. I was expected to sit on a blue water, camper-type toilet. No seat covers, no paper towels to dry my hands. I was surprised there was toilet paper provided. The instructions explained in English and showed pictures of how to use it. No thanks, I'll wait. I washed my hands, ran them dry on my pants, and unhappily slid the door handle open. I skulked back to my seat. I didn't have to go to the bathroom anyway.

"Cindy, can I get in?" I tapped her on the shoulder. She had her earphones plugging up her head. She stood up and let Max out to let me in. He stood right next to her seat, intentionally leaving barely enough room so I had to push against him to pass by. I have to say, great way to sneak some touching time. I heard him inhale me and felt his face close to my hair. His hands wrapped around my waist just enough to look like he was helping me, his arm brushed me, and his hand rested over mine as he sat down. Cindy plopped back down and closed her eyes to listen to her music. I leaned forward and spoke Cindy's name. She didn't flinch.

"Ladies and gentleman we are starting our descent into Oakland, California. It is a mild sixty-five degrees...." The captain's voice disappeared as I looked into Max's eyes.

This was it. True to the end, our Aspen weekend officially became a memory that we would try and recall when we'd talk about how we started dating. My heart pounded quickly in my chest. He grabbed my hand and whispered in my ear.

"Wilson, think of this as the beginning. Not the end." He pressed his lips to the side of my head. I felt his comforting breath bend and sway across my hair. Risky, what he was doing, but I needed it. He leaned back and the warmth of his essence across my hair was replaced by the chill of our reality. He tapped Cindy on the shoulder.

"Cindy. We are landing. We're in Oakland." Max turned back to me then to her again. Her eyes gradually opened. She looked around and noticed everyone had their chairs up and seatbelts fastened.

"Are we landing already?" She was unaware of how loud she spoke. Max indicated to her to pull the plugs out of her ears. She did.

"Yeah, we are," he whispered making a point to talk low.

"Sorry, didn't realize I was talking so loud." She did her ritual clean up of her iPhone and pushed her bag back under the seat in front of her. "I am *so* glad to be home. It's been a *long* weekend," she whined.

I couldn't believe what came out of her mouth, a long weekend? She partied, raged at dance clubs, had one night stands, fought with her brother and dad and totally ignored me most of the weekend. She could call it a fun weekend or a crazy weekend, even call it a trying weekend; but to have her call it a *long* weekend—well, that just wasn't acceptable. It wasn't long enough for me.

One more day would have been perfect. I would have liked to have gone to brunch with his family today, spent some more time in their company—especially his mother's. There was something magical about her. I didn't feel so broken around her. She made me feel accepted and important, even a bit normal.

The plane landed with a couple of rough bounces and it became really loud as it slowed toward the end of the runway. But, all in all, we landed safely and securely in Oakland. I looked out the window and caught Max's reflection watching me. He smiled, watching my expression. As our bodies got pulled to the seats in front of us, he pushed his hand against my shoulder stopping me. He leaned into me.

"I miss you already," he whispered.

Cindy was already taking off her seatbelt and getting her backpack ready to go.

"I've got to go to the restroom. So if we get separated, meet me at baggage claim okay? Max, Mr. Goldstein, see you tomorrow at school." She stood up pushing her way forward. In minutes she was able to work her way out of the plane. Not without pissing a lot of people off. But that was Cindy, her way or no way.

I couldn't believe how lucky we were. Here I was worried about finding a place to say goodbye to him and Cindy gave us the perfect spot, right where we were. Max pushed his lips to my skin. I forced my hands up into his hair. It felt like a lifetime since I'd touched him. His hands slid up around my neck and under my ears. His fingers tangled in my hair. He pulled his lips away smiling, teasing me to push to him, my mouth open, his breath filled me. We inhaled every moment with each other. Our kiss danced and tied every memory of our weekend together. Visions of him flashed vivid across my closed eyes.

His taste of the sweetest milk chocolate, his resonance of untamed desires, and his scent lured me to visions of a breezy crisp snowy white day.

He drew his mouth off mine and stopped kissing me. His sultry green eyes journeyed up and down my face as he pulled away. He told my butterflies to stay active and keep fighting for him. I pressed my body hard against his. My shoulders rose as I knotted my hands back in his hair. His hands clutched my arms and pushed me away. His head dropped to see the last people were leaving the plane.

"We'd better go before Cindy comes looking for us." His hands still held the space between us.

He stood up and slid to the aisle. He reached up to the storage above my head. He looked so good. His dark T-shirt rose to expose his navel, his Calvin's band showed just enough to make me want more. The button on his jeans was unsnapped, making them just loose enough to fit my hand. It took everything in my power not to wrap my arms around him and pull his shirt from his body.

"I need to take a mental picture of what I see. Mmm." I pushed my hands to my face and clicked my imaginary camera. He dropped his chin to look at me. His eyes constricted making his brow furrow. God was generous when he made Max. He was perfect. My butterflies leaned heavy trying to tilt me to him.

"Watch yourself." His jaw clinched, his muscles strained as he plopped my bag down into the seat between us. He pulled his small backpack from above and swung it over his shoulder.

"Here, let me carry your bag for you." He pulled it out of the chair allowing me to slip in front of him in the aisle. Behind him the attendant waited to make sure we left the plane.

"Thank you Max." My hand bounced on the top of each seat as I moseyed down the aisle and out of the plane.

Cindy met us half way down the walkway.

"What took you so long?" She flipped her hair back from across her shoulders. "Oh, Mr. Goldstein." She looked at my duffel bag he was carrying.

"Wilson's bag was stuck in the storage compartment. She couldn't get it out." He turned to me. "Here you go." He handed me my bag. I took it and wedged it across my shoulder against my neck.

"Thanks," I mumbled.

"Are you guys the last ones off the plane?" She looked around noticing there was nobody walking behind us.

"Yeah, none of the attendants would help me. Thanks again Mr. Goldstein." I glanced at him before I looked at Cindy. "Did you get your suitcase?"

"No, I went to the bathroom then waited for you to come off the plane." She studied my expression then Max's. I could see the wheels turning in her head.

"Let's go then, before someone walks off with your suitcase." I paced ahead of them.

"Well Mr. Max Goldstein, it looks like you are Wilson's knight in shining armor." She elbowed him as she walked next to him. A smirk grew across her face.

"No, just her government teacher that was able to help when she asked." He looked down at the ground then back up to her. I slowed my stride and strained to hear what she was saying.

"I saw the way she looked at you. She has *it* for you." Cindy looked like she just discovered gold.

"No, I don't think so." He swallowed hard.

266

"Whatever! She likes you. Her heart must be totally broken knowing you have a girlfriend. Trust me Max, she's into you." She smiled, smug and content. He smiled back and didn't say another word.

My heart crashed against my ribcage so hard, I swear I could see it pounding. She knows. Cindy has figured it out. It was written all over my face, how could she not see it? My knees went weak and my hands numb. This meant trouble. She was like the Santa Ana winds, if even a spark existed, huge wildfires would ensue, devastating anything in its way, including Max.

"I'll meet you at the baggage claim," I told them as I slipped into the restroom. I grabbed my phone out of my pocket and called Max. He answered it on the second ring.

"Hello?"

"Max, you can't let her know about us," I whispered. I heard him put his hand over the phone and tell her he had to take the call. He would see her at the baggage claim.

"I know. Don't worry. I'll make sure she keeps thinking I have a girlfriend," his voice was really low.

"I don't think I'll be able to meet you tonight. She'll know something's up with us if I leave tonight," I rambled into the phone. I didn't know what to think. I was totally caught off guard with her comments.

"Hey, don't say that. I don't want to let her win with us. I'll chalk it up to a student crush you have on your teacher. Let's just wait and see," he struggled with what he meant to say.

"You have to leave before I meet Cindy at the baggage claim. Call me when you're gone." I held the phone tight to my ear. I didn't want to miss any words he said to me.

"I still want to see you tonight. Don't let her scare you off. Not now Wilson. We'll figure it out. Text me when you get back to the dorms," his voice became low and vulnerable, taunting me with my need to see him before he left the airport.

"Max, she will ruin everything. Is that a chance you want to take?" *It killed me to tell him I couldn't see him tonight.*

"Yes it's a chance I want to take. Hey, I understand your hesitation. So I'll tell you what—I will wait for you," he growled slowly as his breath pulled me in. "If you text me I will come get you and if you don't, I will see you Monday fourth period. Fair enough?" he waited for me to answer. It took a moment.

"Fair enough. Max?" I heard him release his breath into the phone.

"Yeah," his voice bounced light with hope.

"Don't forget to text me when you leave. Okay?" I whispered.

"I won't. Bye Wilson," he answered taking a deep, heart wrenching breath.

"Bye Max." I pulled the phone from my ear. This bathroom was much nicer than the airplane's. I used it, washed my hands and pulled the door open. Maybe there was a way to sneak a peek of Max before he left. I just had to make sure I wouldn't get caught.

CHAPTER TWENTY-SEVEN:

I got to see Max grab his duffel bag from the baggage claim. He tossed a wave to Cindy and I watched him pull his phone out of his pocket as he left out the sliding doors. Just outside he stopped. His head hung down, focused on his phone and I watched him text me. My phone chimed with a message as he turned and disappeared.

I'M GONE. PLSE THINK ABOUT 2-NITE. I WANT 2 C U. W8 2 HEAR FROM U. THNKN ABOUT U. I read it twice. He's thinking about me.

THANX. IM THNKN ABOUT U2! WANT 2 C U2. WE'LL C ABOUT 2NITE. MISS U ALREDY.

I walked up on Cindy getting her bag from the luggage corral, she was cursing under her breath.

"There you are. You totally missed Max. He left in a hurry. So sad for you." Her body jerked forward as her suitcase fell to the floor. A twinge of regret fluttered through my chest. Maybe I shouldn't have over reacted about Cindy.

"You're so ice cold about Mr. Goldstein. I don't have *it* bad for him." I started for the sliding doors. The same ones Max left out of ten minutes earlier.

"You heard me telling him? Well you can thank me later. I totally planted the seed for you." She wheeled her suitcase behind her as she caught up to me. My blood began to boil. I didn't want her to even consider Max and me an option. I needed to get her off the idea that she was going to set us up. Besides, with her vindictive personality, she would do it, then turn around and destroy us.

"Cindy there is nothing to thank you for and I can plant my own seeds. I really don't need your help." I stopped and waited to cross the road.

"So you admit that if you had seeds, you would plant them in his garden?" She nudged me with her elbow.

"No, I don't need to plant any seeds in any garden. Mr. Goldstein has a gardener. Didn't you hear him? He has a *girlfriend*." I crossed as the man in a uniform covered with an orange mesh vest blew his whistle and motioned for us to cross.

"Leave it to me, I know how to turn the dirt and pull the weeds. He's gonna be rototilled and ready when I'm done working my magic." She snapped a Z pattern out in front of her. I actually felt throw-up burn the back of my throat. Now I understood what that saying, 'She leaves a bad taste in my mouth,' really meant.

"Okay, *David Blaine*. We've gotta get going. Remember the summary that's due on the first half of Romeo and Juliet? I was so busy checking out the guy's tights, I didn't really follow the story much. It could be the fact that it was older than dirt. I think it was filmed in the sixties." I stopped and looked for her car.

"I know, totally ancient," Cindy answered as she dug out her keys and pressed the locator button. Her car horn beeped and its lights flashed. We were actually not too far off. "I couldn't even hang with the special effects. I thought I was going to throw up when they started dancing. She should have rented the one with Leonardo DiCaprio. Now I would love to cultivate *his* garden." She continued as she pushed another button on her car and the trunk popped open.

I wish she would stop about the freaking gardens. It's played out. She struggled with her suitcase, loading it into the back. No room left for my duffel bag, so I put it down by my feet and let it lean heavy against my shins.

The drive back to Wesley was uneventful. We made small talk about homework. Most teachers didn't assign any over the weekend. But the ones that did—really stuck it to us. Mrs. Clouser, gave us the summary of the crappy sixties movie, Romeo and Juliet. But we only have to summarize half of the movie, because that was all we saw. Mr. Swanks, our trigonometry teacher, assigned all the odd problems from three pages in our math book. And Mr. Kemp, well he didn't really assign homework, just an extra credit lab if we needed it. Of course, I could've used the extra points.

I couldn't stop thinking about sneaking away to see Max. I had no idea where we would go, but just the fact that I could see him tonight started to win the argument in my head. Cindy has no idea Max and I are involved with each other. If she did, she would be all over it. Maybe I could get Joanie to take me to meet him. Or, I could catch the bus and ride it out a couple of stops until I got far enough away to call him.

I could do my summary when I got back to the dorms today and since trigonometry was fifth period I could spend my lunch in the library tomorrow. Totally forget the lab for chemistry. I'll have to ace the next couple of tests to keep my B+.

Chemistry—now that was something I could relate to and I'm not talking about my class. Max and I had it. I could feel it.

He made things mix and bubble in my body, even explode. Not to mention the butterflies he trained to send me reeling when I was around him.

That was it, I was going to see him tonight, but only if I got most of my summary done. There, that was my compromise. Not bad, I could do it. I felt better now that I made up my mind and just in time. Cindy pulled into the driveway of our dorms. The swirling knots that overtook my stomach and started surging up my throat were unexpected. My hands tingled and became damp. The muscles in my back tightened, rippling up through my shoulders and across my neck. Wait a minute, I made up my mind. There was no reason to start freaking out. It was the same old place where I've spent three years of my life. It was where I got my first B in science, where I found out Jasmine Cushing liked the same boy as me. She ended up dating him and telling me later that he was a jerk. It's where I met Max and fell in love with him.

Yeah, I said it, the 'L' word. Does it feel a little too soon? Sure, but I have a real connection with him. He could finish my sentences or jump in front of me if a tiger escaped in the zoo. He had this way about him that reassured me of his desires for me. Just me, the way I was, tattered, bruised, and alone, he saw past all the bullshit.

I loved that. I wasn't going to lie.

"Wilson, come on. Don't want to hang in the parking lot," Cindy yelled from the back of the car as she slammed the trunk. I caught my breath as it jarred me from a suspended state of Max On My Mind. I pushed my bag out from by my feet and climbed out of her car.

That is when I realized I forgot to text Joanie and tell her I was on my way home. She was going to be mad, hurt, and disappointed in me. I think that was what would stress Joanie and my relationship the most. It wasn't guys or other friends. It was the fact that I would forget to do things normal family members did.

I wish my excuses were sufficient, but they never were. The fact that I was never taught or I wasn't *wired* to be that way wouldn't fly with her. She has been my best friend for nine years. And for those nine years she has tried to get me to be more responsive to the common courtesy of a phone call or note. Neither of which I've been able to master.

But on the other hand, maybe that was what balanced us so much. She did enough for both of us. She was rock solid, a predictable constant, and the refuge I could seek anytime I needed it. She knew what it took to keep me grounded. I gave her the excuse to cut loose and show the side of her only a few people really knew. I also gave her the perfect friendship of forgetfulness. Events never really stuck with me. I've always been that way. It was easier to let it go than to catalogue everything that happened in my life. If something pissed me off, I dealt with it and let it go. I didn't harbor anger or let resentment fester into a gnarly mass of hate. I will say, Cindy has pushed me further than most.

I pulled out my cell phone and called Joanie. It only rang once.

"Hey J,"I said fast.

"Hi Wilson. Where are you?" she sounded excited.

"Here in the parking lot. I forgot to call you from Denver. Sorry," I apologized.

"Why are you sorry? I'll be right there." The phone went silent.

"J? Joanie?" She hung up.

I kept walking behind Cindy. I figured at some point she was going to need my help picking up her brick filled suitcase.

Joanie met us on the path. She was smiling so wide it caused her eyes to squint.

"Hi Cindy." Joanie gave her a hug and Cindy answered back with a slight one arm hug and a pat on the back.

"Hi Joanie. I am so exhausted. Glad to be back." She let go and started rolling past her.

I stood there. We both flung our arms around each other. She was taller than me so her arms wrapped around my neck. I squeezed her around her ribcage. I knew I missed her, but didn't realize just how much until now.

"Wilson, I missed you," Joanie whined.

"I missed you too. There's so much to tell you," I said low enough so Cindy wouldn't hear.

She tightened her arms around my neck and squealed before she let go and pulled me along.

Cindy was already in our room and putting her clothes away when J and I came in. Our dorm building was two levels. Lucky for us our room was on the first floor. I have to say there was something comforting about being back. Three years at this place, it starts to grow on you—it's home. Joanie plopped on my bed, wedging her hand against her ear waiting to hear what happened.

"So, how was the weekend?" she asked both of us. I looked at Cindy and she looked at Joanie.

"Well, it was really awesome. Right when we got there I called all my besties and told them that I was there, they all came over that night for a ragin' party." She smiled at me as she winked and tossed her hair back from her face. I looked at Joanie, then back at Cindy.

"I thought they were called your seasonals?" I snapped.

"*Seasonals*?" Joanie looked at me and Cindy.

"Well, yeah they are known in Aspen as seasonals, because they are only there during ski season. Anyway, you'll never guess who showed up to *my* party." She pressed her hands to her chest as she twisted into an excited dance.

"Do you need to go the bathroom?" Joanie asked as she looked at Cindy then me, and back to Cindy.

"No Joan-ee. Mr. Goldstein came to my house and partied with us," she spat. "But you can't tell anyone. Wilson's all paranoid that he'll lose his job or something. Whatever!" She kept putting away her clothes.

"Well, Cindy, that's because it's true. It would be on your shoulders if he lost his job because you told the wrong person about him *unintentionally* coming to *your* cabin in Aspen and drinking with underage students." My breath shortened and the muscles in my back tightened, rippling up through my neck and down my arms.

"See, I knew you had the *hots* for him. You've never given a rat's ass about any of our teachers before. Why him? Why now?" she taunted me as she snapped a red and white striped shirt in front of me to fold it.

She's baiting me to talk. Don't listen. Just stay calm and tell her what any other person would say. Hold it together, Wilson, come on. I had to talk myself down from the frenzy swirling in my body. My butterflies, protective and strong, swarmed heavily around my body, working to find a way to bring Cindy down.

"I don't like him *that* way. Why are you doing this? He's a good teacher, that's all!" We were standing toe-to-toe with each other. My eyes narrowed and my face was stoic. Her smug smile and arrogant stance as she shifted her body was proof enough that she believed she was right.

"Oh, come on you guys. Whatever!" Joanie tried to change the dynamics of our argument.

"I just want Wilson to admit she has the hots for Mr. Goldstein and I'll leave it alone." She flipped her hair back and bounced her hand toward me.

Lava of hate bubbled in my stomach. It was beyond the abilities of my butterflies.

"Fuck you, Cindy. It isn't always about *you* and what *you* can figure out. Not everything has to do with sex. Oh wait, I forgot it's you I'm talking to. Why don't we tell Joanie about the guy you slept with last night? What was his last name Cindy, huh? Oh, you don't remember? Or maybe it was that you never knew! So don't stand there and tell me to admit to something you have no clue about. You are so tainted. Poison, that's what you are, poison." I looked at Joanie and left. Now it was war. Truth be told, it was my perfect excuse to get out of there and be with Max. I'd just taken it to another level, and I was pretty sure she wouldn't follow me.

I was fuming. Why did I let Cindy get to me? My lungs ached from my shallow breathing and my throat stung from the words that scuffed and cut their way out in a desperate attempt to keep my secret. My eyes burned; I hated losing it like that.

"Wilson! Hey wait up," Joanie was screaming. I didn't stop. I wanted to be far enough away before I stopped walking. All I wanted was to get to Max. He could calm the madness that fluxed through my body.

"Sorry, J. I just needed to get away from her," I told her as she bumped into my side.

"Don't worry. Are you okay? Wilson, I've never seen you so pissed. I was waiting for you to clock her upside the head." She swung her arm around my back; catching my shoulder, she pulled me against her side.

"I'm fine. I just couldn't take it anymore. She is such a bitch!" I took a deep breath, trying to clear all the negative energy seeping into my heart. "I can't believe I dropped the F-bomb on Cindy," I continued.

"I know," she barked.

"I've never said that to anyone before." I felt my insides shaking.

"I know," she repeated. I took another deep breath.

I wanted to ask Joanie if what I was doing with Max was wrong. Was it really that bad to want someone who made me feel whole again? He made me feel so safe. I could be myself with him. When I was with him I didn't feel seventeen and he wasn't twenty-two. We were two people who belonged together. I decided not to ask. I just didn't want to know if she had some doubts.

"Where are you planning to go? Because if you plan on just walking around I need to change my shoes." Joanie stopped me and pointed to her slippers. We laughed. "J, I want to see him one more time before school tomorrow. After that, it's going to be different. I just know it." I stared up at her with my puppy eyes. She stared back for a moment before she broke away.

"What do you need me to do?" she asked as she looked down at the sidewalk.

"I need you to be okay with what I'm doing. That's all." I looked down at the sidewalk too.

"I'm okay with it. You're my best friend and I want you to be happy—always." She pulled me into a hug. She always hugged the best: strong, tight, and comforting.

"Thanks, J." Relief flooded my soul.

CHAPTER TWENTY-EIGHT:

Joanie gave me a ride to Peet's Coffee and waited with me while Max came to pick me up. It gave us a moment to talk about my weekend with him.

"Okay, so what happened? Details, please." Joanie turned off her car and faced me with the anticipation of what I was going to say.

"Well, Max showed up at a party Cindy had the first night we were there. He came with his brother, Calvin. Anyway, we ended up in this huge bathroom across from the room I was staying in. I thought he was going to kiss me, but he didn't. He left and I was devastated." I took off my seatbelt and adjusted myself to sit facing her.

"Oh my God. He was being a total tease." She smiled and pushed me.

"Yeah, I guess. He did leave his number in my pocket." I pushed her back.

"Get out!" Joanie hit me again.

"No, really, he told me to call him that night. So I did. We were talking and getting along great when he said he couldn't be with me. So I broke down crying and, the next thing I knew, he showed up." I was bursting inside with excitement. It was like reliving it all over again.

"He showed up?" Joanie adjusted her body and got real comfortable.

"Ah, yeah—he showed up." The butterflies woke up.

"Did you guys do anything?" She licked her lips. She wanted all the juicy details.

"He kissed me right there in the bathroom, against the sinks. Mmm, J, he was really good, too. Like your favorite piece of chocolate cake good." I could feel my face heat and my cheeks tighten above my smile.

"You kissed him back, right? What did you do with your hands? Tell me you kissed him back." She swallowed hard leaning toward me.

"Oh, heck yeah I kissed him back. My hands were up in his hair, of course. You know how I feel about his hair." I laughed.

"Wilson's first kiss! And by an older, hot, smart guy. What happened after the kiss?" she squealed.

"Okay, ready for this? He spent the night with me. He slept with his body against mine. Oh my God, Joanie, he was so sweet and a total gentleman. Didn't try anything with me." My eyes glossed with the thoughts of us together that night.

"Un-frickin'-believable! You are so frickin' lucky, Wilson." She pulled me across and hugged me tight.

"Thanks, J, I appreciate it," I whispered.

"Well, you deserve to be happy!" she sounded like she was going to cry.

"I am happy." I pulled away to see him drive up in a black Mustang. "What is he doing in that car?" I pointed to him across the parking lot. My phone chimed with a text from him.

"I'm here, where are you?" I read out loud to Joanie.

I'M N THE WHITE DURANGO N FRONT OF PEETS W/JO-NEE. WATS UP W/MUSTANG? I sent it back to him.

I watched him lower his head to read what I sent. He looked so good. He had a navy blue hoodie pulled up over his head. I saw him smile as he looked around and spotted us. I waved across to him. He moved his car closer before he got out and came to my side of the Durango. He tapped the window with his finger. I pushed it down.

"Hi, Wilson," he smirked.

"Hi." I answered before I smiled. I was so nervous. I wanted him to be okay with Joanie seeing us together. "Joanie gave me a ride here," I justified her presence.

"Joanie." He looked across to my best friend. "How are you?" He raised his hand from the door of her car and gave a small wave. His eyes narrowed as he looked back at me.

"Fine, thanks, and you?" Joanie grabbed the steering wheel and pulled it back and forth.

"Good, thank you." He looked at her. "J, do you mind if Wilson comes over to my place for a little while tonight?" he asked her for permission. My butterflies begged her to let me go. *How honorable was he?* I looked over at her, she looked at me.

"No, Mr.—Max, I don't mind at all," she told him. "Just don't stay out too late, young lady!" she scolded me before she smiled and gave me a hug goodbye.

"Thanks, Joanie," he told her as he pulled the handle on the Durango, opening my door for me.

"See you, J. I'll call you later," I said as I shut the door and looked in at her from outside the car.

"You better. And don't forget the paper that's due for Mrs. Clouser tomorrow," she shouted as she started her car and put it into gear. She rolled her window up and drove away.

He held the door open on the black Mustang then sped around the car and hopped in. Immediately he started questioning me.

"So what is this about a paper due for Clouser's class?" He started the car to a loud rumble.

"Wait." I pushed across the car to him, wrapping my hand around the back of his neck, his hoodie still covering his head. I kissed him. His lips were warm, inviting, and tasty. I wanted to touch his hair so bad. "Hi," I whispered.

"Mmm, hi, nice try Wilson. What paper is due tomorrow?" he growled low. His words, no matter what he said, teased my butterflies.

"Joanie! She snitched on me. It's a paper about the first half of the movie Romeo and Juliet from the sixties. Not hard at all. I could write it in my sleep." He grabbed my hand and drove to his house without saying another word about Mrs. Clouser's crappy homework.

He literally lived five minutes away. When he pulled into his complex my stomach did somersaults. My butterflies loved it.

"My roommate won't be back until tomorrow. We have the place to ourselves." He parked in a covered carport.

"Whose car is this?" I asked as he came around and opened my door.

"It's my roommate's. He let me borrow it." He crouched down, helping me out of the car. His hand wrapped tight around my waist as he shut my door and led me to the stairs that took me up to his condo.

"I can help you with your paper, if you would like me to," he breathed into my ear across my hair. His body pushed against mine from behind.

"I didn't come to work on my paper." I leaned back against him. He grabbed me around the shoulders and pushed me up the last couple of stairs.

"Yeah, but what kind of influence would I be if I let you get away with that?" He pulled my hair away from the side of my neck and warmed my skin with his lips. I shuddered and tweaked my head back. Chills forced their way up my scalp and across my shoulders.

"Hey, how about a ticklish influence?" I spun to face him.

He had pulled off his hoodie. His hair was disheveled and calling to my butterflies; of course my hands got there first. I loved to tangle my fingers until they got lost in it. His perfect hands pressed hot against either side of my face. His stare seductively climbed from my lips up to my eyes and back to my lips again. His shoulders high against his ears, I closed my eyes and his lips pressed unyielding against mine. His fingers were firm against the back of my head before they wrapped around my back, pulling me tight against him. He was so warm and pleasing. Our moans and breaths caught low in our bodies. He pulled away just enough to push back against my lips with fierce lust.

He started moving me to the door. I shuffled. He wasn't letting up. He kissed me like he hadn't seen me in days. He backed me up against the door to his condo, twisted the knob, and we went in.

I wish I could tell you what color the walls were or what type of furniture he had, but I couldn't. He was determined to get me straight to his bedroom. And to be honest, I was so wrapped up in *him* my eyes never opened and my lips never left his. It was just like the movies—we kissed our way to his room. We just didn't strip on the way. As a matter of fact, when the back of my legs hit his bed, he stopped kissing me and pushed me down onto the mattress. His legs pushed between mine as they dangled down the side and he stood looking at me for a moment.

"I'll be right back," he whispered, low and bothered.

"Okay," I projected.

He left the room. I pushed up on my elbows. *Where was he going? Last time he did that to me he came back with something to eat.* My stomach growled excitedly. But this time he came back with paper and a pencil. He had a book under his arm, and suddenly it hit me what he was going to make me do.

"Okay, so what's all this?" I sat up.

"Well, you have a paper due tomorrow and I happen to have paper. I also found a pencil. What are the odds?" He held up the paper and a pencil.

"What makes you think I will cooperate?" I teased.

"I have an incentive for you." He pushed his legs between mine, tossing the paper and pencil on the bed. "For every paragraph you get done you can choose your prize." He smiled and it caught his eyes. He pushed his hands into the pockets of his Levi's.

"What's the catch? Do the prizes start small then get bigger as we go?" I breathed as I slid my hands up under his T-shirt and hoodie.

"Nope. You choose. But it might make for better sport if you *find* your way to the big prize." He pulled his hands from his pockets and grabbed my arms out from under his shirt.

"Okay, I'll play. What's that about?" I pointed to the book he had flung onto the nightstand next to his bed.

"Cliff notes. In case you get stuck coming up with ideas." He leaned against me, pushing me onto my back. His face was so close to mine I felt the heat of his breath warm my lips. His eyes fixed on mine as his hands slid across the bed and grabbed the paper and pencil.

"Deal?" he asked as he backed off me with them in his hands.

"Fine, deal," I snapped. I grabbed the paper and pencil and walked over to the desk. "You have no idea what you're in for. I can write for days. Hope you're ready!" I flopped into his chair and pressed the pencil to the paper.

My first paragraph was done in five minutes flat. *Wonder what he was willing to give me? He did have a point about build-up. Maybe I shouldn't take advantage of him with the opening paragraph, and just ask for a kiss.*

"Here you go. Check my work, Mr. Goldstein." I held the paper in the air. He read it to himself mumbling.

"Good! What are you going to get for your first prize?" he grinned and crumpled his eyebrows as he ran his fingers through his hair.

"Well, Max, since it *is* the first prize earned in this contest, I would like to ask for a kiss." I stood up.

He came over close. He let out his breath slowly from his nose as it flared. His eyes twinkled as he teased me. He wrapped his arms around me and dipped me low in front of him. His lips pressed hard into mine as my hands knotted in his hair. His arms were rock hard as they held me. He tasted so sweet my butterflies didn't know where to go. They pounded hard up and down my body. He rolled me back to standing and I actually got light-headed.

"Whew." I pushed my hair back from my face, his hand still tucked around my waist.

"You liked it?" he growled against my ear.

"Oh yeah," I answered him as I went back to his desk and hammered out another paragraph.

You would think it would have been easy to get another paragraph done when it comes to Romeo and Juliet, sixties style, but I came to find out it was a little harder than I thought. Do I comment on the production of the movie and how well it followed the book? Or do I focus on the abilities of the actors to bring the characters to life? It was probably better to just write about the characters' triumphs and tragedies. Mainly because that *is* what we are studying right now: Shakespeare and the poetic injustice of Romeo and Juliet. The forbidden love and pent-up angst of two young people from two different worlds. *Sound familiar?*

"Well, stumped, are we? Here, let me see what you've come up with." Max leaned across the desk and snatched up my paper before I could stop him. He held it high as he read it. I stood up and he raised it higher in the air.

"Hey, I wasn't ready for you to read it yet." I kept jumping, trying to reach it, which was totally useless; there was no way I could get it. His hand caught me around the back of my waist as he pulled me closer. I stopped jumping.

"This was the part of the challenge I didn't get to tell you about. I get to check what you've written, and if I like it, I get to choose the prize for you." His eyes studied my expression as they persuaded me to kiss him.

"Did I pass?" I smirked as my lips left his.

"Well, let me see…nope." He tossed the paper back onto the desk.

"How come?" I moped. I pulled the chair out and sat down.

"See here? And there?" He pushed his finger to the page. He leaned over me like he would when I was in his class. Familiar excitement flooded my body, feeding the famished butterflies. "You're missing the main idea that ties this section to your opening paragraph." He pushed his mouth to the top of my head and inhaled my scent. He moaned as he exhaled.

"If I fix that do I get two prizes? One for my paragraph and one for doing what you told me to do?" I tilted up to see him.

"Maybe. We'll have to see how fast you get done." He walked across the room and pushed his iPod into its docking station.

Within a couple of minutes I had my paper in the air waiting for him to look at it. He meandered over and snagged it from my grasp.

"Okay, yeah, not bad. I like how you brought in other characters like Benvolio and the Nurse. Alright, what two prizes were you thinking about?" he huffed, smiling.

I grabbed my paper out of his hands and pushed against him. I wanted to tease him. Kiss him without letting him touch me. That was my prize. I took his hands and pushed them to his back. He obeyed and shoved them into his pockets. I ran my hands up the front of his shirt and locked them behind his neck pulling him down to me. His eyes closed and I tasted him lightly. I pulled away and watched him lean forward He wanted more; I wouldn't let him. His hands loose, he tried to grab me around my waist. I caught his hands and held them away from me.

"Hey. My prize, my rules. You don't get to touch," I scolded him.

"Just a little something?" He gave me a needy look. I pushed his hand to my cheek. His fingers mingled with my hair as he cradled my ears. He watched me as I leaned into him and kissed delicately under his jaw. His other hand steadied my face as he pulled me across to his lips. He couldn't take not being in control. I pulled away and pushed him down.

"That was something. But it's my game and I'm upping the ante. Stay there," I told him. He lay across the bed on his back, propped up on his elbows. His feet were flat on the floor anchoring him to not move.

"What are you going to do?" he growled low.

"You'll see. No touching unless I say so." I grabbed the bottom edge of my shirt and pulled it up over my head. My hair tickled as it fell back onto my shoulders. His mouth dropped open and he swallowed hard. All that was left was my black bra.

"This isn't fair. Come here, Wilson." He bit his bottom lip as his eyes drew across my face, down to my stomach, and back up to my chest.

"Do you like what you see?" I asked in my most sexy, gravelly voice.

"Um hum." His tongue wet his lips. "Come closer," he demanded.

"Nope." I went over to his iPod and adjusted the songs until I found a sexy, slow song. I had no idea who it was. Some indie band, no doubt.

I stood staring at him as he stared back. He was sitting up now, his hands pulling his hair back from his face. I think that was the only place he could put them without grabbing for me. I moved closer. Slowly I unbuttoned the top button on my jeans. He couldn't take it. He jumped up so fast, I screamed; he startled me. With his hands navigating across my stomach and around my back, his mouth tracked down the side of my face, under my jaw, and down my neck to just above my bra. He sent chills throughout my body and my butterflies took notice. I had him exactly where I wanted and I still had another prize to claim.

CHAPTER TWENTY-NINE:

Three paragraphs later we were down to just our pants on top of the bed making out. My report was done and I just had to give props to Romeo and Juliet. It was the perfect aphrodisiac.

Still, time ticked away with every breath I took. Even when I attempted to inhale slowly and deeply, the anxiety of Monday coursed through my body. I wanted to know what to expect. To be prepared for the intensity and torture of being in a room with him and not being able to kiss him.

The reality of our limits clocked me hard upside the head— I'll have to watch him help other girls in my class; I'll have to listen to the other girls tease and paw after him. It made my heart hiccup thinking about it. I tucked under his arm and cuddled next to his warm, firm body.

"What's on your mind?" he whispered as he tightened his arm around me. I exhaled before I answered him.

"Monday and every day after that," I groaned. I leaned my head back.

"We will make it through Monday, and every day will get a little easier." He grabbed my chin and brought my eyes to his. "I promise."

"I hope so," I mumbled as he kissed the tip of my nose. He let out a slight laugh.

It was frustrating that he found it humorous, because for me, I was worried to the core about messing it up for us. What if someone saw the way I looked at him; put two and two together and figured us out? Or just so happened to see us touch? If anything happened to him because of me, I don't think I would ever forgive myself. Cindy has already pressed too close for comfort.

"Wilson, you need to stop worrying. It'll be fine." He rolled me onto my back and pressed the side of his face against my collarbone, turning to kiss the base of my neck. His legs tangled with mine and his hand pushed my hair back from my shoulder.

As much as I should have liked what he was doing, thoughts of Cindy wouldn't stop hijacking my mind—her face as I told her, 'F- you' and left; her vindictiveness that would be boiling over with different scenarios she could create to get back at me. I slid off the bed and stood looking at him. I tucked my hands in front of me, covering my bare chest.

"I should tell Cindy I'm sorry." The words sped from my mouth.

"What? Why?" He sat up, reaching for my arm.

"I said the F-word to her face and stormed out. She wouldn't stop pushing me about liking you. I know it was wrong, but I just couldn't take her crap anymore." I paced back and forth along the length of the bed. He stopped me. His arms wrapped tight around me and he pressed my head to his chest, wedging it under his chin.

"I won't let her hurt you, Wilson. Don't let her ruin our night. Okay?" He jockeyed his head, catching my eyes. "Okay?" he asked again.

"Okay," I answered. I shivered as goose bumps rippled up my arms.

"Good. You cold?" He rubbed his hands across my arms and up my shoulders.

"Yeah, a bit." He snatched a shirt from on top of his dresser and snapped it to unfold.

"Here." He pulled it over my head, sliding it down over my chest and across my stomach.

I loved it when he took care of me. There was something magical about it and it made my butterflies awaken. His long sleeves clung coolly to my skin. I pulled the neck of his shirt up to my face, inhaling as deeply as I could through my nose. I couldn't get enough of his aroma. His pheromones mixed with his scent caused me to quiver deeply. He noticed and teased me, wrapping his hands over mine and pressing his nose to my chest below the bend of my neck.

"You smell so much better than me," he said against my skin, inhaling again. I didn't agree. Instead I broke my hands free and lost them in his hair, pulling him up to my lips. His hands pushed against my back. He was still shirtless so I pressed my fingertips hard against his naked, hot skin.

He pulled his lips from mine. "I'd have to argue that point," I said.

"Wilson, you can argue till you're blue in the face. Your scent is so tempting, there is no way I could smell as good as you." He was confident.

"Well, how do you know?" I tried to hold back a smile, causing my eyes to narrow and my cheeks to burn red.

"Trust me, I know." He snickered and snuck a small kiss.

"What were you like when you were in high school?" I asked before he came in for another kiss.

"I was shorter and completely immature, probably because I was seventeen when I graduated," he snapped back quickly with a smirk.

"Hey, now. I bet you were a total book nerd. Oh wait, maybe you were a dumb jock." I pushed him away and jumped onto his bed.

"Oh, no you didn't just go there with me." He sped to the bed, jumping next to me.

"Ah, yeah, I think I just did," I answered him back. His shirtless muscles flexed as he grabbed my arms and pushed me down against the bed. Pressing his body on mine, he dropped his face real close.

"I was the guy that carried girls' books, helped the teachers set up labs, and pulled a pretty high grade point average all four years," he answered, then smiled as he pushed harder against my body. He adjusted himself to fill the curves of our bodies before he slid down to just below my chest and rested his head on my stomach. "But that was then and this is now." He pushed his fingers behind the waistband of my jeans. I lost my breath. Chills shot down my legs and, without hesitation, I pulled my knees up.

"Now is good," I told him. He pulled his hand away and lifted his head. He stared at me through furrowed brows.

"Now *is* good, isn't it?" He ran his hands up my sides and under my shirt, finding my breasts. His eyes still smoldering and constricted, he pressed his lips to my stomach.

He knelt to the ground, his hands delicately tugging at my knees as he pushed his body between them. When I sat up, his eyes met mine. His hands brushed over my shoulders and down across my chest, then snatched the hem of my shirt.

Never uttering a single word, I gave him permission to take it off. He pulled it over my head, tangling it around my hands, locking me in the fabric that once protected me.

He drew his knee onto the bed and pressed himself against my body. The only place to go was back. With my hands locked above me, my arms fell to cover my ears. His breathing...my heart beat...our kiss... it all filled my head. His warm hands studied my body while his lips traced hot between mine. His tongue tasted the skin across my neck, working to get back to my lips. I wanted to kiss him passionately. He followed the inside of my arms up to where my shirt arrested my hands and untangled them. Now I was free and wildly ready to touch him.

His chest pressed hard against mine as he grabbed my wrists above my head and rolled me on top. I tickled my fingers down the insides of his arms. He wanted me—I could feel him pushing against my body as his arms wrapped urgently around my back. He worked to catch my lips as I tried to work my way down his chin and across his neck. His hands fetched either side of my face and he locked his mouth with mine before he drifted to my cheek, then my neck, and behind my ear. I had lost any of the control he willingly gave me by being on top. I pulled away from him, dragging my hands down his chest and catching the button on the waist of his jeans. I pulled on the flap, trying to release the buttons. He was breathing heavily as I kissed his stomach above his navel. His hands explored my body.

I had never experienced someone touching my body the way he was. He knew what drove me wild, and he made every effort to accommodate. This weekend was-life altering with the things he had done to me—things I'd only heard other girls talk about. And tonight it was my turn to try and give him something before we had to go back to our limiting world.

I unbuttoned his Levi's and drove my fingers around his waist, pulling everything off—including his boxers. I dragged them completely off his body. His body was hard, amazing, and ready for me to explore. I stood next to the bed, staring at him; he grabbed my hand and pulled me down next to him.

"Take off your pants Wilson," he growled at me firm and low against my hair.

"No. I'm not going to do it. If you want them off, you're gonna have to do it," I teased him. I got up on my knees and tried to get off the bed. He grabbed the waist of my pants and slid his fingers around the snap. He had them unbuttoned, unzipped, and off my body just as I escaped. Standing there facing him in just my panties, I slid my hands up to my waist and wrapped my fingers around the band.

"Stop. Leave them on." He pushed up on his elbows, watching every move I made.

"Really, why?" I felt a lump rise in my throat.

"I want to take them off you," he told me low.

"Well, what if I told you no?" I asked barely over a whisper.

"I'd have to respect that. Besides, there *are* ways around them," his eyebrow peaked as he answered. He pulled me onto the bed. His hand slid down under my waistband and across my backside. His fingers tickled low before he pulled his hand out from my panties.

"Yeah, well that must come from experience," the words sped out of my mouth. Part of me was concerned that he would take it wrong. *He took it exactly how I meant it.*

"That? No, that was an attempt to see what you would do. This comes from experience." He twisted me to my back. His eyes smoldered with want. He kissed my lips, dragging his mouth across my face, down my neck and straight down to my chest. My back arched and I lost my breath. His tongue tasted my skin all the way down to my stomach. His hand pushed against my calf, up past my knee and across my thigh. I looked down at him; he watched my expression change as he slipped his hand under my panties. I lost my breath.

His experience was perfect. What he did to me was perfect. He pulled his hand away and pressed his mouth to my upper thigh. I was quaking. He collected the waistband of my panties and this time I didn't say anything. He slid them off down past my knees, where they tangled at my ankles before they were off my body.

My heart pounded hard. I felt my body releasing the thrill of what he was doing. *I was so ready. I couldn't stop, change the subject, or redirect him. Not that I wanted to; but it had been my idea to please him first. I guess that had gone out the window, for now.* His firm hands wrapped above my knees, pulling my body to the edge of the bed. My toes tangled with the plush, white fur area rug next to the bed, anchoring me in the moment. His body wedged between my legs. Kneeling, he brushed his fingers delicately across the outside of my legs. His lips pressed against my inner thigh, then below my navel—teasing me, making me want him to take me to the place where my body becomes one with the universe and explodes with a euphoria that is unexplainable in this world.

He was so good, cool air rippled across me and mixed with warm. I felt him growl deep in his throat, driving me to the place I thought he had taken me before. My body understood what to do. My hands fisted in his hair; all the self-control I had was gone. Chills, goose bumps, and endorphins flooded my body making me instantly ticklish. I pushed myself away as I returned to the universe. It was as if I had run a marathon. As he pushed his chest onto mine, I felt my heart pounding faster than his, and the pressure of him was just enough to clear the chills. It was so strange—I was hot and then freezing, my body worn with the aftermath of his talent. I knew I needed to pull myself together.

"How was that?" he asked, whispering against my ear.

"Unbelievable," I was out of breath. I lay back for a moment, embodying what just happened.

My mind swirled with visions of how to go about pleasing him. I had no idea how to do it. *I was a rookie, with no experience. Worse than a rookie; at least a rookie had played before. Me? I wasn't even registering on the scale of measured experience yet. I had to let intuition guide me with what I thought he would like.*

I pushed him back, straddling his body. Catching his bottom lip between my teeth, I pulled just enough to make him whimper. His hands folded across my back and pressed my body firmly against his. I left his lips and lowered my kiss to his neck, then across his chest. His stomach was hard as I kissed each muscle of his six-pack. His moans and growls pulled at me; he was exciting me again—seeing him naked, kissing his skin. I took a deep breath and followed the trail down to him. My head overflowed with ways to start. *Do I tickle across his waist first? Do I just start and hope he likes it?* I didn't know what to do so I just took a chance and wrapped my hand delicately around him, low. I watched his face as he smiled and his eyes rolled back. Natural instinct pushed me past the fear of my inexperience. I closed my eyes and he caught his breath. Groans of pleasure rose from his body. I let air swirl around him; he went wild. He grabbed at my body catching my arms before he clutched the covers of the bed.

I felt complete power with what I was doing. If I stopped, he would do anything to get me to start again. If I kept going, he would do anything to get me to do it again. I've always aspired to be in control of situations; this instance was no different.

His hand pushed the hair back from my face.

"Wilson..." His head rolled back and forth.

I didn't know what to do. I really didn't think about what happens to me when he reaches his euphoric state. I watched his body shake. His muscles throughout his body flexed tight then loosened. He growled and panted deep bellowing moans, pulling me down against him and kissing me across my neck.

"Well I guess I wasn't too bad then, huh?" I laughed. It was more than a nervous reaction. I didn't know how to do what I did and I was a little intimidated by his experience. But I have to say, it felt damn good to make him shiver like that.

"No, it was good, really good," he laughed with me. His arms tightened around me. We were in the moment.

"Really? Because you know, I've never done *that* before." I didn't make eye contact. He pulled at my chin making me look at him.

"I know. You drove me wild, I couldn't hold back. Look at me." He pushed his arm out into the air. Naked and cold, I burrowed into the covers of the bed.

"Hey now, wait for me." He pulled the covers loose from his side and slid next to me.

Our exposed bodies against each other warmed to a nice, comfortable temperature under the down comforter. He pressed against my back, fitting perfectly around me—his arm, protective across my waist. Our hands coupled, locking our fingers together.

"What time is it?" I hated asking him.

"It's nine-thirty," he whispered.

The last thing I wanted to think about was time. I wish we could freeze the night in a capsule and live there for as long as we wanted. But La-La Land had enough girls trying to get a ticket in. I had to be realistic and figure out how to maximize every moment we had left tonight. That made it so difficult. It wasn't like we could spend endless hours together, the way girls around me got to do with their boyfriends. Ours was a forbidden love that had to be handled just the right way.

"We have about an hour before I have to get back," I told him. He already knew.

Dorm curfew for juniors and seniors was 10:30 p.m. with lights out at 11:00. It was better than the freshman and sophomores who had curfew at 9:30 and lights out at 10:00. That extra hour was invaluable. However, tonight it gave me the time I wanted…and stole it from me all in the same moment. I pushed the blanket back off my legs and got up.

"Where ya going?" He reached across but didn't catch me.

"Just getting dressed." I wanted him to pay attention to what I had to say, and if I talked to him half-naked he wouldn't be able to focus. I scooped up my panties and pulled them on. My jeans were bunched up on the floor; I shook them to release the legs and wiggled into them.

"Here, let me help you." He sauntered toward me. His fingers caught the front of my pants. Pulling at the button, he snapped it tight below my navel. His hair blocked his expression. His fingers still behind my waistband, he slid them around to the small of my back. I shivered.

"Max," I whispered slowly through my exhaled breath.

"Shhh. Don't say it." The muscles in his jaw constricted, his brows converged above his narrow, pained eyes as he raised his head. He brought his forehead to rest on mine. "I know how hard it is going to be—being in a room with you, not able to hold you and kiss you, or talk freely with you," his voice was low; his breath smelled sweet, like Jolly Ranchers swirled in

Ghirardelli chocolate. His hands clung to my back, pressing me close to him.

He got it. The whole picture of us tangled in the vines of the forbidden fruit. We can't go to dinner together in public. We won't kiss goodnight at the door. Holding hands was totally out of the question. We will have to maintain the student-teacher facade for another six months. Just until after graduation, then we could be ourselves. I pushed my lips to his. "I'd better text Joanie to come get me." My butterflies became frantic. "I'll have her meet us back at Peet's." Their wings hit and tore, fighting to break the bubble of regret surging up into my throat.

I broke away and pulled my phone from my pocket.

"Wait, Wilson. I need twenty more minutes with you." He grabbed my phone and closed it. My heart climbed up into the back of my throat. Maybe it was the butterflies succeeding at escaping the churn of emotional turmoil deep in my body.

Max stared at me, his inviting green eyes filled with the apprehension of actually calling out the amount of time we had left together before my chariot turned into a pumpkin pulled by little white mice. Twenty minutes wasn't much time. He slid his hand around my waist and pulled me in. His long fingers brushed my hair back as he pressed his palm to the side of my face. My hands clutched at his waist. My eyes watered. He slid his thumbs right under them to catch my tears.

"You are so beautiful. I'm so lucky," he whispered.
I didn't say anything. I didn't want to ruin the moment with stupid words that would bumble awkwardly from my mouth.
So I breathed deeply and leaned against his chest, tightening my arms around his waist. Tomorrow was going to be okay.

EPILOGUE: MONDAY

Everything was silent when I woke up Monday morning. I half expected Cindy to still be pissed at me. I wouldn't blame her. Instead, she was already gone. Probably better that way. I don't think I could handle another fight with her.

Last night, when Joanie picked me up from Peet's Coffee, it was excruciating to drive away and leave Max in the parking lot. My heart was torn from my chest and it left a huge gaping hole. My butterflies poured out, desperate to stay with him. It was Max who had tamed them, and they were loyal.

I had a dream last night—more like a nightmare. The warning bell for fourth period had rung and I was heading into my government class. Max's class. The door was heavier than usual but I didn't care. I was going to see him and I could feel my butterflies jump to life. Except when I walked into class, an old, gray-haired woman stood behind his desk. She was frail and little, dressed from head to toe in black. She noticed me right away and shuffled over. She asked me if I was Ms. Wilson Mooney before she handed me a folded note. My knees went weak. I felt the blood drain quickly from my cheeks. My butterflies froze. I recognized the lined paper—it was the same type Max had used to give me his number, the same one I flushed down the toilet.

The paper was soft and the folds were flat but worn, like he'd opened and closed it too many times. My hands trembled as I walked back to my desk, waiting until I was sitting to open it. The room was filled. There was someone I knew at every desk: Cindy, Joanie, Bonnie, and Jacky. My heart pounded fast and loud when Max's mom came over and told me to take a deep breath and open the note. Tears were streaming down her face as she reached to touch my cheek. Her hand was so cold it cooled through my skin and muscle, all the way down to my bones.

My eyes dropped to the folded paper in my fingers. I fumbled to open it, taking care not to rip the fragile, worn edges. I brought it to my face. Pressing it to my nose, I smelled him. Lavender flooded my senses. As I pulled open the last fold, I saw it was in *his* handwriting. The words bounced and jumped off the page, breaking apart as the tears landed on his thoughts written on the lined, creased paper. Mistake, age, student, and too young were the words that clawed their way into my head before they poisoned and ripped their way down to my heart. They destroyed every butterfly that struggled to survive. Every last one—dead.

I looked up to an empty room; I was alone. I stumbled to leave, clutching the handle on the door, when I saw my mother in the doorway. Her arms were outstretched; was it me she wanted? It couldn't be me. I turned to look behind me and that's when I saw Cindy. She ran past me into my mother's arms. They clung to each other, an embrace I had waited my whole life to get from her. It wasn't for me.

My eyes sprang open. I was back in my dorm room with Joanie, still asleep. My heart leapt from my chest, clogging my throat, making it hard to take a deep breath. I knew it was a dream; it was just hard to swallow the messages it sent to me. I could justify Cindy in my dream—she and I were on the outs. I could even see the fear of losing Max. What with him being my teacher and me not being eighteen. But my mother…I never saw her coming.

The only thing that made the first part of the day half bearable was the thought of seeing Max during fourth period and after school. I wondered if my butterflies would be there, waiting to come back. I had to admit, a small part of me wondered if he was going to have a substitute today. And if it was a little gray-haired lady in black, I wasn't stepping foot in his room.

Cindy didn't sit with us at first break. She made it pretty clear she was still mad. I even tried to make eye contact with her during Humanities: nothing. She was good at making me feel terrible and guilty. It was lunchtime when I figured she knew about Max and me and was just waiting for the right moment to destroy us. Joanie and I skipped lunch and went back to our room. I needed to talk to her before I faced Max. She was my rock and I needed to be grounded; it was the only place we could talk in private.

We sat on my bed and she knew exactly what to say to make me feel okay. I told her about my dream and she reasoned every scary image away with a positive twist. I loved her for that. I called her my best friend but she was more than that. She was my mother, my sister, my best friend, and the only family I truly had. When I get married, she will be the one to give me away and stand next to me as my maid of honor. She was everything to me.

We were on our way to Max's class when I shoved my hand into my pocket. My cell phone wasn't there and I *always* carry my phone with me. It was like leaving my room without shoes—it just doesn't happen. I told Joanie that I'd probably left it on the bed where we were talking and that I'd catch up with her. I ran back as fast as I could. I didn't want to be the last one walking into government after the bell rang. I wanted to mingle with the crowd of girls going into his class, making it easier to get to my desk without anyone noticing me.

I pushed our dorm room door open as Cindy pulled. We ran into each other. She didn't say anything, even when I tried to apologize for dropping the "F" bomb. She just stared through me, smirked, and kept walking. I spotted my phone on my bed. It was open. My body flushed a cold sweat from every pore. Why hadn't I cleared all my messages? I spun around the room looking for evidence of where she'd been. Maybe she hadn't seen my phone. I snatched it up, scrolling through our texts, seeing if our words were as descriptive as I remembered. I couldn't believe I had just given her the biggest weapon of all; one that could annihilate everything Max and I had.

As I ran to his class, adrenaline pumped fast throughout my entire body. I struggled to convince my mind that she hadn't seen it. She had government with me and I wanted to catch her before she went in. When I turned the corner to his classroom, I saw the door slam shut. I cased the room as I peered through the diamond-wired window, looking to see if she was slinking her way to her desk like a shark hunting for kill. She was laughing and talking to Jacky when they both looked across the room. I followed their gestures. There he was. Max. His back was to the class; he was erasing and rewriting something on his whiteboard. My knees went weak and I shuffled away from the window. I had to go in, had to be there to show Cindy that nothing was going on between Max and me. I grabbed the handle as the second bell rang. I was late and everyone was going to see me walk in. I wanted to vomit; get the anxiety to leave my body. I needed to remember what every day before the weekend was like when I came into his room. I took a deep breath, swallowed the last bit of regret, and pulled the door open.

Can't wait for more?

Watch for...

Wilson Mooney

Eighteen at Last

Available 2012

www.wilsonmooney.blogspot.com
www.writtenandready.blogspot.com
Or find me on Twitter! @delaogk

www.ingramcontent.com/pod-product-compliance
Lightning Source LLC
Chambersburg PA
CBHW030025180626
46810CB00001B/208